RAMPAGE

ALSO BY JOHN SANDFORD

LUCAS DAVENPORT NOVELS

Rules of Prey
Shadow Prey
Eyes of Prey
Silent Prey
Winter Prey
Night Prey
Mind Prey
Sudden Prey
Secret Prey
Certain Prey
Easy Prey
Chosen Prey
Mortal Prey
Naked Prey
Hidden Prey
Broken Prey
Invisible Prey
Phantom Prey
Wicked Prey
Storm Prey
Buried Prey
Stolen Prey
Silken Prey
Field of Prey
Gathering Prey

VIRGIL FLOWERS NOVELS

Dark of the Moon
Heat Lightning
Rough Country
Bad Blood
Shock Wave
Mad River
Storm Front
Deadline

KIDD NOVELS

The Fool's Run
The Empress File
The Devil's Code
The Hanged Man's Song

OTHER NOVELS

The Night Crew
Dead Watch
Saturn Run

BY JOHN SANDFORD & MICHELE COOK

THE SINGULAR MENACE

Uncaged
Outrage
Rampage

THE SINGULAR MENACE • BOOK 3

RAMPAGE

JOHN SANDFORD
& MICHELE COOK

ALFRED A. KNOPF 🐎 NEW YORK

THIS IS A BORZOI BOOK PUBLISHED BY ALFRED A. KNOPF

Visit us on the Web! randomhouseteens.com

Educators and librarians, for a variety of teaching tools, visit us at RHTeachersLibrarians.com

Library of Congress Cataloging-in-Publication Data is available upon request.

ISBN 978-0-385-75313-5 (trade) — ISBN 978-0-385-75316-6 (ebook)

The text of this book is set in 11-point Simoncini Garamond.

Printed in the United States of America
July 2016
10 9 8 7 6 5 4 3 2 1

First Edition

RAMPAGE

TRAPPED . . .

No way out.

The smell of oil and rust and wet rot was all the sharper for the total darkness. They were trapped in the bow of the ship, heavily armed hunters above them on deck. Shay's pistol was cocked and cold in her right hand, and she held X's collar in her left.

Someone not far away was moving back toward the stern. The wolflike dog twitched against her grip, ready to fight.

Harmon, the ex-soldier, invisible in the dark, touched Shay's sleeve and whispered, "We need to go up. Get between the support beams and the deck."

"What about X?"

"He's gotta climb with us. . . ."

Combat boots rang on the metal stairs, and then a voice, unintelligible, and the faint glow of a flashlight, still a hundred feet away, behind a stack of shipping containers. The rumble of the engines was muted this far forward, but the vibration caused the old freighter to creak and moan. Shay and Harmon were wearing soft running shoes, and the freighter's metallic complaints would cover the sounds of their movement.

A man's baritone voice, hard with a hunter's intensity: "Hey—there's one! Rick, he's heading aft, he's heading aft. Get him! Get him!"

Shay and Harmon had released a group of prisoners—human experimental subjects—from the ship's holds. Now the security men were chasing them down.

The echoing voices seemed to move away . . . but there was another soft, unnatural rattle from nearby.

"Still there," Harmon whispered. "Too big for a rat."

Shay: "Look at X. He can see them."

The dog was straining into the darkness, his one cybernetic eye glittering like a firefly.

Harmon: "Don't shoot unless you have to—I'm gonna hit them with the light."

Harmon had an LED flashlight, small but powerful. Two seconds after he'd warned her, the light beam lanced into the dark . . . and found a pack of zombies: four of the recently freed human experiments.

The Asian men, round faces slack beneath shaved heads, blinked into the light, BB-sized bronze knobs on their scalps, which were striped with red surgical scars. They were dressed in loose green cotton shirts and pants, like hospital scrubs, and plastic slippers.

The three in back retreated, each holding on to the waistband of the man in front of him, shuffling backward into the darkness again. They made hoarse, growling sounds as they went, "Owwwww . . . owwww . . . awwww . . ."

Shay blurted, "Oh my God . . ."

The fourth put up his hands in the universal sign of surrender and asked in fragmented English, "You are help us?"

At Shay's nod, the man turned and called softly to the others in another language.

"Korean," Harmon said. "I don't understand it, but I know the sound."

Shay thought the man might have been calling the others back, but the three faded into the dark.

Another man's voice, far away: "Check the bow. Harvey, Stan, check the bow. There must be some of them up there. . . ."

"We gotta go *now*," Harmon said. He shined the flashlight up at the underside of the deck. The interior of the hull, as it came to the bow, was braced with rusty steel crosspieces spaced a foot or so apart, like shelves in a bookcase. The crosspieces were a foot deep, and the hull rose at an angle, rather than straight up. Almost a stairway.

"Gotta go," he repeated.

The fourth zombie stood staring at them, gold pins winking from his scalp. Shay said, "You have to hide. You understand me?"

"I go with you."

"Can you climb?"

"I go. . . ."

Harmon and Shay were both climbers, and scaling the rusty crosspieces would not normally have been a challenge for them. But with a dog and a zombie and guns in their hands . . .

Harmon said to Shay, "Lead the way. Get X up there. I'll help this guy."

"Come on, boy," said Shay, and the dog went with his girl as he always did, up toward the underside of the deck in the faint, hand-cupped illumination of Harmon's flash. X was moving at Shay's hip until a front paw missed the fifth brace and his body pitched forward into the gap. Shay caught him around the belly and pulled him back with a snapping motion like a cobra's. The dog gasped but regained his footing.

The Asian man, an awkward climber, came next, steadied by an occasional touch from Harmon. As they came up under the deck, Shay felt a draft of cooler air that stank of the muddy river. She leaned into Harmon and whispered, "Feel the air? Where's it coming from?"

"Dunno . . . but let's go that way."

They edged along the supports and, ten feet back toward the stern, found a service ladder and a hatch. The hatch was not entirely tight: the rubber seals had either ripped or worn away, allowing a thin stream of night air into the hull. A wheel hung from the center of the hatch. Harmon let a bit more light seep through his fingers and muttered, "Looks like it hasn't been opened for a while. Take the flash. Don't drop it."

He turned the light off and handed it to Shay, who cupped her fingers over the lens and turned it back on.

Harmon was a large man, and strong. He stood on the ladder, got a grip on the wheel, and tried to turn it. It moved a half inch, then stopped with a nearly inaudible *clank*. "Get the light closer. . . ."

A latch that fit into the wheel mechanism was preventing the wheel from turning. Harmon tried to pull the latch free, failed, then began hitting it with the heel of his hand. After a few blows, it began to move, and he managed to push it the rest of the way over. With the latch open, the wheel turned reluctantly but steadily, and a minute later, Harmon pushed the hatch up enough to peek out at the deck.

"We're right where we came aboard," he said. "And . . . we're moving backward."

"What?"

"Shhh!"

Down below, more footsteps, and this time, a brilliant beam probed the interior of the hull, where the prisoners had just been. Then a man's gruff voice: "We're clear here."

The footsteps started away, then another man shouted: "There! There they are! Stan, go left, three of them going left!"

The Asian man whispered, "They catch my friends."

X's throat vibrated—it would have been a growl, but Shay had her arm around his chest and squeezed. The dog understood the warning and went silent. The footsteps and the light from the flash began to move away.

"Now what?" Shay whispered.

"We've got a way out now—we could be over the side in two seconds," Harmon said. "Maybe we hang here, see where they're going."

"What if they turn around and go out to the ocean . . . like, all the way to North Korea?"

"Probably want to get off before then," Harmon said.

"Funny," she said.

Shay Remby was a slender sixteen-year-old, a rock climber with serious muscles in her shoulders and arms, currently with brutally cropped black hair. A few weeks earlier, her hair had been long and a striking fiery red—but a few weeks earlier, she'd never fired a gun, never handled a firebomb, never left a man standing on a toilet with a noose around his neck . . . and only a few days earlier, she'd been a sworn enemy of the man who now stood with her in the dark rusting freighter.

The trouble had begun when she ran up against the Singular Corporation of San Francisco. Singular was experimenting on human beings—on human brains. If the company succeeded in its research efforts, the consciousness of one person could be transferred into the living brain of another. If the transfer was made from an old body to a young one, life could be prolonged almost indefinitely. There was no limit to the number of bodies that could be used. The minds of the donor bodies would be wiped in the process—a deadly science in which one life was sacrificed for another. Nobody expected there to be volunteer donors.

The cost of the program was astronomical. The beneficiaries were necessarily the richest and most powerful people in the world. And the program was necessarily top-secret.

That is, until Shay's brother, Odin, without really knowing what he was getting into, stole information from a lab that revealed the existence of the Singular research program. Singular was frantic to eliminate the leak. Shay and her friends were doing anything, everything, to turn the leak into a flood and expose Singular's crimes—preferably before Singular eliminated *them*. . . .

The Asian man clung to the crosspieces, a foot below Shay and X, and asked in his rough English, "You are who take Fenfang?"

Shay, surprised, nodded, then realized he couldn't see her. "Fenfang, yes! How do you know her?"

"I was at prison when you take her. . . . I see you then. Your hair is not same. Is Fenfang okay now?"

Shay said, "We can talk when we get out of here. . . ."

She didn't want to tell him there had been a firefight a half hour earlier, off the boat, and Fenfang had been shot. Shay didn't hold out much hope.

They could hear boots on the deck overhead coming closer to the hatch, then passing by and receding.

After a moment, Harmon whispered, "Security check."

The Asian man asked, "Are we in the ocean?"

"No. We're going inland," Harmon said. "We have to get off the boat and bring the cops down on them before they get rid of those prisoners."

"Let me get up on the deck," Shay said. "Check the possibilities."

Harmon pushed the hatch lid up, and Shay climbed past him onto the deck. The cloudy night sky was a smooth, creamy color to the west, over San Francisco, but here, straight up, there was nothing but deep, starless darkness. Ahead of the ship, she could see the lights of a bridge high over the water and could hear the righteous thump of a decent rock band.

Shay took a fast look around, listened, then stepped to the edge of a bank of steel shipping containers and peeked around. A hundred yards ahead, on the near shore, bright lights had been strung over a concrete pier that jutted out over the water. Thirty or forty people were dancing on the pier, and more moved back and forth between a bar and the dance floor. Another bunch of people sat on folding chairs, watching the dancers, chatting.

She moved back to the hatch and dropped down the ladder.

"I know how we can get the cops on the boat. Lots of cops. In ten minutes."

A moment later, Shay cracked the hatch again and stood on the ladder with her head poking out. Harmon muttered, "If you hear anyone, pull back."

Shay got on the phone. Twist answered on the first ring: "Where are you?"

"We're still on the ship. We're going inland, away from San Francisco. Where are you?"

"Looking for you."

"How's our friend?" She was staying away from names, in case they were being monitored.

"She didn't make it."

"Oh no . . . Oh God." Shay turned to look down at Harmon. "Fenfang . . ." She shook her head.

"Ah, Jesus."

From below, the Asian man asked, "What is trouble?"

At the same time, Twist said, "Tell me where you are."

"We can't have gone far." She looked up the river and said, "We're going to create an emergency."

Twist heard her out and said, "That plan has so many problems I can't even begin to list them all. But . . . it could work."

"Look for us after the fireworks," Shay said, and closed the hatch.

1

The ship was a dark shadow moving up the river, traveling slowly but steadily away from the scene of Fenfang's murder.

Shay's group was tracking it: her older brother, Odin, a computer hacker who'd precipitated the fight with Singular; Twist, the rich, thirtyish artist who ran a hotel for street kids and runaways and had helped Shay escape a pair of pimps on her second night in Hollywood; Cruz Perez, one of the teens at Twist's hotel; and Danny Dill, a former hotel resident and now a marijuana grower from California's north coast. Cade Holt, another teen living at the Twist Hotel, guided them through the night from a hideout in Northern California. Still aching from a beating delivered by Singular security people, he was talking to them through throwaway cell phones as he looked at satellite photos on Google Earth.

Twist was driving the Jeep, Odin in the passenger seat beside him, when Shay called in her plan. He had begun to point out all the crazy flaws when Shay hung up. Cursing, Twist filled in Cade, who relayed the news to Cruz, who was following in a Toyota truck, and Danny Dill, trailing him in a Volvo. Cade said, "If it's an old freighter, it can't be moving fast. It's only been gone a few minutes. One or two miles an hour . . . it won't be to the Antioch Bridge yet."

"What's the Antioch Bridge?" Twist asked.

"It's a bridge across the channel—they'll be heading right toward it," Cade said. "Let me look it up. . . . Ah, Wiki says it's got a hundred and thirty-five feet of clearance, so they'll be able to go under it. That looks like the best place for the pickup, if they really pull this off. A road goes right down to the river."

"Get us there," Twist said.

Cade guided them back through town. The tight convoy moved at the speed limit: they couldn't afford to be stopped by the police. For one thing, the backseat of the Jeep was still wet with Fenfang's blood. They'd rushed her to the hospital . . . too late.

Cade was calm enough, had been since the shooting. "You'll be coming up to a left turn . . . past a marina . . . it'll take you down to the water."

Twist said, "Have cars Two and Three circulate; I'll run down to the water and look around. Keep an eye out."

Twist took the turn, passing an open gate and a PRIVATE PROPERTY—NO TRESPASSING sign, and he and Odin found themselves on a blacktop road crowded with vehicles. At the end of the road, well off to their left, they could see lights and hear music.

"That's the party," Twist said. "That's the target."

Twist turned the Jeep around, and Odin said, "This has to work. The Singular guys cannot get away."

Odin and Fenfang had begun a romance a few days before the girl was killed. She'd died in Odin's lap, and he was reeling from the shock, emotions roiling. But the idea of trapping Singular was focusing his mind.

Twist and Odin got out and looked downriver. "Is that it?" Odin asked.

"I think so." There were moving lights coming their way, but slowly. "Gotta be sure, lots of ships going back and forth. . . ."

Twist got on the phone to Cade: "Tell cars Two and Three to head back, look for the ship. It looks from here like it's a half mile away. . . ."

"Going now," Danny said to Cade's instruction. A minute later: "We got it. That's it. It's right on the shoreline. They're turning, though. Jeez, I don't know if it's wide enough to turn here."

"The river's wide enough," said Cade, who was looking at a satellite image. "If they get turned, they'll be able to move faster."

A minute later: "They're turned—they made it," Danny said. "They're heading back up the river. . . ."

Cade warned Twist: "One, it's coming right at you."

"Got it," said Twist.

Harmon boosted X through the hatch, then climbed out on the ship's deck beside Shay. The Asian man followed. Harmon murmured to Shay, "You see those metal boxes bolted to the rail? The square ones?"

"Yeah?"

"They should have life rings in them. Get them. You'll be exposed, so move slow. And listen. Soon as I finish with the gun, we'll go over the side."

"Gotta be at least fifty yards to the shore. Maybe more."

"Not much choice," Harmon said. "We'll be okay with the rings . . . unless they shoot us, of course."

"We'll go off the far side of the boat, away from the shore. They'll be looking the other way, if they're looking at all."

The Asian man chipped in: "This is very, very dangerous. Very."

Harmon and Shay looked at him and said, simultaneously, "Yes."

"I go also?"

Harmon shook his head. "It would be best if you stayed, because you speak good English. What we are going to do will bring many American police officers here. You can hide down this ladder until they arrive. Then you tell them everything that happened to you."

"They will believe me?" he asked, and patted the knobs on his head. "And fix this?"

"Yes . . . we think so," Shay said. She turned to Harmon. "You still have that Sharpie?"

He fumbled in a thigh pocket, found the pen, and handed it to her. Shay said to the Asian man, "I will write this on your arm so you can call me. . . . Pull your sleeve up."

He pulled his sleeve up, and she wrote a phone number on his arm above his elbow. "Don't let anybody see this."

He nodded.

"You're Korean? Or Chinese, maybe?"

"My memories are confused, but I know them in Chinese."

Shay nodded; it made sense. "Do you know how or where you were captured?"

"No. But I think I am a soldier. I see myself with a gun," the man said.

From the deck, Harmon took the semi-automatic rifle out of the sling on his shoulder and called quietly, "If we're gonna do this . . ."

"You're a brave man," Shay said, touching the prisoner on the shoulder.

The man bowed and said, "Be lucky with this plan."

"Yes," Shay said with a thin smile. "We will need to be lucky."

The man moved back down the ladder but paused on one of the rungs to watch the girl and the dog go to the gunslinger's side.

"Party time," Harmon said.

Colored lights were strung all along the pier, and a five-piece band was knocking out disco tunes. "Old people dancing," Shay said.

"Hey! That's 'I Will Survive,' 1980s finest," Harmon said, peering through the night at the party.

"I wasn't born yet, so I wouldn't know," Shay said.

Harmon grunted, "Get the rings."

He jacked a round into the rifle's chamber and began unscrewing the flash suppressor. He wanted the flashes to be seen, the brighter the better.

Shay crawled slowly across the deck—moving fast would catch the eye—to one of the rectangular metal boxes welded to the rail. The box opened with a simple thumbscrew: if a ring was needed, you wouldn't want it to be hard to get at.

She turned the thumbscrew, popped the box: a thin white ring buoy was inside, with a short rope attached to it. She looked once toward the ship's bridge, saw no one, pulled the ring out, and slid it back across the deck to Harmon. "I'll get the other one."

There was a similar rectangular box on the opposite rail. She crawled over to it, and Harmon, behind her, said, "We're getting close."

Shay pulled the ring out and moved back to him.

"Tie it to your belt," Harmon said. He was tying the rope of the first ring to his own belt. "As soon as you're in the water, take your jacket off and throw it over the ring. The white's too visible."

Shay tied the ring to her belt, took the cell phone out of her jeans pocket, and zipped it into a water-resistant chest pocket in her jacket.

"Here we go," Harmon said. "I'm going to fire into the concrete abutment at the base of the bridge. Any ricochets will angle out into the water, but it'll look like we're shooting at them."

Shay checked her knife in the sheath at her back, shoved her pistol into its holster, and got a good grip on both the life ring and X's collar. Harmon braced his left hand on the rail, and faster than Shay could count: *Bang-bang-bang-bang-bang . . .*

The gun held a thirty-shot magazine, and Harmon let it all go. Shay heard screaming from the party and half stood to look over the rail as Harmon slammed a second magazine into the gun tossing the first one overboard.

As he lifted the gun to his shoulder, they heard another gun, not far away, and several slugs banged off the shipping containers overhead.

Harmon said, "Sonofabitch, hold on. . . ." Moving in a crouch, he stepped to the corner of the pile of shipping containers and peeked toward the stern of the ship. Three stories up, silhouetted in a lit window at the ship's control level, he saw a man with a rifle. He said, "Trying to push our heads down. He'll see us if we go over the side."

"So—"

Before Shay could ask the question, Harmon stepped from behind the container stack and fired a dozen shots at the control level. Glass shattered, a man cried out, and the ship began to drift. "Get ready to jump!" Harmon called. He fired a half-dozen more shots at the control level and then emptied the gun at a safe angle past the party onshore. The party had dissolved in chaos, people running, screaming, chairs tipping over, the band members abandoning their instruments and jumping down from the stage to run for cover.

Harmon heaved the rifle over the side and said, "Go! Go now!"

The water was a long way down, and dark and forbidding, but there was no choice. Shay got X's paws on the rail, then squatted on the rail herself, and Harmon snarled, "Go!" and she launched herself and pulled X with her. X followed without resistance, over the rail and fifteen or twenty feet down into the murky water. She gasped a breath before she hit, went under, kicked back up. The water probably wasn't too cold, if you were measuring with a thermometer, but it felt like ice, a shock, and her clothes tried to drag her under—her jeans and her sneakers.

Shay focused on pulling in the life ring and holding on to X. When she had the ring, she lifted it up over X's head, and the dog put his paws on the inside of it, as though he'd done it before. She remembered Harmon's direction about her jacket and pulled it off, threw it over the ring, and, wrapping it around X's head, said, "Okay, boy, you're okay. . . ."

The ship was nearly past them, and she looked for anyone tracking them from the outside rail, but it was difficult to see much of anything in the dark. A hand caught her shoulder, and she turned to Harmon, who sputtered and asked, "You okay?"

"Clothes want to pull me down," she said. The ship was past them now, heading under the bridge.

"We'll be hypothermic in five minutes, we gotta get moving toward shore. Kick. Like a sidestroke . . ."

"Look at the ship! Look at the ship! It's gonna hit the bridge!"

It didn't sound like a car accident.

It sounded like the world's biggest bass drum, and then there was a screeching, scraping howl as the ship's metal hull bit into a concrete abutment under the bridge.

The sound seemed to go on forever, and they treaded water for a moment, then Harmon said, "Gotta swim, gotta swim."

There was no current. Shay launched into a sidestroke so she could tow X along in the ring, but they'd gone less than a dozen yards when the dog ducked his head beneath the rim of the ring and swam away from them, directly toward shore. She lost sight of him and was now thinking about his robotic hind legs: would the electronics Singular had placed in his brain and body short out in water?

She shouted, "X, go faster, faster!"

• • •

Two minutes, three minutes. Harmon was right about hypothermia. He was pushing his ring next to hers, and he asked again, "How are you?"

"Cold . . . ," she said, and her teeth chattered.

"I'm going to push down on my side of your ring. You push down your side, and when it's under, heave yourself up on top of it, if you can."

"Okay . . ."

They both heaved, and Shay managed to crawl on top of the ring . . . almost lost it sideways, but righted herself.

Harmon: "Now just a breaststroke . . ."

"How are you?" Shay asked.

"I've got more bulk than you, so I won't get hypothermic as fast. . . . Keep paddling. . . ."

They heard X bark. Shay lifted her head and caught sight of what looked like a gray shadow, but he was on his feet, out of the water. She kicked harder. Two minutes later, Harmon's feet touched bottom, and he said, "I'm walking." Shay rolled off the ring, clambered up the rocky shore, and hugged her wet dog.

Shay called quietly, "Twist?"

There was no one to meet them.

Shay checked her jacket pocket. The phone inside seemed dry, and when she hit the switch, it lit up.

She called Twist. Before she could say anything, he asked, "Where are you? Are you hurt?"

"We're under the bridge. . . ."

"We realized we'd be trapped if we came in too close. Head out toward the street. You gotta sneak past the marina, then across an access road, past a whole bunch of boats in a parking lot. There are a lot of people from the dance wandering around. If the cops show up before you get out, get in among the boats and keep moving toward the street. Call when you get there. We're parked behind a building a couple of blocks away. That's the best we could do. You gotta hurry; about a million cops are gonna be here in the next five minutes. Man, that ship hit the bridge, and now everybody in the world's on the way. . . ."

"We're coming."

Harmon took Shay's arm, said urgently, "Look!"

She turned back to the ship, saw a body hurtling toward the water, then another.

"Oh my God! They're throwing people off!"

"No, no. I think they're the Singular guys, getting off the ship," Harmon said. "They know what's about to happen. That means they're gonna be right here with us. Let's go. . . ."

They jogged out toward the street. Off to the side, they could hear people yelling for help: the partygoers.

There was enough ambient light to make good time, and Shay held on to her phone and kept X at her side. They ran past the marina, across the access road, and straight on. There were sirens, lots of them.

The first cop cars turned before they got to the boat lot, rolling down toward the marina where the party had been. Another pair were on the ramp going up the bridge. . . .

"It's happening!" Shay said. "It's happening! They're going for the ship!"

"Keep moving," Harmon said.

Then a police car turned down the road toward them, its lights sweeping past as they dodged into a cluster of cabin cruisers.

The car stopped, blocking the street. "Did they see us?" Shay whispered.

"I don't know—I think we were covered," Harmon said.

The police car idled where it was for another minute, then started rolling toward them. Moving slowly. They faded farther back into the cover of the boats. A minute later, the car was past them, continuing toward the water. They'd been squatting behind a boat trailer, and now they began threading their way through the parked boats again.

Harmon called quietly, "Stay away from the bows of these boats—there'll be a trailer hitch out in front of some of them. If you hit one running, you'll break your leg."

Fifty yards more, then Harmon slowed and grabbed Shay's damp shirt. "Getting close to the street. We need to call Twist again."

"Not yet," Shay whispered, and pointed at X, his ears erect, his muzzle sniffing the air. "Somebody's coming behind us."

Harmon turned, listened, then pushed her shoulder down. "Lie flat. Keep the dog quiet. It's one of the guys from the boat."

They froze in place, beneath a boat, with an axle between them and the approaching man. He'd chosen the same route they'd taken, for the same reasons: it was open enough to move through quickly and still provided cover.

The man kept coming, and just as he got to the boat, he suddenly dropped into a crouch, looking ahead . . . and then his eyes turned toward them.

Harmon said, "Freddy, I'm pointing a pistol at your head."

"Goddammit, Harmon, that was you, wasn't it? Back on the ship."

"Yeah. Where're you going?" Harmon asked.

"A long way from here. I'm done," Freddy said. "So are most of the other guys. Ginsburg and me are hooking up and heading for Mexico and then maybe farther south, the tri-border. Maybe go to Africa—there're jobs there."

"How'd that happen?"

"The ass is falling off the company," Freddy said. "We've all been talking about you—and what you told Butch and Jim. We think you're probably right. When we signed up, we didn't know what we were getting into, but it's getting pretty clear now. There's some bad shit going on, and Thorne's lying to us. That research ain't legal, no way."

"No way," Harmon agreed. "You got a ride out of here?"

"No, we're running. Man, I walked through Baghdad in the dark, right in the middle of the war, so I won't get caught here . . . if you let me go."

"You got a gun with you?"

"A nine."

"Keep it in your pocket. You try to ambush us farther up the line . . . well, we got the dog with us. He can see in the dark and he'll tear you to pieces. I'm telling you, Freddy, he'll kill you."

"I'm not messing with you anymore. I'm out of it."

"Go, then," Harmon said.

Freddy started to move away, then hesitated and said, "I appreciate this, letting me go. So I'll give you something. There's another Singular base that you guys don't know about. It's in the desert, a little less than two hours by private jet, southeast of San Francisco. There's a good private landing strip and some nice ranch houses, a little lake with some bass in it, but not much else. I flew it four times as security and to pass out drinks and keep an eye on the passengers. I got the feeling it was in Arizona, east of Phoenix, or maybe New Mexico? The passengers going down were okay, but coming back up, most of them had had some kind of surgery done on their heads."

Shay asked, "Old people? Rich people?"

Freddy said, "Didn't see you back there. You the chick who kicked Thorne?"

"Yes."

Freddy chuckled. "He is *really* pissed. You won't want to spend any time with him, you know, in private."

"I wasn't planning to," Shay said. "So, old people? Rich people?"

"Yeah, I'd say so. Wrinkles and bling."

"Who were the pilots?" Harmon asked.

"Two guys named Walt and Barry. No last names. Got a feeling they flew for the agency at some point. Hey—gotta go. You guys take care. And, honey, stay away from Thorne."

They saw no one else as Shay forged a path to the far edge of the lot. She signaled a stop with her free hand, and she, Harmon, and X crouched behind the last boat so she could call Twist.

"Come now. Last boat."

"Coming."

At that moment a white SUV skidded to a stop twenty-five yards away. A door popped open and a man got out. He moved like a military operative—like Harmon, like Thorne, like Freddy—and rather than try to hide himself, he shouted boldly into the dark, "Pickup! Pickup! This is Red! Pickup! Pickup! This is Red!"

Harmon hissed to Shay: "Stop Twist."

Shay called Twist back and said, "That SUV in the street is Singular. . . ."

"Got it. Too late to stop now. I'll blow right past him."

Five seconds later, Twist went by in the Jeep.

Red glanced at the passing Jeep. When it was out of sight, a man came jogging down the road, in the open, and jumped into the SUV. Then another showed up, and a third. Sirens were getting closer, lots of them, and all different flavors: cop cars, ambulances, fire trucks.

Red was still in the street, shouting, "This is Red! Gotta go, gotta go!"

Another man broke cover, slid into the SUV, and shouted, "I'm the last one!"

They heard Red ask, "Where's Ginsburg and Freddy?"

"They're running on their own. So's Butch."

"Ah, shit." Red got into the SUV and took off. At the first chance, he turned a corner and was gone.

A moment later, Twist called and said, "I'll pick you up where the SUV was. Thirty seconds."

The Jeep was moving fast, but pulled over at the last second. They piled into the back, led by X.

As Harmon yanked the door shut, Twist said, "Cops everywhere. We've gotta get out of here."

Shay leaned forward and placed her hands on her brother's shoulders and murmured, "Fenfang." She didn't know what else to say.

"They shot her. She was running right to them and they killed her," Odin said bitterly.

"I'm sorry," Shay said, and pressed her face into his neck. "I'm so, so sorry."

"How did this happen to her?" Odin asked. "She lived in China. She was going to college and was living her life, and she ends up in

America, with her head cut open like some worthless lab rat. . . . How did that *ever* happen?"

"There's no making sense of it," Twist said as he cranked the wheel and took them onto a well-lit boulevard. "Stop trying, all right? You gotta stop trying. . . ."

"I've got her blood on my hands," Odin said.

"No, you don't," Twist said sharply. "This isn't your fault."

"Oh God," Shay said. "He does."

Odin had spoken literally: he was holding his palms out in front of him, and splotches of dried blood were visible as they passed under the streetlamps. "We'll stop somewhere so you can clean up," Shay said.

Harmon had already set his pistol on the floor and was pulling off his wet jacket. He held it over the seat to Odin and said, "This will work."

Odin took it. Then he squeezed some water out of a sleeve, rubbed his hands together, and choked back a sob.

The Chinese prisoner who'd lost the knowledge of his own name was hiding in a hold when the ship hit the bridge. He'd heard the gunfire and, in the silence following it, mumbled a vaguely remembered Buddhist mantra for the well-being of the two Americans and their dog. He'd been crouching, listening, and the impact sent him sprawling.

He waited, then crept to the top of the stairway and peeked out. The ship hit the piling again and began scraping along it. He stepped out onto the deck and looked up: he was peering at the bottom of a bridge. He could hear sirens in the distance.

That, he thought, could only be good. He ran light-footed back down the stairway to the first hold and turned the steel latch on the door. The door popped open, and he found a cluster of prisoners, now silent, staring at him. They looked, he thought, like gulag prisoners in some old 1970s film.

"We are free," he said in Mandarin.

They didn't understand.

He repeated himself in the elementary Korean he'd picked up in captivity. Some of them shuffled forward, feet dragging. Others just stood and stared, eyes like owls'; one had his arms extended, shaking with palsy. Two of them began whimpering. *Zombies:* that's what their captors had called them, and the Chinese prisoner understood the word. And he agreed, though it applied to him as well. . . .

Five minutes later, twenty cops were looking down at them from the bridge. The ship was still out of control, but there wasn't much current, and it turned slowly in the water, repeatedly bumping into the bridge pilings. Fifteen minutes after the first impact, two small coast guard boats roared toward the ship, coming from the inland side of the bridge. A moment later, the Chinese prisoner went to the rail as a coastguardsman called up with a megaphone, "Ship's captain! Ship's captain!"

He shouted, "Nobody here! Nobody here!"

"We will board you. We will board you!"

"Yes!"

A grapple-and-pulley device flew over the rail at the middle of the ship and hooked on. The Chinese prisoner bent over the rail and saw that the pulley rope was attached to a ladder, which was being drawn up the side of the ship. Soon a coastguardsman came over the rail with a gun. He didn't point it at the freakish group in surgical scrubs now clustered by the rail . . . but he didn't point it far from them, either.

He called, "Who are you? What's going on?"

The Chinese prisoner called, "We are . . ." He groped for a word.

Then he shouted, "We are slaves! We are slaves! They cut our heads off! They put wires in our heads!"

"What?"

More coastguardsmen swarmed the ship, and two went up to the control deck, restarted the ship's engines, and carefully edged it away from the bridge to a pier a few hundred yards away, where they dropped the gangway to the pier's deck. They were met by a group of local police officers, several Border Patrol agents, and more coastguardsmen, along with TV reporters from a half-dozen television stations.

The word *slaves* had gone viral on the police and media networks: the Chinese prisoner had chosen exactly the right word to get attention.

The TV stations were also alerted that another "slave" had been shot to death and was at an area hospital, and newsrooms around the Bay Area were scrambling to get reporters on the scene.

The first of the various law enforcement officers up the gangway confronted the experimental subjects, who were loosely watched by four armed coastguardsmen. An overweight, sloppily uniformed police captain looked at the men and what he thought were, on second and third take, a couple of women, bronze studs sticking from their scalps, and asked hoarsely, "What happened to you?"

The Chinese man stepped forward and said, "I only speak the English. We are took from our lives and made to experiment with. They shaved our hair and they drilled holes in our heads and they put wires inside. . . ."

"Who's 'they'?"

"The North Korean people and the American doctors."

The police captain looked at the ranking coast guard officer and said, "I don't know a lot about your ranks. I was in the army, myself. But you're, like, a lieutenant?"

The lieutenant nodded and said, "Yeah."

"I'll tell you what, Lieutenant, this is way, way above our pay grades. We need to get some serious shit down here and we need to get it quick. I'm hearing there's another one up at the hospital, shot to death. As far as we know, the water could be full of bodies. . . ."

The lieutenant raised a hand to quiet the captain and asked the Chinese man, "The people who ran the ship, where did they go?"

He made a diving motion with one hand and said, "They jump."

The captain turned his head toward his shoulder radio and said, "Raul, we probably got some runners up onshore. Get some guys out there to drag the area."

Back to the coast guard, happy not to lead, he asked: "What do we do next?"

The lieutenant said, "I think we get these people to a hospital . . . one with a security ward."

The captain said, "Good. That's good. I'll get some guys with guns to take them, make sure nothing gets screwed up. And this whole ship is a crime scene. We gotta nail it down."

A Border Patrol agent asked, "What about the media?"

They all looked toward shore, where the media vans were gathered. "Not much we can do about that," the lieutenant said. "No comment from any of us, a press conference to be announced later."

"But how do we get these . . . subjects . . . off the ship?" the agent asked. "Without the media climbing all over them?"

The police captain looked at the mutilated people, who were clearly frightened as they huddled in their tight little group. "You know what? Somebody needs to get dropped in the shit for whatever the hell is going on here. I say we walk them right by the cameras. Screw anybody who has a problem with that."

The lieutenant said, "Yes." And, "I'll back you up if there's any fallout, Captain. I mean, look at them. . . . How *did* they get those things in their heads?"

The captain turned and said to the Chinese man, unconsciously speaking in American pidgin, "We take you hospital, okay?"

"Okay," the man said. "We need hospital. We all need hospital."

"But you're okay now; you're safe," he said.

They didn't look safe. They didn't look happy, or sad, or okay, or safe. They looked like zombies. They looked like something terrible had been done to them. The Chinese prisoner told his fellow prisoners, in his poor Korean, "We go now."

The group shuffled toward the gangway, all clinging together. Owl-eyed and blank-eyed, their feet dragging. One of them groaned, then another started.

A blitzkrieg of video camera lights hit them, and then pretty much everyone . . . screamed.

4

With Twist at the wheel of the Jeep, and Odin, Shay, Harmon, and X crowded inside, they fled west on Highway 4, led by Danny Dill in the Volvo and trailed by Cruz in the Toyota pickup. Cade, calling from Danny's house in Arcata, fed them directions.

"We really whacked the hornet's nest," Harmon said. "I gotta give you credit, Shay: it's possible this is gonna drag them down."

"Not soon enough," Shay said, grim-faced. "Fenfang and West, both dead."

Harmon hung his head. Marcus West had worked intelligence for him at Singular until learning the truth about the company's research. The young former soldier had risked everything to help Shay, Twist, Cade, and Cruz free Odin and Fenfang from a secret facility, only to be shot dead by Singular's head of security, Thorne.

Twist glanced at Harmon in the rearview mirror and sensed a regret that would plague the man for the rest of his days. Twist said: "We need to decide where we're going. If we go back to Danny's, we'll probably be safe, but it's not the best place to operate from now that Singular's hurt. It'd be good if we had access to the media."

"Like in L.A.?" Shay said.

Twist asked Odin: "What do you think?"

He shrugged, withdrawn. "I don't care."

Harmon said, "Whatever happens in the next few days, Singular still has access to a lot of police assets. Believe me, we hacked into everything you can imagine. If they picked up one of our license plates during the night, they could track us through police license-plate registries all the way back to Arcata. The problem there is, if they sent in a bunch of guys like Jim or Stan—"

"Who?" Twist asked.

"Navy SEALs," Shay said. "Tell you later."

"Anyway, they send in people like that, Danny's place is so isolated that they could take us all out and disappear before we could call for help," Harmon said.

"What we need is a fort," Twist said. "I *got* a fort."

Shay: "The Twist Hotel."

"To get us out of there, they'd have to massacre about sixty kids," Twist said. "They really don't need that right now. Once we're there, we'd have five-minute access to the biggest media array in the world. People I know. We can operate."

Odin spoke up: "We'll need to get word to Fenfang's family."

Twist nodded and said, "There's a Chinese consulate in L.A., I've seen it. They can help with that."

Harmon asked, "Where would I stay?"

"We got room," Twist said.

Shay said, "I'll call Cade—see what he thinks."

When she got Cade on the phone, he said, "Man, cracked ribs or not, I'd ride a rodeo bronc if it'd carry me back to L.A. Work it out."

They stopped to use the restroom and get snacks and discuss the approach. Cruz called a friend and offered a thousand dollars of Twist's money to check out the Twist Hotel and let them know if it was safe. A half-dozen Sureños from Cruz's brother's set would filter through the neighborhood around the hotel, talking to business owners, checking for watchers, either from law enforcement agencies or Singular.

Danny called Cade and gave him complicated instructions for how to set the alarm systems on his house, along with a long list of things to bring with him. Cade would pack up all their stuff and drive to L.A. in the truck Harmon had left there.

They were energized. They were going home.

They arrived at dawn.

The Twist Hotel had six parking places, three of them in use—almost nobody who lived there could afford a car. Three was just the right number for the refugees from the San Francisco fight. They pulled in one after another, and Twist got out and looked at the old pink stucco building and said, "Ahhh."

There was a door to the hotel off the parking lot and Twist had the key, but instead of going in the short way, he led the group around to the front, where he bounded up the stairs and pushed through the front door, the one with the taped-up bullet hole in the glass, walked into the lobby, and shouted: "I'm home!"

At that time of the morning, there were only a handful of people around, mostly teenagers headed for jobs in the hotel kitchen, but they came running to greet Twist and the others. Then Twist led the way to the front desk and said, "I need rooms for my friends."

"Hope you don't need too many," said the kid on desk duty. "We only got four empties."

"We only need three," Twist said. He got keys for Harmon, Danny, and Odin and then said to the kid, "I'm calling a general meeting here in the lobby at one. Put up a poster."

"I can do that."

And to the rest of them: "I'm going up to my studio. Somebody show Harmon and Odin around."

"Wait," the kid said, and came out from behind the desk to hand Harmon, Odin, and Danny a flyer that went to every new guest. On it were the ten Twist Hotel Rules, meant to keep the peace in a building with sixty street kids—everything from "Nothing That Attracts the Cops" to "No Ringtones (vibrate or die)." Harmon rubbed his forehead, reading and rereading rule number one: "No Guns (check knives at front desk)."

"Man, I gotta keep my piece," Harmon said.

Twist snatched the flyer from Harmon's hands, crumpled it in a ball, and pitched it over his shoulder.

"Rules apply to anyone under thirty—you're good," he said. "But, Miss Shay . . . your knife, please."

Shay took her blade from her waistband and handed it over to Twist, who dropped it in a holding drawer already crowded with knives and various improvised sharp weapons.

"Anything else?" Twist asked, eager to get up to his room for a shower.

Harmon said, "Ah . . . I'm not the only one packing."

Twist smote his forehead at the oversight and held out his hand again to Shay. She rolled her eyes and produced the pistol. Twist walked over to Cruz, waited again with open hand, and collected the .45 that came out of his belt.

Twist turned back to Harmon, handed him the weapons. "Get a gun safe and keep 'em in your room."

Harmon nodded, and Twist went on his way.

Shay said to Harmon, "Narc."

Danny had lived in the hotel as a young runaway and knew his way around, so he took Odin up the stairs to their rooms on the second floor. Shay and Cruz took Harmon to his room on the third floor and explained about the showers down the hall.

"Given the situation, I hate to leave my gun in the room," Harmon said. "You're always in the can with your pants around your ankles when the bad guys come through the door."

"There are private toilets and shower booths. You'll be all right," Cruz said. "Take the gun with you, if you're worried. But . . . wrap it in a towel, or something."

"Will do," Harmon said.

"I'm gonna crash. See you at the meeting," Shay said.

Shay shared a room on the fifth floor with a girl named Emily. Cruz was another flight up; he had a single. In the stairwell, Cruz took Shay's hand and said, "Now that we're home, it'd be nice to spend some time with you. In my room. Alone."

She kissed him on the angle of his jaw. "If Twist found out, he'd have to kick us out. . . . You know, rule number two."

"That 'No Sex' thing is mostly . . . propaganda . . . for the younger kids."

"We'll talk about it," Shay said.

"Talk?"

"Shhh . . ." She put a finger across his lips. "I'm exhausted. We'll talk about breaking the rules tonight."

They spent a few minutes sealing the promise, then Shay waved him off. She rattled her keys in the lock and walked through the outer room, which was crammed like a thrift store—Emily supported herself by finding and selling good used furniture and clothing—and into the bedroom, where she found Emily sitting up in bed with a genuine antique Louisville Slugger baseball bat in her hands.

"It's *you*—you made it back," Emily said. "And you're all right!"

"Maybe a little better than that," Shay said, still feeling Cruz's touch.

They all were back downstairs before one, where most of the hotel's teenage population was waiting. There was a mishmash of styles, from simple wash-faded T-shirts and jeans, to full-on punk with lots of leather and piercings, to dorky fast-food uniforms. All the kids had the windburned look that came from being on the street, and there were a dozen skateboards sitting around.

Twist showed up right at one o'clock, stood on a table, and twirled his cane, but before he could say a word, a long-haired skater said, "The old dude's got a gun."

Everybody looked at Harmon, and Twist said, "Yeah, he's our new security guard. Give me any shit and he'll shoot you."

Then Twist caught the kids up on the story as it went so far. To Shay, standing at the back of the crowd with X and Cruz, it hardly sounded real, though she'd lived it.

Twist was saying, "I checked the Net and the story has gone national. We're bringing the bastards down. We've got more work to do, but instead of hiding, we need to be at the hotel. We don't think they'll come for us here again, but we need your help. You're our security blanket.

"If strangers show up looking for us, we've got to know right away. If they try to push through, slow them down. If they're cops, don't fight them, but confuse them. Everybody run, screaming, in every direction, up and down the stairs, pull the fire alarm. Slow them down so we can hide or get out.

"We *don't* want anyone to get hurt. That's the big thing," Twist said. "If guys show up with guns, run, clog up the hallways, but don't fight. Everybody use their phones to take pictures. If they get violent, everybody call 911 . . . and tell them that the cops are coming."

One of the kids said, "Twist! You oughta keep the elevator up at the top and lock it out. You don't let any of us use it anyway. That way, they'd have to go up the stairs, and we could build something on the stairs to screw 'em up."

"That's not bad, Sookie, that's not bad," Twist said. "That's the kind of thinking we need here. . . ."

They talked and plotted for an hour, and when they started repeating themselves for the third time, Twist ended the meeting and said, "All the people who came down with me—Shay, Harmon, Cruz, Danny, Odin—let's meet now in the belfry."

The belfry—Twist's studio—was on the hotel's top floor, which they reached in the creaking old freight elevator. On the way up, Twist said, "We're all over the news. Or at least, the prisoners from the boat are." He looked at Odin. "And Fenfang is. Cade released the movie we made with Fenfang telling her story. He identifies her as the woman in the hospital, the woman shot last night. The video's been picked up everywhere. . . ."

Lou, a tall Ethiopian woman who managed the hotel when Twist was away, was actually streaming the video when they walked in. Fenfang was shown sitting on a balcony outside Danny's home in

Northern California, the forested background carefully shot out of focus to conceal the location. She'd taken off the wig she'd worn since her escape from Singular, revealing the golden electrical connections sticking out of her scalp. An X-ray made by a doctor friend of Twist's showed the thousands of wires and neural devices that had been implanted in her brain.

"My cousin Liko and I were captured in North Korea, where we were traveling with an American missionary man," she said. "After some days, they took us out of the jail to a hospital, where they kept us in more jail rooms. Then they came and got me and took me to a surgery room. There were Americans speaking English, and also Koreans. They put me to sleep, and when I woke up, I had these wires in my brain. They kept me in the hospital jail for many days, I don't know how many, then they took me back to the surgery room. When I woke up, I did not have new wounds on my head, but I had a foreign voice in my mind, the voice of U.S. senator Charlotte Dash. They put Senator Dash in my mind so that when she died, she could live again with my body. . . ."

Odin, propped against a wall, was watching and then closing his eyes, not knowing which was worse.

Shay said to Twist, "What's Singular had to say?"

Twist shook his head. "Nothing. They haven't said a single thing. Neither has Dash."

"Which means they've lost some control," Harmon said. "They should be out with a statement by now. Denying everything. They should be releasing their cover story about Fenfang being a spy, they should be trying to discredit us."

"How do you discredit a boatload of zombies?" Shay asked.

Harmon said, "The good old two-dude defense."

"What's that?"

Twist said, " 'Some other dude done it.' "

Harmon: "Yes. Thorne set up that ship, and I'd bet my life that there's not a single document you could trace back to Singular."

Twist turned to Odin, a speculative look in his eyes, and Odin asked, "What?"

"You're gonna hate me for saying it, but this video needs a postscript—of you, telling people about Fenfang being shot," Twist said.

"How's that gonna help?" Odin asked, his face clenched and his arms starting to flap, as happened when he was angry. "She's six hours away from us, in a hospital with no one to do right by her. Singular will probably figure out a way to steal her body. . . ."

"Take a breath," Shay said to her brother. "We'll get Twist's media contacts to get us some information on what's happening at the hospital, but right now, Twist is right. There needs to be someone who gets out there and talks about how Fenfang died trying to help other prisoners, before the bullshit starts."

She turned to Twist. "You know what else? Odin should make an appeal to the Chinese government for them to do something. . . ."

"Yeah, he should tell them that Fenfang was one of their people and she was kidnapped and operated on and then shot," Twist said. "Murdered. How many Chinese people are there, a billion? More than that? You get it going viral there and there'll be no stopping it. There'll be echoes all over the world."

Odin looked away, and back, and then to Twist. "Maybe I could do something."

"Gotta be soon," Twist said. "Gotta be when the story is hot."

Cruz said, "Cade should be back later this afternoon. We could shoot it then."

Odin looked up at the video screen, where Fenfang was frozen. Tears began running down his face, but he made no noise, just watched the Chinese girl he'd fallen in love with. *Talk about what Singular did to her.*

Odin said: "I'll do it."

5

Senator Charlotte Dash walked away from her jet with an assistant running after her, the assistant carrying a leather legal bag the size of a suitcase. A half-dozen other planes were parked at the edge of the private landing strip, four of them pure jets, like Dash's, two of them smaller propeller planes. The pilots would be waiting in staff quarters, on the edge of a man-made lake.

As they climbed into a waiting Hummer, Dash asked the driver, "Is everybody here, Clive?"

"We have one more plane incoming. Ian Wyeth. He's forty minutes out."

"Damn it, he should be here already. Take me to the bunkhouse. I'll wait there."

"Yes, ma'am."

To her assistant, a twenty-eight-year-old Harvard grad with the skills to run a Fortune 500 company, Dash said, "Candice, you'll wait in the bunkhouse for me. My meeting at the Big House shouldn't take more than a couple of hours."

"Of course. I'll work on the infrastructure estimates."

"Do that." Dash looked out the window at the desert mountains that overhung the ranch. "I should sell this place. Never did like it down here, out in the sticks. Do some research, see what a sale would involve. Don't call any real estate people, though. I don't want people snooping around."

"On it," Candice said.

The bunkhouse was actually a guesthouse built to look like a log cabin, and at five thousand square feet, with four bedrooms, six bathrooms, and a great room full of mounted animal heads, it was what most ordinary people would have considered a mansion.

Dash led the way in, the door opening when a sensor picked up her key card. While Candice settled in with a stack of papers and a laptop at a massive library table, Dash took the elevator to the second floor, showered, and then worked on her makeup and her shoulder-length blond flip. She'd learned that when the shit was hitting the fan, it paid to *look* cool and put together.

The driver called when Wyeth's plane was on approach. Dash said, "When you have him in the car, bring him here, and I'll ride up to the Big House with him."

Ian Wyeth was a neurosurgeon, a tall, thin man with short gray hair and gold-rimmed glasses who usually wore pale suits and Hermès ties. He'd flown his own plane in from St. Louis. Dash waited in the cool air inside the door until she saw the Hummer pull up, then called to Candice, "I'm going! I'll call you when we're done!"

Inside the Hummer, Dash told Clive to give them a minute alone, then asked Wyeth, "Have you seen all the videos these people are putting out?"

"Yes. Disturbing."

"You're *disturbed*? They've told everyone about the taps on my head, shown the world an actual close-up of the place where you drilled a hole in my skull and capped it like a manhole cover! I've spent my morning giving the media the runaround, but what do I do when the majority leader asks me about it? Or the president, for that matter?"

Wyeth's expression was utterly calm. "Show them the top of your head," he said, and brushed a piece of lint off his shoulder. "I worked it out on the way down. Do you still have your wigs? Either here or back in Santa Fe?"

"I've got them in both places, but I don't need—"

"Listen. We shave your head. I can remove the taps themselves, while leaving the leads in place. I'll simply cut the tap head off, curl the wire and tuck it into the incision so we can reaccess it. As for the 'manhole cover,' I'll remove it and plug it with some flesh-toned silicone. Then I'll show you how to use a special makeup designed to cover up scars. You'll just need a touch of it and it'll all be invisible. I've even worked out how you'll deal with the media."

Dash relaxed. Wyeth was one of the smartest people in the research group. She said, "Tell me."

He explained, and she said, "You're sure about the makeup?"

"I've seen it on hundreds of people. It'll be just fine. I brought some with me and you can try it before you leave."

"If you're right, you might've saved my hide," Dash said. "This business out on the coast is going viral, and fast. . . . The whole project is at risk."

The surgeon looked at her, didn't believe it. "When I talked to Cartwell, I got the impression that he still thinks it can be contained."

"He's wrong," Dash said, blue eyes hardening as they spoke of

Micah Cartwell, Singular's longtime CEO. "These people, these crazies, they know how the Internet and the media work. They paraded these experimental subjects out in front of uncontrolled media, and then they dumped that interview with the Chinese woman—there isn't any question that she was shot to death—and the whole thing is so peculiar and dramatic that it won't just go away. Now the Chinese are asking questions about the woman who was killed. . . . I run the Intelligence Committee, for chrissakes. You can see where it's going. It's a feeding frenzy."

"Maybe Cartwell should be . . . replaced," Wyeth suggested.

"There have been conversations along those lines. Actually, Ian, we're talking about moving the whole operation offshore. You know, Honduras, El Salvador, Guatemala. We could buy protection in any of those places, to do anything, and in terms of accessibility, you could fly there almost as fast as you could fly here."

"Varek mentioned that to me. He says Honduras has an old military base with some appeal. . . ."

"We'll go over it in the meeting," Dash said, and motioned Clive back to the vehicle for the quarter-mile drive. "When do you want to do . . . the thing . . . with the taps?"

"Right after the meeting. Take an hour."

If the bunkhouse was a mansion, the Big House was practically a resort. Twenty thousand square feet, with an indoor swimming pool and theater. Most important, it even had its own surgery center, secreted behind a false wall.

Dash led the way inside and all the way to the back, to a soundproof and bug-proof conference room, where thirteen people waited in leather wingback chairs like thrones, with coffee or soft drinks and yellow legal pads.

The principals of Singular.

The people who drove it.

All but a handful were well known, at least to the American public; of those who weren't so well known, one was a North Korean illegally in the United States, two were American government operatives— one with the Central Intelligence Agency and one with the National Security Agency—and two were executives with Singular. The rest were entrepreneurs: to a person, billionaires.

The best-known attendee was there electronically: the vice president of the United States looked down from a six-foot-wide video screen.

Dash sat down and took the bull by the horns: "Let's see the hands of those who think this current situation might be recoverable."

Four hands went up: two of the businessmen, plus the two public faces of Singular's medical research company, which gave the immortality project cover—its CEO and president, Micah Cartwell, and chief counsel, Imogene "Jimmie" Stewart.

Cartwell interjected: "This ship is a manageable problem, as we have no demonstrable connection to it. We operated it through a shell company. . . ."

A billionaire named Iront, big in tech: "But what about the employees? There are a number of employees who know about the connection, and some of them are not reliable—or are no longer reliable. I understand the men who ran the ship have scattered, but the news feeds say that they left behind DNA and fingerprints, which are being explored now. . . . Are you saying that none will turn state's evidence? I find that unlikely."

Stewart: "We are working to contain that right now. . . ."

One of the four women present said, "The FBI has been asked to reinvestigate the laboratory at Sacramento, where there are dozens of employees, including many who must have encountered the experimental subjects. . . ."

The man from the NSA said, "The Chinese government has requested access to the body of this woman Fenfang. . . ."

A software genius named Varek Royce, startlingly thin, his hair ragged, with oversized glasses stuck to his face, was sitting in a wheelchair and was further strapped into an exoskeleton from his waist up. The exoskeleton made it possible for him to move his arms and hands.

Nothing, however, was wrong with his voice. He was looking up at Vice President Lawton Jeffers, showing not a whit of the deference the vice president usually received.

"Goddammit, Lawton, I've got more than a billion dollars in this project, and it has been fucked up! Fucked up! You were supposed to cover us. I've got fifty million bucks into your career, and what have you done for us? I got two years, then I'm gone. I figured I was no better that fifty-fifty to get fully recorded, even when things were running good, and now this comes along. You are killing me. Really—killing me!"

Ian Wyeth broke in: "Our progress on the recording side is spectacular. We'll get you recorded. . . ."

"Yeah? And what are you gonna do when the whole structure comes down on top of your head?" Royce demanded. "What if *this* place gets busted? If anybody ever finds that little graveyard out back, Dr. Wyeth, *you* will be more constrained than I am—in a federal prison!"

"We gotta calm down and work through this," Jeffers said from the video screen.

The arguments continued and finally boiled down to a question from an exec named Cleverly, who faced Cartwell and demanded, "We've heard all the problems. They seem to be multiplying exponentially. Do you have any solution for this? Anything at all?"

Cartwell was sweating profusely. "Yes. Yes, we do, and it's under way. We are gearing up a major PR offensive, and we've contacted a number of lawyers to oppose any move by the FBI. We are planning executive action against these vandals, Shay Remby and her brother and the artist Twist. . . ."

An hour later, after a series of brutal exchanges, the meeting broke up. Stewart, who competed in triathlons on her weekends, hustled into the waiting silver Hummer feeling as spent as she ever had. Cartwell was a minute behind her. They settled into the seats, and she asked, "What do you think they're . . ."

But Cartwell gave a tiny shake of the head, and his eyes cut toward the front seat and the thick-necked driver.

Stewart continued, without a break, ". . . planning for Sarah's wedding? Is it going to be a big deal, or are they going to keep it in the family?"

"Given the groom, I think they'd be better off keeping it as close as possible," Cartwell said with a tight smile. There was no wedding; there was no groom. Nor would there be any more talk where the driver could hear it.

Three minutes later, they were at the airstrip, where the King Air twin-engine turboprop was waiting. The Hummer driver dropped them right at the plane's wingtip; the two pilots were already aboard.

Cartwell asked the head pilot, "How long into San Francisco?"

"Depends on how fast they can turn us around in Flagstaff," the copilot said. "Probably, with the turnaround, you better count on four hours."

"Do we really have to stop in Flagstaff?"

"That's procedure when we fly people in and out of here," the copilot said.

"Understood," Stewart muttered.

They were off the ground in five minutes, launching into the dusk, a few stars popping out overhead. Twenty minutes later, they could see the glow of Phoenix well off to the east, and an hour after they left New Mexico, they were turning for the approach into Flagstaff. Flagstaff went well, and they were off the ground again in thirty minutes.

The copilot came back and said, "That was quick. We'll get you into SFO in two hours, or a little more."

While Cartwell and Stewart flew on into the night, Wyeth carefully snipped the tap heads off the wires that led from Dash's scalp down into her brain. He did it while Dash sat upright in a comfortable chair in the surgery center.

"We'll just fashion some new taps that we can push onto the wire ends. Not a big deal," he said as he worked. Every time he snipped a tap, Dash felt a flash of pain, like an electric shock from a toaster. When he'd cut all the taps free, he touched the tiny holes with dabs of antiseptic.

"No chance I'm going to get a brain infection?" Dash asked.

"Oh, no. The wires lead to little plates that sit on your skull, under your scalp. This wire only leads from the surface of your scalp to the plate—there's no direct connection from the outside to the brain itself. That's completely sealed off. Worst case, you'll get something on your scalp that looks like a pimple. I doubt you'll even get that."

With the tap heads gone, Wyeth removed the quarter-sized cap Shay and Cruz had captured on film when they'd invaded Dash's house in Santa Fe. He injected a flesh-toned silicone and sculpted it smooth with his fingertips. Then he carefully shaved the senator's head with a safety razor until it was pale and white. "You'll have to do this every couple of days or so. You'll need some makeup mirrors."

"Got those," Dash said. "But I hate to lose my hair again. I hate it."

When her scalp was thoroughly shaved, Wyeth brought out a half-dozen small jars of makeup, and together they matched the makeup to the color of her scalp. "Just a tiny dab where each tap head was, and the cap. Then smooth it into the surrounding scalp."

When he was done, Dash stepped to a mirror, and with Wyeth holding a smaller mirror above her head so she could see the reflection all the way around, she said, "Well, I have to say, I can hardly believe it. I don't see *anything*."

"Nobody else can, either. You can take your nice, clean scalp and really stick them, if you play the media like I suggest. . . ."

Dash grunted. "I can do that." She took a last look and said, "This is gonna work."

Cartwell and Stewart hadn't talked much after takeoff. The meeting had been a nightmare, and it had been clear who was going to get blamed for the San Francisco ship fiasco. Cartwell had tried to defend himself, but the vice president had shouted him down, his face looming huge on the oversized video screen.

"Getting trashed on the national news! They're calling them

zombies! Zombies! The Chinese ambassador has a call in to the president. . . . He's asked me to look into the matter and advise him!"

He'd ended with a threat: "Micah, you get this straightened out or you're gone."

Cartwell had spent most of the flight to Flagstaff on the phone to Sync and Thorne, his heads of security now that Harmon had defected, demanding updates and action.

As they lifted out of Flagstaff, Stewart said, "I have to tell you, Micah, I've got to take care of myself. I'll try to stay on while we wind down the public side of the company, if that's what's going to happen. But I reserve the right to bail out at any time."

"We can fix this," Cartwell insisted. "There's no direct trail to us. . . ."

"Micah, they're gonna pick up some of those SEALs you hired, and they'll take them into separate rooms, and some of them are going to talk. When a single one of them talks, it's over. What I want, what I may *need* if I have to get my own attorney, is money. I want you to authorize a bonus. Let's say . . . three million. Call it hazard pay."

Cartwell was sitting across from Stewart and slightly ahead of her, so he had to continually turn his head to talk, and then he'd turn away in irritation. He couldn't stop thinking about the vice president. The way the man had eviscerated him in front of all the others. . . .

Stewart had been lifting her voice to make her points clear and to be heard over the engines—". . . probably not going to hold up . . . going to have to find another solution . . ."—when she heard herself shouting.

Not because she was speaking louder, but because the engine noise had suddenly quit.

Then more shouting, but this time from the cockpit: "Restart! Here's the sequence. . . ."

She could feel the plane falling beneath her: not quickly, but distinctly. From the cockpit: "Look for an alternate, look for an alternate. . . . Restarting sequence. . . ."

"No alternates! No alternates!"

Cartwell turned to her, ashen with fear, and said, "I'm afraid they've already found another solution."

Stewart looked out the window. They were over the mountains, she knew, but all was darkness, and they were falling faster now.

A few seconds later, a fireball lit up the mountains, but no one was there to see it.

6

Twist and Shay were laying out a painting on the studio floor in the early morning, the light over the mountains warming the windows. Shay was surprised that Twist wanted to paint right now, after all that had happened, but Twist said he needed the routine, color on canvas, something normal, so she showed up at nine o'clock and started mixing paint.

The others were involved with their own projects—Cade was back, and he and Odin and Danny had worked on the additions to the Fenfang video until long after midnight—or still asleep. "We've got to keep the pressure up, but we don't have to do it before noon. . . . I can get a few hours up here," Twist had said.

He'd even suggested another building-hung poster like the one on immigration he'd been doing when he and Shay first met: this one would be a stark picture of Fenfang, her head angled to show the mass of wiring on her scalp, an anguished look on her face.

Shay said, "Sometimes your imagination horrifies me."

Twist, fists on his hips, said, "Listen, you think Fenfang herself wouldn't have approved it if it helped pull these killers down?"

"I wasn't thinking of Fenfang. I was thinking of Odin."

Twist went back to the painting. "Yeah, you got a point. He's not as tough as Fenfang was. I don't know what to do about that."

They were still talking about it when Danny Dill burst into the studio. "Have you heard?"

Twist said, "Sounds bad. What happened?"

"Corporate propjet crashed in the Sierra Nevadas. Everybody's dead, they think, though they haven't gotten to the crash site. Singular's president and chief counsel, plus the pilots. It's on TV."

"Oh, shit . . ." Twist scratched his head. "Wait. I take that back. I don't know what it means."

"Let's get Harmon up here," Shay said, taking out her phone.

Harmon arrived five minutes later, wearing gym shorts, a T-shirt, running shoes, and his silver aviators. There were sweat spots on his chest and armpits, and a lump that looked like a gun under his loose T-shirt.

"What happened?"

Danny said, "Plane went down in the mountains. Micah Cartwell and Jimmie Stewart were on board."

"Oh boy. That's no accident," Harmon said. He took out his phone and pushed a couple of buttons.

"Who you calling?" Twist asked.

"My old boss Sync. I think he still might talk to me."

"Put it on speaker—I want to hear," Shay said.

The phone rang. Then, without a greeting, a man said, "Harmon. Tell me you didn't have anything to do with it."

"We didn't."

"Goddammit. Well, I didn't think you did, though I had to consider the possibility," Sync said. "I'm headed out. . . ."

"What's happening?"

"As close as I can tell, there's another executive layer that we didn't know about, and they're cleaning us out. Cartwell and Jimmie went down to a meeting at the New Mexico site. . . ."

"What's at that site?" Harmon asked.

"That's right—you didn't know about it. It's where the company does the implant surgery on the clients. I was never there myself. It was mostly a medical site—no computers, nothing to see. They'd bring in a neurosurgeon from St. Louis and some staff from Eugene. Anyway, there was a meeting there yesterday. Cartwell was all shook up; he called me from the plane. . . ."

Shay had grabbed a sheet of paper and scribbled a note that she now held up to Harmon's nose: "The place in the Southwest that Freddy was talking about!"

Harmon nodded. "You know who runs the new layer?" he asked Sync.

"No, but I can tell you something. Thorne was at the Sacramento lab sometime after midnight last night, after the crash, and he wasn't worried about Cartwell. He was taking care of business, I'm told, backing up the database to the cloud somewhere and then wiping the research computers. He must've known what was coming. When I heard that Cartwell and Stewart were dead, I tried calling Janes up in Eugene. Can't get him. Not at the lab, at his house, on his cell. So they've either taken him out, too, or moved him."

"Thorne's not smart enough to run a major op. . . ."

"No. He takes orders. From me, I thought, but now I don't know who he takes them from. Anyway, he was smart enough to fool us. So if you want to know who runs the next layer, you'll have to ask him. He's in and I'm outta here."

"You got a plan?" Harmon asked him.

"If there's nobody waiting for me. I got some cash. My girl'll take me. This'll be the last time I use this phone."

"Wait. Remember the belly dancer with the jelly bean? If you get out, leave me a note there. I might want to talk someday."

"I'll do that," Sync said. "Is the redhead listening to this?"

Harmon glanced at Shay, who'd cut her hair and colored it black after the Sacramento raid on Singular, and winked. "Yeah, she is."

Sync said, "Listen, girlie, you're pretty goddamned talented at this. Forget the tree-sitting animal rights shit. Find a job where you need brains and a gun. I'd hire you."

"Thanks a lot," Shay said.

Harmon said to Sync, "You don't know the half of it." And then, "Where is this place in New Mexico?"

"Gotta go," Sync said without answering, and he was gone.

"Tell us what all that means," Twist said.

"It means he's trying to run and hide," Harmon said. "We've got enough history that I kinda hope he makes it."

"What about his girl taking him in? Isn't she the first one they'll look for when they find out he's gone?" Danny asked.

"His girl's not a girl," Harmon said. "It's a sailboat, and it's in an obscure marina somewhere in the Bay Area. I'm the only one who knows about it, I think, and I don't know where it's at. A Pacific Seacraft 37, rigged for long-distance single-handed sailing. He could sail it to South America or Africa or Australia or the Med or anywhere else—if he can get it out in the Pacific."

"What about the belly dancer with the jelly bean?" Twist asked.

Harmon grinned. "*That's* a girl. She used to work in a tearoom in Aqaba, Jordan. Instead of having a ruby in her navel, she'd stick a red jelly bean in there. The place is actually a semi-undercover bar run by a bedouin who used to work for the Jordanian intelligence agency. This bedouin is sort of a mailbox for people like Sync."

"And you," Shay said.

Harmon nodded. "And me."

The whole group started assembling in the studio at noon.

"Fenfang's video is getting a lot of hits, and we've got messages from the FBI and the Chinese embassy, asking for information," Odin said. He and Cade had posted it on the revived Mindkill site—Cade was on offense against any moves by Singular to bring it down—and the two had also managed to funnel it through contacts to another dozen high-traffic pages.

"What do we say to them?" Shay asked.

Twist said, "I think we talk to the Chinese embassy, but not the FBI. I'd rather pick the agents we talk to, instead of talking to whatever agents come along."

"Sync said Thorne was putting the computer files up in the cloud somewhere," Harmon said. "That means that they're transferring the operation somewhere else."

Shay: "I bet it's going to New Mexico—wherever this place is that they do the surgeries on the rich people."

"They can't be talking about Dash's house in Santa Fe if it's a big-deal secret," Cruz said.

"No," Shay said. "That Freddy guy from the ship said it has its own airstrip and lake. Dash lives on a mountainside in a city."

"We can start looking for it," Odin said. "The plane that crashed—it must have filed a flight plan. Any idiot could get into the flight plan files."

The door at the end of the studio popped open, and Cade walked in. He had his grin going, but his face was still a mass of purple bruises, with more bruises on his neck, disappearing into his faded DON'T WORRY, BE HOPI T-shirt.

They gave him a quick summary of Sync's call, and Cade said, "I'd prefer to spend the afternoon sitting down—ribs, man—so I'll find the flight plan. The guy on TV said the plane was leaving Flagstaff. . . ."

Twist brought up the idea of another building-hung poster with Fenfang's face. "She's already somewhat viral, but if we could put together a really iconic image, something everybody could remember, like that Obama HOPE poster. . . ."

"Ah man, I *hate* that," Odin said.

Twist said, "Hey. We're not talking about some cheesy ad campaign. We're talking about a . . . a . . ."

"A tribute," Shay said.

"Yeah, that's what we're talking about," Twist said.

Odin said, "I've been commenting under a bunch of different names on all the big news sites, trying to keep things going, throwing out questions about Singular and Dash. . . ."

They agreed to keep pushing all the publicity buttons and suggested that they get all the computer-savvy hotel teens to get online to expand the commentary, under a variety of names, as Odin was doing. "If we do it right, we can make it look like thousands of people are demanding information. . . ."

• • •

Later in the afternoon, Twist called Shay and said, "Dash has called a press conference about the Fenfang video. C-SPAN's gonna have it live in twenty minutes."

"Don't know how the hell she can deny it," Shay said. "I'll get Odin."

They gathered under the big flat-panel TV in Twist's studio. Dash was five minutes late for the press conference, but when she showed up, she looked confident and ready.

She stepped up to a cluster of microphones and said, "You all know why I'm here. Some irresponsible animal rights radicals on the West Coast have released a video of a young woman who accuses me of stealing her brain, or some such nonsense. I really don't know what she means by that, I don't have any idea of what's going on, but I do have an idea of why she chose me: because she knows I wear a wig.

"How she found that out, I have no idea, although I have to say that as chairman of the Senate Intelligence Committee, I may have been under surveillance. I've been told by the media—not by the intelligence community—that she may be connected with Chinese intelligence services."

She looked around at the throng of media representatives and seemed to grow angrier.

"Why did she choose me to attack? Probably because of my position, and because of my wig. Why do I wear a wig? Because I've been fighting cancer. I've tried to keep that quiet, as a personal matter, although I long ago informed the house majority leader and other members of my committees about my medical challenges.

These challenges do not affect my intellectual capabilities in any way, nor does the treatment. The treatment does affect me in the sense that immediately after my chemo treatments, I suffer some nausea, which is controlled by rather benign drugs. And it made my hair fall out, which is why I wear the wig.

"Now, this Chinese person said that I have electronic implants in my skull, which were used to transfer my brain—my mind, I guess—to her brain. But as much as it angers and hurts me to do this, I want to show you the reality of my situation."

Dash reached up, grasped the front of her wig, and slowly peeled it off her head. Her scalp was smooth and white, without a sign of the plastic cap that had been there when Shay, Cruz, and Fenfang had raided her house. Or the brass-colored connectors.

"Oh my God, she had everything taken out," Shay gasped.

"She must be wearing makeup, something heavy, like for covering up tattoos," Cruz said. "Bet if a doctor examined her, a real examination, they'd find the wires."

Dash turned in a slow circle so all the media people, with their cameras, could see. After a few seconds, she pulled her wig back on and stepped away from the microphones for a moment to straighten it, using a mirror held by an assistant.

She then returned to the microphones and said, "I asked my doctors in New Mexico to provide me with an X-ray of my head, and a printout will be provided to you by my office.

"So, you have humiliated me. I'm not speaking now of the Chinese woman, whoever she is, but of you media people—with your irresponsible, unsupported reporting, you've dragged me out here to show everybody what happens when you're ravaged by cancer. Congratulations.

"That's all I have to say, and that's all I'll ever have to say on this subject. This press conference is over."

Some of the reporters shouted questions at her, but she trudged off the stage and out of sight.

As a C-SPAN commentator summarized the event, Twist said begrudgingly, "She's not bad. Not as good as the handicapped veterans at Singular's press conference after we lit up the Hollywood sign, but not bad."

"You sound like you admire her," Odin said with a spark of anger.

"Well . . . she's tough," Twist said. "Not honest, not worthy, completely immoral, and a killer, but still, tough."

"We have photos of that pop cap thing in her skull and some of the electrical connectors," Shay said. "And we have the video of her in her house. . . ."

The video had been shot with small hidden cameras strapped to armbands worn by Shay and Cruz after they broke into Dash's house with Fenfang and demanded that Dash open a safe that Fenfang knew of from the memories implanted in her head. Inside, they'd found a contract that detailed the half-billion dollars Dash had paid Singular to try to beat the cancer that was killing her.

"We need to edit the video and get it out there," Twist said. "It clearly shows how complicit a U.S. senator is in Singular's program. . . ."

"And it shows a U.S. senator being attacked in her house, which has got to be some kind of a major crime," Harmon said.

"That's exactly why we have editors," Twist said. "She lies a lot; we may have to lie a little, about where the video comes from. Remember, though, those reports about her being attacked in her house . . . she told the cops she'd been attacked by robbers. She can't backtrack now and say that she was attacked by us. Or that the video comes from us."

"I'll buy that," Harmon said.

7

Cade and Odin headed for Cade's room, where they would continue their computer search for the New Mexico facility and look at the Dash footage again. Danny had friends in Westwood that he wanted to see, and Harmon wanted to explore the hotel and talk to the other kids. Twist said he had "things to do," and Shay found out later that he had a date with an actress who'd had a number of minor roles in major movies—roles that usually involved a brass pole.

Cruz nuzzled Shay's neck in the stairwell outside the studio and suggested they take the next couple of hours to go to his room and break some rules. X was behind them, sniffing at a nasty stain on the concrete.

"Here's what I'm thinking we'll do," Cruz said, and whispered into her ear in Spanish. Shay rolled her eyes but grinned and said, "Oh, señor, I don't think so." They kissed again, and she tapped the heavy plastic bandage on his left arm, where he'd been badly bitten by one of Senator Dash's guard dogs as they'd fled the house. She said, "Maybe we should wait until you have total and complete use of all your limbs."

Cruz started trying to rip off the bandage right there.

"Hey, hey, stop that," Shay said. "I could cut it off with my knife, if I had it. . . . You take X. I'll find something to cut it with in the studio. Meet you in your room in five minutes."

Cruz moved furiously. First to the bathroom, then to his room to chew a stick of gum and make the twin-sized bed with the sheets he'd last washed . . . three weeks ago? He scratched X on the spot between his ears he liked, then told the dog that he was going to need to "chill" for a while and directed him to the corner farthest from the bed.

"Stay over there, and there's a burger for you later."

Shay came through the door with a smile and an X-Acto knife. She sat Cruz down on the bed and carefully cut the bandage off. X sauntered over and watched.

The bite had gone deep, and there would be scars, but the skin was scabbed over and healing. Cruz rubbed his arm and turned his wrist over for the first time since he'd been attacked by Dash's dogs.

"You wanna keep?" Shay asked, and held up the two chunks of bandage. "A little memento of our time together breaking and entering?"

Cruz said he wasn't sentimental that way, then put his free arm around her waist and pulled her down onto the bed. A couple minutes later, shirts were off and she was kissing the tattoos on his chest: the RIP in memory of the brother who'd been shot in a gang war, and the words of revenge he'd had inked in Spanish but never followed through on because he'd found Twist, and the hotel, and another way of going. . . .

Cruz's phone buzzed in his jeans pocket. It was Odin, asking if he'd seen Shay. Cruz lied: "No . . . what's up?"

"See if you can find her," Odin said. "We've got something you guys ought to look at."

"I'll check around," Cruz said. He hung up and said, "Well . . . what do you want to do?"

Shay: "Oh, man . . . we should go."

"Don't want to."

"Neither do I. But it sounds important."

Cruz flopped back and groaned, "Go ahead and shoot me."

"Didn't bring my gun," Shay said. "I could stab you. . . ."

The X-Acto was on the floor at the end of the bed.

Cruz sat up and dropped his feet to the floor. "All right. Let's go see what's so important."

They got buttoned up and zipped up and put their shoes on, and Shay hurried down to the ladies' room to throw some water on her face, then ran back up the hallway, where Cruz "found" her.

They were headed for the front stairs and down to Cade's room, where they ran into Harmon coming up from the basement. He was with Dum and Dee, the nearly seven-foot-tall twins who handled hotel security for Twist when they weren't playing their horns in bands around town. All three men were carrying dust-covered bicycles.

"What're you doing?" Shay asked.

"Working out some defensive positions, in case we get hit," Harmon said. "There are a dozen old bikes down in the basement. We put them in the hallway, loosely tied together with a chain. If we get hit, we freeze the elevator and throw the bikes onto the stairs, front and back, in a big pile. You ever try to climb over a pile of bikes? It's almost impossible. . . ."

Shay shook her head. "Whatever you say . . ."

"I say," Harmon said. "Where're you guys going?"

"Odin and Cade found something. You oughta come along."

Harmon handed Dee his bike.

There were five computers in Cade's room, and Odin and Cade were using all of them.

"What's up?" Shay asked.

"Okay," Cade said. "We got the news reports on the airplane crash, which said the plane was flying out of Flagstaff, Arizona. Odin cracked the FAA site . . ."

Odin said, "Yes, I did."

". . . and we found the flight plan, and we also found the flight plan that took them *in*to Flagstaff the same day. If you believe those flight plans, they were on the ground for ten hours or so. We couldn't find any people checking into a motel with their names, or with Singular credit cards, so then Odin comes up with the bright idea of checking the fixed-base operator—that's who takes care of private planes. Took us a while to get to the FBO's computer, but we found that the plane refueled twice—once right after arrival and once right before departure."

"Which means the plane went somewhere in between, without a flight plan," Harmon said.

Harmon thought for a moment, looked back and forth between Odin and Cade, then asked: "Can you get into IRS files?"

"Yeah, but it's tricky," Cade said. "Why?"

"Or maybe the New Mexico tax records. If you own a piece of property that you have to pay tax on, you can deduct that from your income tax. So if they're going to a private place in New Mexico, somebody's got to own it."

"Dash," Shay said.

Harmon said, "That's what I'm thinking. New Mexico is a very good place if you want major privacy. There are ranches out there that cover hundreds of thousands of acres, with almost nobody on them. Nobody snooping. Some of them have landing strips. Dash certainly could afford a place like that. . . ."

Cade said to Odin: "Ten dollars says I crack New Mexico's tax department before you do."

"You got it," Odin said.

While the rest of them sat around and chatted, Odin and Cade pounded on two computers each, and twelve minutes later, Cade said, "Got it. I'm in."

"Damn it." Odin handed him two limp fives that had been sitting on the bed next to his leg. Surprised that Cade had gotten in first, Shay raised an eyebrow at her brother. "He's actually better than he looks," Odin said.

"And I look pretty friggin' good, if I do say so myself," Cade said. He moved the laptop so Odin could see it and, as he typed, said, "Dash, Dash, Dash, where are you, Senator Dash? Ah—there you are."

They all gathered to look over Cade's shoulder as he scrolled through a massive income tax return to find the page for property tax deductions. Dash owned more than two dozen properties scattered around Albuquerque, Santa Fe, and Taos, but Harmon touched a line that listed a deduction for $210,000 for a property in far southwest New Mexico. "I recognize the name of the county," he said. "I've been there researching Indian sites. I can tell you, $210,000 in taxes means it's a big chunk of dirt down there. Really big."

The tax return listed a post office box as an address, which didn't help, but they went to the county appraiser's office online help page, and, after some more thrashing around, got a legal description of the property.

"Yeah, it's big," Harmon said. "A hundred and sixty thousand acres—that's two hundred fifty square miles."

"If it was a square . . . ," Odin began. He looked at the ceiling, his eyes defocused for a second, then continued, "It'd be fifteen point eight miles on a side. You could hide a jet landing strip on that."

"I can do square roots in my head, too," Cade said.

"Yeah, but yours are estimates," Odin said.

In another ten minutes, they had a precise location that they could transfer to the satellite views on Google Earth, and thirty seconds after that, they were looking down at a ranch that included a lake, a long blacktop landing strip, and seven buildings.

Harmon whistled and said, "I bet that strip's longer than most of the municipal landing strips in New Mexico. I'm not saying you could put a jumbo jet down, but you could put any business jet in there."

Cade took a virtual tape measure out of the Google toolbox and stretched it down the landing strip. "I don't know how accurate this measure is, but it says it's seven thousand feet long."

Harmon said, "You could land an Air Force C-130 on that."

"Which means a plane big enough to move a lot of prisoners," Shay said.

Cruz put a hand on Shay's back and said, "You are so smart."

"Yeah," Shay said. "We gotta think about getting out there. See what we can find."

Lou stuck her head in and said, "There you are. Shay, Dylan Brown from KABC is calling here, trying to get in touch with Twist and 'that red-haired girl.' He wants you on his show tonight to talk about Singular. I got a number for him."

"That's good," Cade said. "We'll put the show up on Mindkill afterward."

"Better call Twist," Shay said to Lou. "He knows about this stuff."

"I hesitate to do that," Lou said. "He's on a date."

"Jeez, Lou, it's important," Shay said.

"So you call him," Lou said.

Shay called, got switched to voice mail. Hung up, called again. Hung up, called a third time. Twist picked up and shouted, "WHAT?"

"Dylan Brown from KABC is trying to get in touch with you. He wants you and maybe me to be on his show tonight. We've got a number for him."

Silence. Then: "Give me the number."

Shay gave him the number and Twist hung up. Four minutes later, he called back. He wants us on his show at six-thirty. He wants your hair red. Go get some red hair."

"Twist—"

"I'm turning off the phone now." *Click.*

Shay looked around. "Where do I get red hair?"

Cade spread his hands. "Emily."

"Of course," Shay said.

Emily called in a favor with a hairdresser at a place everyone called Bon Bon, which was a shortened form of the real name, Bonjour Bonheur, French for Hello Happiness.

The hairdresser, Agrippine, was a severe dark-haired woman with a beauty mark on her upper lip. She looked at Shay and asked, "Why would you want to change?"

"It's a movie thing," Emily said. "They want her to be a redhead—and that's her natural color."

"Ah. Oui. I see." The woman was digging around in Shay's hair, where her natural red color was showing at the roots. "You want a match?"

"Yes."

"Perhaps, I think . . . with a small green accent?"

"No. Just a match," Shay said.

"I think a green accent would be terrific," Emily said.

"Striking," Agrippine said.

"Distinctive," said Emily.

"You're not helping here," Shay said. "I just want a simple match . . . nothing else."

The first step, Shay found, was to scrub in some stinky stuff that, after it had worked its magic, turned her hair translucent orange. "What! What!"

"Relax," Emily said, pushing her back down in the chair. "It's the necessary first step. Agrippine knows what she's doing." She popped her gum to punctuate the statement.

"She'd better," Shay said. "Or you best know how to sleep with your eyes open."

"I spit on your threats," Emily said.

Two hours later, they were back on the street. Shay could hardly believe it, but Agrippine had precisely matched her original hair color.

"You know the most amazing stuff."

"It's a gift," Emily allowed.

Twist was back at the hotel. He glanced at her and then smiled. "You're you again."

"More or less."

"We've got an hour before we have to leave. Let's get the group together and figure out what Dylan might ask and how we're going to answer."

Harmon drove them to Glendale in Twist's Range Rover, with Twist giving Shay performance tips all the way across town:

"Don't look at the cameras. Ignore them and talk to Dylan. The cameras are set up so they can shoot you straight in the face, and shoot Dylan separately, and both of you together, and so on. Smile when you're being polite to him, but go serious when you're filling him in on Singular. Don't cut him off when he's talking—it'll not only piss him off, you'll both be talking and nobody'll know what either one of you is saying. . . ."

And so on.

KABC was a beige building with what looked like a flying saucer parked on its roof.

Harmon, who'd stuffed his gun under the seat, said, "I'll be close. If you call, I'll be out front in less than ten seconds."

"Shouldn't be a problem," Twist said.

X would stay with Harmon, though the dog didn't like it. When Shay shut the door, X whimpered at her, wagging his tail in forlorn hope.

"Be right back," Shay promised.

An intern named Carly took them to a studio with a high ceiling and lighting equipment and cameras everywhere. There were several sets, including the weather girl's station, which was nothing more than a box and a green screen. A sound tech rigged them with wireless microphones.

They waited through a forecast from the weather girl, who had the aging-cheerleader look of an NFL sideline commentator, saying it would be hot and sunny with no rain even slightly possible. The usual news in L.A. Then a commercial came up, and while that was running, the intern herded them across the studio floor to a simple set with chairs in front of a green screen. Dylan Brown hustled through a side door and nodded at Twist and shook Shay's hand. He was a short man with spiky hair and an expensive suit worn without a necktie; he might have been any age between thirty and forty. He said to Twist, "I'm going to ask some hard questions. No offense."

"We'll answer anything that doesn't put us in jail," Twist said.

Brown nodded without smiling and asked Shay, "What happened to the long hair?"

"It was too warm down here, so I cut it," she said.

He looked at her for a moment, and then a woman standing behind a camera with a clipboard in her hand said, "Thirty seconds."

Brown said to Shay, "Twist is an old pro at this. You're not. Look at me and answer the questions. That's all you have to remember. If you can't answer or don't know the answer, say so."

The woman started counting, "Five, four, three . . ."

At "zero," Brown peered at a camera and said, "We're back, with the L.A. artist known as Twist and with Shay Remby, the redheaded girl you may have seen swinging down a building or climbing the Hollywood sign. The two have been on a campaign against the research company called Singular, which they claim is pursuing a scientific form of immortality and doing illegal experiments on human subjects. The night before last, one of those alleged subjects, a young Chinese woman, was shot to death shortly before a ship apparently holding at least a dozen illegal aliens, Korean and Chinese, crashed into the Antioch Bridge, near San Francisco. Authorities have been tight-lipped on the status of those illegals, but word has leaked that they were apparently the subjects of grotesque experimentation. Then, last night, a private plane carrying Singular's president and legal counsel crashed in the mountains. They were both killed, along with the pilot and copilot."

Brown turned to Shay and asked, "Were you there when the Chinese girl was shot? Were you on the ship?"

Twist jumped in: "Dylan, we had some ground rules. . . ."

Shay held up a hand to him, turned to Brown, and said, "Yes. I was there. I won't tell you who else was there, though. The people you called illegal aliens are not. They were kidnapped and brought here against their will from North Korea, where Singular used them as human lab rats. Now they are more like zombies. Zombies! That's what's left of them after Singular did their experiments. We don't know why the authorities are hiding this information from the public."

Beside her, Twist was rubbing his face with both hands.

"And the girl who was shot?" Brown asked.

"Her name was Fenfang. She was a wonderful person, a university student back in China until Singular kidnapped both her and her cousin and experimented on them. They tried to implant another woman's memories into Fenfang's brain. So when she escaped, Singular was afraid of all she knew, and wanted her dead. They shot her in cold blood."

Brown said, "Twist seems very reluctant to talk about this. Why are *you* talking?"

"Two reasons. Mostly because what Singular is doing is . . . evil. I don't know what else to call it. And they have to be stopped. My brother was kidnapped by Singular. He had some flash drives that had information about the experiments that Singular was doing on humans. They waterboarded him in a prison they were running in Sacramento, trying to make him tell them where the flash drives were hidden. That's the same place they murdered one of their own men, Marcus West. He wasn't killed like they said: he'd been wounded, and he was waiting for an ambulance when they executed him because he was trying to help my brother escape."

"Murder and waterboarding. Extremely serious charges," Brown said. "What's the other reason you're talking?"

"I'm sixteen," she said. "I don't think anybody will come after me, or any of the rest of us, once the truth comes out, but if they do . . . I'm a juvenile. Twist isn't."

"So you're saying you've broken some laws. . . ."

Shay said, "I never wanted to break any laws—I wanted to expose a bunch of killers. Now I'm waiting for the real law enforcement people to get involved."

Twist was nodding and said: "We want the authorities to do the right thing, and we believe they will."

Brown said to Shay, "Yet this whole episode started when you and your brother led a raid by animal rights radicals on a laboratory in Eugene, Oregon. . . ."

Shay shook her head. "No. I wasn't there. I'm not an animal rights activist and never have been. But that's no longer the point. That's like getting all upset when a squatter sneaks into a house and finds it full of dead bodies, and so you arrest the guy for being a squatter. You have to concentrate on the important stuff. . . ."

Brown grinned at her and said, "I'm trying to do that."

"Good," Shay said. "Try harder."

Brown grinned again: he liked how this was going. "Okay. Now, somebody, either you or people aligned with you, claimed that Senator Charlotte Dash had implants on her skull, and you've released video of the supposed implants. Yet Senator Dash appeared at a press conference, talking about her loss of hair due to cancer, and removed her wig. There are no implants on her skull. . . ."

Twist said, "She'd covered them up well, hadn't she? It was a great performance."

"How so?"

"Dash said, 'My doctor took X-rays and we're showing them to you.' And all you media guys say, 'Well, I guess that settles that.' Why didn't you ask the obvious question? Ask Senator Dash: 'Will you submit to X-rays at some recognized hospital?' You just took her handouts and decided everything was fine."

"*I* didn't," Brown said. "And I think that needs to be done." He looked at the camera and said, "How about it, Senator Dash? X-rays at Walter Reed?"

They finished two minutes later, after talking some more about the shoot-outs in Sacramento and San Francisco. When the floor producer called, "We're out!" Brown turned to Shay and said, "I'll tell you what, Shay—"

He didn't get to finish, because the woman blurted, "Dylan, the FBI is here. They want to talk to your guests."

Twist stood up, glaring at Brown. "You sold us out?"

"Of course not," Brown said. "Haley . . ." He nodded at the woman and said, "Take them out the back way. I'll go talk to the feds. Slow them down. Let's move it."

The woman hustled Twist and Shay down a hall lined with small offices and people peering at video screens, and Twist was on his phone to Harmon.

As soon as they walked through the back door, they saw the Range Rover heading for them. Harmon paused long enough for them to pile in next to X and had them rolling again.

"The FBI showed up," Twist told him. "Dylan's holding them off, but we gotta move, because he won't hold them long."

"Got it," Harmon said. "I saw them. Guy and a woman, dark suits, sunglasses. Looked like feds—but how do we know for sure who they're working for?"

"Exactly," Twist said. "That's the problem."

Harmon: "This is a dead end, but I found a route out through the parking lots. . . ." They bumped over a curb and through an empty parking space, then wound around a parking lot and out onto the next street over from the TV station.

Shay held on to the seat in front of her and said, "I hope that helped. I hope that was worth it. . . ."

9

They were almost back to the hotel when Twist took a call from Lou, who said, "You better get back here."

"Uh-oh. Is the FBI there?" He punched up the speaker so they could all hear.

Lou said, "The FBI? No. It's guys from the Chinese consulate. Odin's trying to answer their questions, but he keeps blowing up."

"Three minutes," Twist said. "We'll be there in three minutes."

When Twist was off the phone, Shay asked, "What's our strategy? Do we tell them everything?"

"Why not?" Twist asked. "The general idea is to get as many people involved as we can, as many people pissed off as we can. I don't know much about the Chinese, but from what I *do* know, they seem to get seriously pissed off when their citizens are hassled in other countries. Of course, if they ask if we did anything criminal, we deny everything."

"I'll drop you out front and go park," Harmon said. "I'd rather not get involved, in case they find out what my last job was."

• • •

At the hotel, they found six kids on the front steps, but the kids weren't looking out at the street, the way they usually did when they were lounging there; instead, they were all on their feet and looking into the hotel.

When Twist, Shay, and X pushed through, they were told that two guys were in the lobby, waiting for them. "We figured we should block them in," one kid said.

"Until you got here," said another.

"That's great," Twist muttered to Shay as they went in. "We've captured two Chinese diplomats."

The men were sitting on a couch with Lou and Odin, surrounded by fifteen more kids. The men were smiling, but their smiles weren't happy smiles—they were the kind people put on when they're trying to avoid a mob attack.

Lou looked relieved to see them and said, "Here is Twist."

The men stood up and extended their hands, and Twist shook them and said, "I'm sorry if this was . . . uncomfortable. We're a little worried about our safety here. Not worried about you, worried about other people. Let's go up to my studio and talk."

The taller of the two men said, in faultless English, "I think that would be very good. I am Dang Hui from the Los Angeles consulate, and this is my associate Guan Zhi."

Twist led them all back to the elevators. Cruz had been standing at the back of the crowd with Danny and Cade, and when Twist went by, he said quietly to Cruz, "When we're out of sight, tell the kids they did good."

"You want us to come up?"

"Better stay down here. A couple of feds—supposed feds—

showed up at the TV station, and we split out the back. If they show up here, we'll want to isolate them. . . ."

Cruz nodded.

Nobody spoke on the way up to Twist's studio. Shay checked out the two men while everyone else stared up at the floor numbers clicking past. The men were both tall, dressed in dark suits and ties, with tight haircuts. Once in the studio, Twist and Shay dragged a couch and some chairs around, and Twist asked if the visitors would like a beer or a Coke, and they both took Cokes, as did Twist.

Odin took a seat next to Shay and said to the men, "I'm pretty unhappy about your attitude. . . ."

Twist said, "Whoa, whoa, whoa. Let's start over. How can we help you?"

Mr. Dang said, "We wish to know as much as we can about Fenfang, who, we are told by your videos, was a Chinese citizen."

"You need to get her body . . . ," Odin began, but Twist waved him down.

"What we know is what she told us. She and her cousin, a man named Liko, were students in the town of Dandong, on the Korean border. To make money to go to school, where she wanted to study computer science, she and her cousin apparently traded Chinese merchandise on the North Korean black market."

Odin picked it up: "An American missionary named Robert Morris paid them to take him into North Korea so he could report back on the conditions facing people over there. Something went wrong, and they were captured. They were put in jail, and then all three of them were transferred to an experimental laboratory."

"How did she get here?" Mr. Guan asked.

"They brought her in on a freighter ship, along with other prisoners, and she was taken to a laboratory in Sacramento. Understand, this was mostly an American . . . thing," Twist said. "I think the Koreans mostly provided laboratory subjects."

"They did some experiments there, surgery," Shay said.

The two men glanced at each other, and then Mr. Dang said, "There have been American news reports that she crossed the border from Canada after flying in from Hong Kong."

Twist shook his head. "That's a story invented by Singular after Fenfang escaped with us. One of the men involved in creating that story changed sides when he found out what was going on—that people were being experimented on and were dying. If you help us publicize this . . . we can provide exact details of how it was done. If you have security cameras in the airport in Hong Kong, you could probably identify the woman who played the part of Fenfang."

"We have cameras," Mr. Dang said. "We would need the time, the date, and the airplane flight number, if possible."

Odin glanced at Shay and then said, "We can get those."

"Excuse me for asking," Mr. Guan said, "but how? How would you get those?"

"We have a certain amount of access to Singular," Twist said.

"So you have proof this woman is not a Chinese spy," Mr. Dang said. "This is very good, because I can promise you, she was not. But your FBI does not necessarily believe this."

Shay said, "There may be elements within the FBI that are cooperating with Singular. . . . We are very careful about talking to the FBI."

Mr. Guan smiled and said, "Yes. So are we."

Odin: "If you give us an email, we will get the information on the woman who impersonated Fenfang."

Shay added, "The people who were experimented on . . . I think most of them are Koreans, North Koreans, but there is at least one more Chinese man who was kidnapped. He was on the ship that's been seized by American authorities in San Francisco. You could ask to meet with him. He told me he thought he might have been a soldier."

Mr. Dang took a small leather notepad from his suit pocket, wrote on it for a moment, turned the page, wrote some more, tore out the second page, and handed it to Odin. "An email you can use. When would we get the information about this woman you say is a false Fenfang and the Chinese man in San Francisco?"

"Before you get back to the consulate," Odin said.

"If all you say is true, we will file a protest with your State Department," Mr. Dang said.

Twist: "That's fine—but we would prefer it to be public. A public protest. I can give you some names of local television stations. . . ."

"We would not be the ones who make the protest," Mr. Dang said, flashing a smile. "That would be done from much further up in our . . . establishment. I will pass along your request, but much depends on the state of . . . other matters . . . between our two countries."

"I assume you'll speak harshly with your friends the North Koreans," Twist said.

Mr. Dang smiled again and said, "Mmmm."

They talked for another five minutes. The men were interested in the general outline of what Singular had done and what the company's goals might be. When they were satisfied, they stood up, and Mr. Dang asked, "Will we have trouble going through the lobby?"

"Not at all," Twist said. "But I'll go down with you."

• • •

"Well, they were certainly polite," Shay said when the diplomats were on the sidewalk, headed back to their car.

"You know what bothers me?" Twist asked, looking after them. "They weren't angry enough. About Singular, about the experiments, about Fenfang or the prisoner who might be one of their soldiers. It's just another problem to be solved, a protest to be filed. I hope this isn't about to deflate."

They found Harmon, and he got his laptop and brought up his notes on the Fenfang impersonator. He didn't have the flight number, but he had the approximate departure time from Hong Kong, and the approximate arrival time in Vancouver, and the date. With that information, they found a flight number they were confident was correct.

They sent along the information, with the feeling that they were dropping a pebble into a well. They might get a splash, but they might not; their pebble might just sink out of sight.

10

The Chinese man lay on his hospital bed, feigning sleep. He still didn't know his name, and the people who ran the ward had begun calling him Eight, because the chart at the end of his bed identified him as UNKNOWN #8.

Fifteen experimental subjects from the ship were being held in a locked ward at St. Crispin's Hospital in San Francisco, a ward normally used for violent psychiatric patients. The ward had been cleared, the regular patients distributed to other wards and hospitals, before the experimental subjects—twelve men and three women—were brought in.

Although he'd spoken to the police when they'd boarded the ship, Eight had avoided using English in the hospital, the better to overhear the conversations of the attending doctors and nurses. A Korean translator had been brought in, but only three subjects had been well enough to talk. The Korean translator knew a little Chinese, but not enough for a full interview.

Eight was disturbed by what he was hearing in the muttered conversations among officials who'd come to listen to the Koreans: there was a possibility that the experimental subjects might be returned to Korea as illegal refugees, rather than being treated as victims of a crime who needed urgent care—anywhere *but* North Korea.

If they were sent back there, Eight knew, they'd all be killed, one way or another.

The ward was organized like an intensive care unit, the patients isolated from one another by privacy curtains. Sometimes the curtains were open, sometimes closed; a small television was attached to a bar above the end of each bed, with earphones for each patient.

When he was alone, Eight clicked between news channels, looking for information. The first night they were in the hospital, he saw several stories about the ship and the raid, and more the next morning, but with little in the way of facts.

There were fewer stories during the afternoon and evening, and none the next morning, except one brief mention on a local program.

They were being lost, Eight thought.

On the third day, the patient in the next bed suffered convulsions just after sunrise. Several nurses responded, and two physicians. The physicians wore knee-length white lab coats with large pockets. One of them pushed aside the privacy curtain between the convulsing patient's bed and Eight's as they worked on the man. The doctor's pocket was right there, and inside it, a cell phone.

Eight dipped his hand into the pocket, took the phone. An iPhone. He knew iPhones. Didn't know his name, but the iPhone was immediately familiar. He turned off the ringer and the locator, slipped it under his pillow, closed his eyes again.

• • •

Shay needed some time alone, so she climbed to Twist's studio at six o'clock in the morning with X, leaving Cruz asleep, sneaking out of his room like a thief in the night. He'd been exactly what she needed last night. She'd felt safe and alive and normal for the first time in a long time. But she'd woken early and needed to move—needed to occupy her brain. . . . She had work to do in the studio and went about opening cans and bottles of paint, mixing it to match swatches that Twist had laid out.

And though she worked quietly, Twist eventually emerged from his bedroom suite, yawning, in a pair of striped pajama bottoms and a T-shirt. "Early," he said. "You make coffee?"

"No. I was afraid the smell would wake you up."

"Okay. So make some coffee. I'm going to take a shower." He wandered over to look at the paint she was mixing, touched one can, and said, "More red."

"Then it won't match the swatch," Shay said.

"Screw the swatch. I got it wrong. Just a couple of shades toward the red end."

"If you say so, famous artist."

"Right." He yawned again and wandered back into his bedroom.

Fifteen minutes later, he was out again, dressed in fresh black clothes, cane in hand, awake now. He cruised a line of large canvases slashed with different colors of paint, a coffee mug in his free hand, then said, "I don't think I'll do any mural-sized stuff for a while. Let's get some wall sizes put together. There's a pile of stretcher bars down in the storeroom; get the two or three longest sizes up here, and we'll see what we can do. I'll roll out some canvas."

Shay went down a flight to the storeroom, took two six-footers and two five-footers, along with some corner and cross braces, and carried them all back up the stairs. Twist was unrolling a gold-colored canvas on the floor; he looked at the braces and said, "You know what? Let's get a sheet of that four-by-eight Dibond up here and pull the table saw out of the corner. Have I shown you how to switch blades?"

Shay shook her head, and Twist said, "I'll go with you, show you where I keep 'em. . . ."

They were poking around the storeroom when Shay's cell phone went off. She glanced at it and said to Twist, "Call from San Francisco."

San Francisco was Singular's home base. "Who has your number?" Twist asked.

"Nobody outside the group. But . . . I'm gonna answer. Even if it's just a threat, I want to hear it."

To Shay's "Hello," a man with a thick Asian accent said in a whisper, "This is the man from the ship."

"Hey! Hi!" She pushed the speaker button so Twist could hear. "Where are you? Are you out?"

"No, I am in hospital and I steal this phone. A nurse here say we go somewhere else tomorrow. Some people say we go back to Korea."

"What? That's not possible."

"I think it is possible. I wish to leave here. But I need help to get out. You are the only help I know."

Shay was instantly ready to help. "All right. Do you know how to turn the phone off?"

"Yes. I know everything about iPhone," the man said. "I know to turn off phone finder, but my name I don't know. They call me Eight."

"Don't make any more calls. We're coming, but we're in Los Angeles. It will take six or seven hours to get there."

"Thank you."

"Don't tell anyone we're coming. And be careful with the phone. . . ."

"Yes."

"Do we really want to go back to San Francisco?" Twist asked. "We got out of there by the skin of our teeth. We're pushing our luck."

"We can't leave him," Shay said.

"Why not? We don't owe him," Twist said. "Not more than we owe any of the others."

"Some of the other people are effectively dead. This guy isn't," Shay said. "C'mon, man."

Twist scratched his nose, sighed, and said, "All right, fine. Get everybody together; we'll talk it over."

"We've got no time. If they move these people tomorrow . . . I mean, it's a six-hour drive."

"No choice about that," Twist said. "We're not flying anywhere. I believe the TSA would snatch us right out of line and call the FBI. Even if we could find a plane, we couldn't rent a car."

"I'll get the guys," Shay said.

They all had still been asleep, except Harmon, who'd run his five miles and was scanning the Internet, and Odin, who was lying on his bed in the same clothes as the day before and looked bad. Shay was aware he hadn't slept much since Fenfang's death and that he'd already been sleep-deprived from the nightmares he'd suffered since the waterboarding.

And she thought: Maybe there existed some appropriate therapy he could get someday, but probably not. Odin had experienced too many lousy interactions with caseworkers and therapists in foster care, who could never quite make sense of his high intelligence and his mild autism—and the depression that had set in after their mother's death. Well, *supposed* death. She'd been a researcher in an early iteration of Singular and then died in a sudden accident that felt like a cover-up, given all they knew now.

Shay stood in the doorway and told her brother about the phone call, and he simply rose from the bed and said, "We have to go get him."

In the studio, with all of them gathered around the coffeepot, Cade suggested that it might be a trap—but Shay knew the Chinese man's voice and believed he was acting alone. Cruz said, "Sometimes you can't help everybody," and Emily agreed: "If you get lucky and get him out, you save one person. How many do you risk if it's a trap? Or even if it's not a trap but the place is surrounded by Singular people?" She looked around the studio. "What if Singular is listening to us now?"

Odin: "Singular is frantic to deny their involvement with the prisoners, so I doubt they're there. And if they want us, I'm sure they know where we are. No need to bug us."

"Could have bugged this place weeks ago," Danny Dill said. "And Harmon's friend, the one he talked to, said there's another level out there. . . . They could be listening."

Lou said, "Nobody got up here to bug it. I promise you."

"Could have flown a bug in," Danny said. "The feds do that to dopers—fly in a little drone, park it in a tree, drop a bug down. . . ."

They all looked at the building windows, and then Twist said: "No way to know. And even I'm not paranoid enough to worry about it." Twist looked at Harmon. "Do you think we should—could—help this guy?"

Harmon shrugged. "We'd have to check out the hospital. A regular hospital won't be hard to penetrate, although the last few feet, to get this guy out, might be. If he's in a locked ward, to get in without sticking a gun in somebody's back . . . that could be tricky. But given some time to look the place over, yeah, we could get him out."

Shay, pacing with impatience, said, "We've got to leave right away. . . ."

"We won't need everybody," said Harmon. "If Danny and Emily are willing, they'd be best for a recon, since Singular doesn't know them. Shay, you and I do the actual retrieval, because we've worked together. Twist and Cruz drive, safer with a backup car. Odin and Cade stay here, because Singular knows their faces too well and we need them to probe that hospital with their computers, get us everything they can find."

"Sounds reasonable," Twist said.

Odin: "I want to go."

Cade: "So do I."

Twist: "We *need* you to stay here. The rest of us can't do what you can, and we need that stuff."

Shay: "It's settled. Out of town in half an hour—grab clothes for overnight, food, whatever. If we move, we can get to San Francisco while it's still light outside."

Six hours later: Berkeley.

St. Crispin's Hospital was a white four-story Spanish-style building with what looked like a thousand small square windows. The main entrance was on one side of the building, facing a major street, and the emergency room on the other. They were there at five o'clock, in heavy traffic, cruised the hospital once, their two vehicles linked by walkie-talkies, since they were still nervous about telephones.

Cade and Odin had been busy on the computers while the others drove north. A half hour after they left Hollywood, not yet out of the L.A. metro area, Odin forwarded a hospital map he'd gotten off a website supposedly restricted to doctors. The restriction was not a problem for Odin or Cade, and the maps showed each floor of the hospital, including the locked wards on the third floor.

Cade forwarded a list of rules for visitors—visitation hours were liberal, from six in the morning until ten at night, so getting in would not be a problem.

Odin's map showed that in addition to the locked wards, there were a number of surgical-recovery units on the third floor.

"We need some names of people who are in those units, or who checked out today, and any information we can get on them," Twist called back. "They need to be either unconscious or, better, checked out, so we can visit by mistake."

"We'll get it," Cade said.

They got names when they were halfway up the Central Valley, with checkout times and conditions, right from the hospital computers. They got brief biographies of the relevant patients as they drove through Oakland, fifteen minutes from the hospital.

"I don't want to say I'm nervous, but I might need to stop and buy some fresh underwear," Emily said as they circled the hospital for the third time. She'd be the first one in.

"Ah, you got a great line of BS," said Harmon. "You'll do good. Gimme the patient's name again."

"Larry Tengle. Eighty-seven. Room 3187. Heart-valve replacement," Emily said. "Checked out two hours ago, taken to a rehab facility."

"And inside the door . . ."

"Is a gift shop that sells flowers. Small bouquet," Emily said.

"Take your time with the flowers, pick a good one. . . ."

"So I can check out security and cameras."

Twist was driving. He picked up the walkie-talkie and said, "Putting Emily in."

Cruz called back: "Gotcha."

They pulled into a traffic circle at the front of the hospital, dropped Emily, then continued back to the street.

11

Emily felt as though everyone on the hospital steps were watching her. She knew they weren't when a man in a suit nearly crashed the revolving door into her face without even realizing it.

Once inside, she paused and looked around. Straight ahead was an information desk, and off to the right, the gift shop. She went that way, checked out the flowers, found a small, cheap bouquet, and lingered for a few minutes at the magazine rack, looking at a *Vogue* and, over the top of the *Vogue,* out into the lobby.

There were cameras, four of them that she could see. She paid for the flowers and the magazine, went to the information desk to ask for directions to room 3187, was sent down a wide hallway to a bank of elevators, and took the first one to the third floor.

The hall the elevators opened onto led to a wide lobby dominated by a circular desk, where two nurses were working on computers. More nurses buzzed around the desk like bees around a hive. Four corridors radiated out from the desk.

From the maps sent out by Cade and Odin, Emily thought Larry Tengle's room was down a corridor to the left, while the locked ward was down a corridor straight ahead. Trying to look as though she knew where she was going, she rounded the desk and headed straight, past a patient pushing a wheeled IV stand.

Nobody stopped her; nobody even paid attention to her. Their lack of attention was almost insulting, like they were waiters in a snooty restaurant.

The doors to the patients' rooms were open, and Emily saw an assortment of people, almost all of them gray- or white-haired, sitting in beds, a few of them asleep, most of them talking with visitors or watching televisions she couldn't see.

At the end of the hallway was another closed door. She was about to open it when a man came through. He was wearing a gray suit and tie and carried a leather portfolio. He glanced at her, stopped, and asked, "Can I help you?"

She asked, "Are there more rooms through there? I can't find Mr. Tengle." As the door swung slowly shut behind the man, she saw a short hallway beyond him, blocked by another door with a sign that said SECURE AREA, and a keypad on the wall.

"No, that's a ward. What room are you looking for?" He was friendly enough, unsuspicious.

"Uh, 3187."

"Made the wrong turn," the man said. "Go back to the desk and take a right."

"Thank you." She gave him a shy smile and walked along with him for a few feet, then asked, "Are you a doctor?"

"Yup. I am."

"Like, a surgeon?"

"Radiologist."

"Oh. I know about those," Emily said. She turned the cuteness up to eleven. "A radiologist told Mr. Tengle that he needed a new valve in his heart."

"Yup. That's us," the man said.

"So you spend all day looking at hearts?"

"I spent this morning looking at brains," the man said. "But I'll probably get some hearts and spines this afternoon. Maybe some guts."

"I'd love to be a radiologist, but I don't think that's going to happen," Emily said.

"You in college?"

Emily almost forgot she was on a secret mission and replied candidly, "I wish. Right now, I'm working in sales, trying to save some money to go to college, probably in-state. Otherwise, tuition is, like, the price of a Ferrari."

"Well, sounds like a plan," the man said, and then, "You're right about the tuition. I've still got loans up to my knees." And, "Hope you find Mr. Tengle." He sped up and disappeared down the hallway.

Emily ducked into a room where an elderly man was asleep, his head tipped back on a pillow. A plastic tube snaked up to his nose, feeding in oxygen. After getting her courage up, she took out her cell phone, brought the camera up, then walked confidently back to the door at the end of the hall, pulled it open, stepped up to the keypad, took a photo of it, and then another, as Harmon had told her to.

She tried the door handle to the secure area, but it was locked.

A few seconds later, back outside the first door, she walked along the hallway toward the elevators and sent the two photos to Harmon. As she rounded the nursing desk, she put in a call to Twist: "I spotted the door, but it's tough. A very long hallway, and you've got to go by a nursing desk with lots of people. I don't think you could get back out past them. Better send in Danny from the back."

"Doing that," said Twist.

On the first floor, a bald man was waiting for an elevator, a worried look on his sunburned face. He was dressed in a reflective safety vest and heavy boots. Emily held the bouquet out to him and said, "I don't need these flowers, as it turns out. You want them?"

"Oh, wow. Thanks," he said.

He seemed really pleased, and that gave her an extra lift as she went back out into the sunshine and started breathing again. She'd done her part, and hadn't messed up.

With Danny in the backseat, Twist drove to the emergency entrance at the rear of the hospital.

Harmon was examining the photos from Emily. "I'm looking at the wear on the numbers. They don't change codes very often in hospitals, and sometimes not at all, because too many people need to know them and they don't want people stopped by a wrong code in an emergency. They'll almost certainly have the same code on all the doors, for the same reason."

Danny was looking over his shoulder at Emily's photos, and the wear on the keypad buttons was obvious. "So . . . two-five-six-nine?"

"Looks like it. Or some combination of those numbers. There are twenty-four possibilities. . . ."

He wrote them all on a slip of paper and passed it to Danny. "Start at the first one, and let them roll. Shouldn't take you more than a couple of minutes, even if it's the twenty-fourth one."

Danny smoothed down his reddish brown dreadlocks and straightened his gold-rimmed round glasses. He was twenty-six and wearing a T-shirt that said PLAY NICE.

"How do I look?"

Harmon checked him out. "Like you OD'd last night and want to go home."

Twist: "Perfect."

Another long-haired man was standing outside the emergency room entrance. As Danny walked up, the man said, "You got a match or a gun?"

"Uh . . . why would you need a gun, chief?"

The man held up an unlit cigarette. " 'Cause if I don't get a match, I'm gonna kill myself."

Danny dug in his pocket, pulled out a Bic lighter, fired up the man's cigarette.

"Saved my life, duder."

Danny went on through the doors. Inside, two dozen or so people were scattered around a waiting room. A male nurse behind a desk asked, "You checking in or checking somebody out?"

"Got a friend I'm waiting on," Danny said. Pointing down a hall-way, he asked, "Can I get to the cafeteria that way?"

"Yep, you got it. Stay away from the green Jell-O."

Danny went that way, down the hall, past a lot of unmarked doors, to an elevator that said FREIGHT ONLY.

He pushed the button, waited, rode the elevator up to the second floor, then walked back in the direction from which he'd come on the floor below. On the first floor, the stairwell door was unmarked, but here it had an exit sign above it, and he went through the door onto a narrow landing. He took the steps up and, on the third floor, found himself behind the secure area's back exit.

The keypad showed hardly any wear; he began running the numbers on Harmon's list, hit it on the fourteenth try. He heard the lock click, turned the door handle, pulled the door open an inch, pushed it shut.

He took his phone out and sent the combination 6-2-5-9 to Harmon. Once he had the code, he was supposed to head back out, but he decided to press his luck a bit further.

He punched the code in again, opened the door enough to peek through. He could see beds with patients, and the patients he could see were Asian. Other beds were concealed by privacy curtains. He could see no nurses or hospital personnel at all.

He slipped inside the ward. He could see seven patients; two reacted to his presence, following him with their eyes, and the other five were either asleep or staring blankly ahead. At the end of each bed was an electronic slate with a name in large letters: CHONG, UNKNOWN #3, PARK, KIM, SUK, UNKNOWN #4, another KIM.

He walked back down the line of beds, now checking those concealed by curtains. The third one he checked was occupied by a thin man with the same bronze knobs on his head that Fenfang had had. The electronic pad said UNKNOWN #8.

"Eight?" he whispered. "We're the people you called."

Eight whispered back: "Get me free."

Eight was dressed in a hospital smock. He wouldn't be walking out like that. Danny whispered, "We'll have to get you some clothes. . . ."

Eight said, "My foot. My foot is chained."

Danny looked: Eight was shackled to the bed with a leather restraint with a locking nut in the middle, and when Danny twisted it, he could feel a steel cable inside the leather.

"We'll bring cutters. When is the best time?"

Before Eight could answer, the door at the far end rattled, and they heard somebody step inside. Eight whispered, "Under the bed."

Danny crouched and looked under the bed: there was some motorized equipment beneath it, but enough space to hide him. He slid under, then scrunched as close to the back wall as he could get.

A moment later, a man a ways down the row of beds said, "Ask him if he has pain now."

There was a burst of an unfamiliar language—Korean, Danny thought—then a translated reply. "No, not now."

More Korean, and then English from the translator: "He wants to know what will happen to him."

"The authorities are discussing that."

More Korean.

"He wants to stay here. He says if he goes to Korea—he means North Korea—they will kill him."

"That's not my job to decide," said the English speaker. They apparently moved on, and the English speaker said, "Ask him about the pain. . . ."

Danny could see, just below the curtains, feet coming down the ward as the doctor or nurse checked each patient capable of speaking and the translator relayed the patients' answers. At Eight's bed, the curtain was pulled back, and the translator said, "This one says he is Chinese and he doesn't speak Korean. I can understand that he is not in pain, but you should get a Chinese translator here."

"Okay. Next." The curtain was closed again.

The pair continued down the ward, and after finishing with the last patient, the English speaker said, "Dinner in half an hour."

The Korean translator said something loudly enough to carry across the full ward, apparently telling those who could understand him that dinner was on the way. The door at the end of the ward rattled again, and the two were gone.

Danny slipped out from under the bed and said, "Gotta go," to Eight, who said, "You come back after twenty-two hundred."

"We'll be back for you."

A few seconds later, Danny was starting down the stairs.

As he did, he heard the stairwell door on the bottom floor open. He looked over the railing and saw what looked like a cop's hat. Danny didn't want to deal with that, so he went through the door on the second floor.

A young woman was walking toward him, pushing a canvas bin full of dirty scrubs, and Danny said, "I'm lost. How do I get to the lobby?"

Barely looking at him, she thrust a thumb over her shoulder and said, "That way. Take a right at the first hallway—that'll get you to the elevators."

All too easy, Danny thought as, ignored by everyone, he walked down the hall, caught the elevator, and swaggered outside.

By nine-fifteen, they were set to go. Cruz looked at Shay and grinned, muttered into her ear, "Maybe later we can make out in the bleachers."

Shay was wearing shorts and sneakers and a red-and-gold sweatshirt from Berkeley High with a GO JACKETS insignia across the chest. She looked younger, harmless.

"How can a jacket go anywhere?" Twist wanted to know.

"We're the Yellow Jackets," Shay said. "You know, like bees."

She'd gotten a Cal Bears hoodie for Eight—the hospital was a half mile from the university—a pair of board shorts, and flip-flops. All the clothes were loose-fitting enough to cover a range of sizes, and the flip-flops would fit almost any adult.

Harmon looked at his watch, nodded, and Shay pulled on her backpack. The bolt cutters inside weren't the industrial-sized cutters she'd needed to break Fenfang's chains, and thinking about that now . . . and about the messed-up way Fenfang's life had come crashing down . . . made her ready.

12

Cruz and Twist would both park in the emergency room lot, five seconds from the ER door and twenty seconds from the front entrance.

"Twenty seconds is forever when you're in trouble," Harmon said. "If there's a problem, we'll try to call ahead, tell you where we're coming out."

Twist said, "If worse comes to worst, hide. Bathroom stall, linen closet. The biggest problem would be if you get tangled up with the local cops—they could have a lot of people here in a hurry."

"If there's a Singular security man in there—or somebody from the next layer of Singular, whatever that is," Cruz said, "he could have a gun."

Harmon nodded. "Good thought." He chewed his lip for a moment, then said, "I didn't want to take a gun in. That gets us in deeper trouble if we're stopped by the local cops." He looked at Shay. "Where's your piece?"

"It's in my pack," Shay said.

"Then you carry. I won't. You look like such a child. . . . If we get in trouble with the locals, ditch it," Harmon said. "If we run into somebody who looks like Singular, give it to me."

Shay slipped the pistol inside the waistband of her shorts, beside her knife, on the way over, Twist driving, Harmon riding shotgun. In the parking lot, Shay looked up at the sky: a clear, cool night, but the stars were washed out, nothing like the diamond stars in the desert.

Harmon muttered, "Ready?"

"Yeah."

As they got out of the truck, Shay could feel it in her stomach and smiled despite herself.

Harmon asked, "What?"

She shook her head and said, "Nothing," as they walked across the parking lot toward the door.

"Bullshit," he said. "You're starting to like it, aren't you?"

"Not exactly," she said. "It's not exactly like that."

Harmon said, "I'll tell you something, kid. It gets addictive. You don't exactly like it, but you can't stay away from it. That's what Sync was getting at the other day."

"I just want to finish high school," Shay said.

"More bullshit," Harmon said. He pulled open the emergency room door. "Now behave yourself."

"Yes, Daddy."

Inside the ER, nobody asked where they were going. A young couple on a couch talked in Spanish to a sick child; a man sat by himself, holding a wet towel to one eye. They walked down the hall toward the cafeteria, took the elevator to the second floor, walked down the hall to the stairway to the third floor. Two cops were standing at the nurses' desk behind them. They weren't paying much attention, but still.

"On the way out, we better go all the way down, if we can," Harmon said.

On the third floor, they listened at the secure door, then Harmon punched in the code and they eased it open. The ward was only dimly lit, all the beds now behind the privacy drapes. Televisions were turned on behind a few of the curtains, but there was no sound, except at the far end, where they could hear the laughter from a talk-show audience.

Without speaking, they counted down four beds and pulled the drapes apart, cringing at the unexpected noise of metal hooks scraping over the metal rod like a shower curtain. Eight was sitting there, propped up, light from his television shining on his face. He put his finger to his lips. Then he gestured forward and whispered, "There is guard. I think on last bed."

Then a man's gravelly voice: "Is somebody here? Hey. Is somebody here?"

A minute later, they were both under the bed, as Danny had been.

The guard, whoever it was, walked down the aisle along the line of beds. From where they were, they could see only the cuffs of a pair of dark pants and two heavy shoes. He paused at the end of the line, then walked back to where he'd been, and they heard a bed creak. The guard, Shay thought, was either sitting or lying on a bed, watching television.

Harmon pushed her gently on the back: *Out.*

Shay crawled out and took the pack off her back, unzipped it.

Harmon slipped the bolt cutters out. The leather restraint looped around Eight's ankle turned out to be a problem. Instead of cutting through it, the bolt cutters *chewed* on it.

Shay held up a finger, reached to the small of her back, and pulled her knife out of its sheath. Harmon lifted an eyebrow but took the knife and sliced easily through the leather, exposing the steel cable. Shay took the knife back, and Harmon cut the cable with the bolt cutters.

Eight eased off the bed, and Shay took the new clothes out of the pack. A minute later, Eight had pulled on the Cal Bears hoodie, the board shorts, and the flip-flops. Shay flipped the hood up over the bronze-colored terminals on his head.

Shay gave him a reassuring smile, even as she thought, *He's probably going to die. . . .*

Harmon put the bolt cutters back in the pack, and Shay pulled it on again. They were about to leave when a cell phone rang and the guard answered it.

"Yeah? . . . No, everything's okay here. . . . No, nobody came through the door. . . . I don't know, I didn't actually try to open it. Sure, I can check. I'll call you back."

Harmon gestured for Eight to get back in bed, and they pulled the sheets up over him and yanked down the hood so nothing showed but his mutilated head. Eight closed his eyes to feign sleep, and Shay and Harmon got back under the bed.

Crouched over and barely breathing, they could hear the guard pulling drapes back from around the beds as he walked down the line. As he drew closer, Shay noticed that Eight's hospital gown was lying on the floor next to the bed. She reached out and pulled it under just as the drapes were jerked open. The guard checked Eight, who seemed to be sound asleep, and moved on to the next bed.

At the back door, he rattled the door in its frame, then opened it, apparently looked down the stairway, pulled the door shut, rattled it again, and walked back up the hall, pulling the privacy drapes back across the beds.

When he got to the end, he made a call. "I checked and they're all asleep or watching TV. The door was shut and locked. . . . Yeah, that was me. . . . Yeah. . . . Well, if it happens again, call me. I got nothing else to do."

Shay slid out from under the bed, followed by Harmon. Eight sat up and dropped his feet to the floor. Harmon caught both of them by an arm and pulled them close and whispered, "There's a silent alarm on the door. There must be an extra code to clear it once you're in. When we go, we have to go quickly."

Eight nodded and pulled up his hood. Shay knelt and looked out from under the privacy drape. She couldn't see any feet on the floor.

They crept to the door, and Harmon quickly punched the code into the interior keypad, quietly twisted the handle, then eased the door open. As he was easing it closed behind them, they heard the guard's phone ring again. Harmon closed it the rest of the way, then said, "We gotta run. Hurry, now, all the way down."

They ran down a flight of stairs to the second floor and were running down another, to a landing above the first-floor door, when the door popped open above them and the guard shouted, "Hey! Hey, there! Stop! Stop!"

They went through the first-floor door and hurried toward the ER entrance, and Harmon called Twist and said, "They're coming after us, meet us at the ER door," and then told Eight, "Go ahead of us—hurry, there'll be a car waiting for you. . . ."

Eight moved fast down the hall, and Harmon said to Shay, "Take my hand."

"What?"

"Hold hands with your daddy. And keep your head down. Don't look up at the cameras."

She took his hand and he pushed her close to the corridor wall as they walked toward the ER; a second later, the guard burst out of the stairway door, spotted Eight walking away, shouted, "Hey!" and ran after him.

Harmon turned to look when the guard shouted. The guard ignored them—a fortyish man with his daughter—but as the guard ran past, Harmon lashed out with a hammer fist, striking him on the nose. The guard screamed and went down on his knees, blood exploding from a broken nose, and cried, "Help!" Harmon and Shay hustled down the hall. They saw Eight go through the exit and a nurse hurrying toward them.

Harmon turned his face away from her and pointed. "That guy was yelling. He needs help. . . ."

The nurse shouted something back at her colleagues and then ran. An orderly burst through a door from the ER's working area and followed after the nurse. Five seconds later, Shay and Harmon were crossing the sidewalk and climbing into the Range Rover with Twist and Emily.

"Eight's with Cruz and Danny," Twist said, calmly pulling out. "Everything go okay?"

Shay looked at Harmon, then shrugged and said, "Yeah, pretty much. But I wouldn't stop for that traffic light."

Harmon laughed.

13

They were back in Los Angeles as the morning light was breaking over Mount Wilson. They'd taken turns sleeping and driving during the trip back but were still cranky, stiff, and tired when they arrived.

Eight had talked with Shay and Harmon for part of the ride, but the experiments had left his mind grievously wounded. As he'd told them on the ship, he felt he might have been a soldier. Harmon asked whether he knew anything about QBZ-95 assault rifles, a trick question of sorts, and Eight proceeded to explain everything from how to load a thirty-round magazine to the improved ejector port on a later version.

"You're a soldier in the People's Liberation Army," Harmon declared. "That's the primary firearm they use. You left-handed?"

Eight wasn't sure. Harmon dug a pen and a small notebook out of the console and asked Eight to write something. "One to ten, anything," he said.

Eight started with his right hand, made some complicated lines, then switched to the other hand and made the same complicated lines more elegantly.

"That's what I thought," Harmon said. "The ejector port you mentioned, it was moved in part to help with lefty shooting."

Eight smiled. "It is good to know something about me."

The reality was, he had few life memories, though when he was sleeping, he'd said, he sometimes dreamed of growing up in the back of a small grocery store. The store had a telephone where people came to make calls, and it rang incessantly in his dreams. He thought the store might have sold a lot of rice: his dreams were accompanied by the pleasant, earthy odor of grain.

They'd told Eight about the Chinese diplomats.

"I want to show them what they do to me," Eight said. "I want to go home."

"We'll get them back to the hotel," Harmon said. "You can decide then whether you want to go with them."

Eight said there was no need to think it over, and then he fell into a deep sleep. Ten miles from the hotel, his eyes popped open and he said he would like to answer more questions because it made him feel alive. Shay said that something very important was still unknown to them.

"On the ship, at the very end, did any more prisoners come aboard?" she asked him. "We went to hide before the ship began to move. . . . Did they bring any new people down to the hold?"

Eight shook his head.

Interesting. It had been the arrival of a Singular convoy of three RVs holding experimental subjects that trapped them on the ship.

Shay said to Harmon: "The prisoners in the RVs . . . if they didn't get them on the ship, they must have put them back into the RVs and driven away. They're still out there."

Harmon said, "They wouldn't take them to any known Singular facility."

"New Mexico?" Shay said.

Harmon nodded and said: "Maybe. Or maybe they . . . got rid of them. If we've spotlighted all their major labs, maybe they'd have no way to finish their experiments."

"But we haven't. They still have labs in North Korea, and they might be in other countries we don't know about. They could be hiding them in New Mexico until they can get someplace else."

Harmon thought that sounded plausible.

"We gotta get down there," Shay said.

"Somebody does," Harmon said.

"What do you mean, 'somebody'? Dash is a U.S. senator on the Intelligence Committee. You think the FBI is going to poke their nose in there on our say-so?"

"Probably not," Harmon admitted. "Not without a lot of preliminaries, which would give Dash time to move everybody out."

"It's on us," Shay said. "It's on us."

At the hotel, Twist put Eight in Cruz's room and assigned Cruz the role of Eight's full-time shadow. Before they all broke up to shower and sleep, Twist told them, "I'll call the Chinese consulate, see if we can set up another meeting this afternoon. Until then, don't talk to me. I need a nap."

Odin said, "We should talk before the Chinese get here."

"Studio at noon, then," Twist said. "Good night."

• • •

Shay hadn't had a chance to talk privately with Cruz since she'd left his room twenty-four hours before. Now they walked down the hall together, and Cruz said, "I really want to get together again."

"Me too."

He kissed her temple, then led Eight on to his room while Shay headed to hers. Emily was coming out of their room with a towel and a bottle of soap. "Shower, then sleep."

"Just sleep for me," Shay said, and was out in a matter of seconds.

Shay was up at eleven, hit the shower, got dressed, and walked out to a Starbucks for a straight cup of coffee for herself and a grande no-fat, no-foam latte with a double shot for Emily, along with cranberry and blueberry scones. Emily opened her eyes when the smell of the coffee hit her. "You really are a princess," she said. "I was wondering how I'd make it to the stairs without caffeine. I hope to God you got a double shot."

"Of course," Shay said. "Better move your butt, though. Meet in twenty."

More like forty, with the group drifting into the studio, scraping chairs into a circle, yawning, still sleepy, several of them with cups of bad coffee cadged from the cafeteria. Twist said, "I got an answer from the consulate. They'll be here at two."

Shay filled them in on what Eight had said—that the experimental subjects they'd seen around the RVs before the firefight at the dock had *not* been put aboard the ship.

"So there are still a bunch of people out there, unless—Harmon mentioned this—Singular killed them. But I think there's a good possibility they've been taken to New Mexico. As far as we know, it's the last Singular property in the United States."

"It's hard to believe that they'd do that—just kill them," Emily said. "I mean . . . it's hard to believe."

"That's because you haven't been with us on this whole trip," Odin said. "What they've been doing to these people . . ." He glanced at Eight and shook his head.

Eight looked at Emily and said: "We are nothing to them. After they do this to me"—he gestured at the knobs on his scalp—"they take me for examination and they laugh and talk like I am a rat. Not like I am a man, but like I am a rat."

Emily nodded and looked away, wiped a tear off her cheek.

Shay said, "If there's a chance there are more experimental subjects there, I think we need to go. To see if we can rescue them. Or at the very least to document that they are there—on Senator Dash's property. But we need to go soon—before it's too late."

"We have no idea what we'd be walking into," Twist said.

But Shay cut him off. "So let's figure it out."

They talked about it for more than an hour. Cruz got one of Twist's drawing pads and began making a list of equipment they'd need.

Much would depend on the terrain around the ranch. Odin and Cade were tapping on their laptops, talking to each other about the maps they were reviewing.

Odin: "The land around the ranch houses is pretty flat—it's a long floodplain along the Los Lobos River, that's where the landing strip is. But it's a V-shaped valley, with mountains on both sides, narrowing to the V where the mountain ranges hook up. The mouth of the valley to the south, that's pretty open and flat. . . ."

Twist eventually called a halt to the planning: "We can get back on it later this afternoon. The guys from the consulate will be here soon."

Three Chinese diplomats arrived precisely at two o'clock: the two who'd come before, plus an older, gray-haired man, whom Mr. Dang and Mr. Guan treated with deference. The kid working the front desk escorted them up to the studio, where the group was waiting.

When introductions had been made—they learned that the gray-haired man was Mr. Shen, but his title was not given—Twist gestured at Eight, who was still wearing his Cal Bears sweatshirt with the hood pulled over his scalp.

"Gentlemen, this is the man we believe is one of your citizens," Twist said. "He does not know his real name but has been going by the name Eight since the American authorities took him off the ship. Eight escaped from the hospital in San Francisco last night, where they are holding the experimental subjects."

One of the Chinese asked, "Escaped? By himself?"

"The details aren't important," Twist said. "Let's just say he made his way here."

The older man looked at Eight and said something in Chinese, and Eight immediately responded, and at length, talking for three or four minutes. Then, suddenly, Eight removed his hood, and the three men reared backward. Mr. Dang, who had done most of the talking in the previous meeting, got up and examined Eight's scalp so closely that his nose bumped a knob.

The three diplomats spoke to each other in Chinese for another minute, then Mr. Guan said, "I have an instrument here. . . ."

He took an iPhone from his pocket and what looked like another cell phone, although it was half the size of the iPhone, and square. They were connected with a cable. Speaking in English, he said to Eight, "We would like to take your fingerprints."

Eight said, "Yes. Please."

As the group watched, the diplomat took each finger on Eight's right hand and pressed them, one at a time, to the face of the smaller screen. When he had done all five, he looked at his iPhone app for a moment, then pushed a button. In English, he said to the group, "If . . . Eight . . . was a soldier, we will know in a few minutes. I've transmitted his fingerprints to the Ministry of National Defense."

Twist: "Well, what do you think? Is he Chinese?"

Mr. Dang nodded pensively and looked at Eight. "I think you are from the mainland."

Eight said something in Chinese, and the diplomat nodded more firmly and retreated to his chair.

Eight said to the group, "I say I wish to go home."

Mr. Shen said to the group, in good but accented English, "If all you say is true, then we will make strong representations to your government on behalf of our citizens."

Twist: "I hope you will do it publicly. I hope you will make your representations to the press. The problem is, Singular has more prisoners, and they will kill them if they have to. They are in the process of killing them now, with their experiments. Compared to some of the rest of the subjects, Eight is in very good condition: some of them have no minds left."

Mr. Shen said, "How does this happen in an advanced country?"

Odin: "We think people very high up in the government are involved in this, and they have influence over the police forces. . . . That's why we need your help. We need people at the highest levels to look at this; we need the president. He would do it if representatives from China addressed him directly."

Mr. Shen said, "This would not be entirely up to those of us here in this room. We would need further consultations with our government."

"Make them quick, or it'll be too late," Odin said undiplomatically.

Mr. Guan looked down as his phone chimed. He read for a moment, then spoke to the other diplomats in Chinese and then directly to Eight in English.

"Your name is Peng Bao. You were—you are—a lieutenant with the People's Liberation Army, stationed in Dandong."

"That's where Fenfang was from," Shay said.

The man continued: "When you disappeared, your blood was found where you were last seen. It was believed by the police that you were killed by smugglers and your body thrown in the river."

Peng Bao bobbed his head and spoke for a moment in Chinese, then said to the group in English, "I thank them for this, but I have no memory of this name. My name is Peng Bao. Peng Bao. Peng Bao. I do not know."

Harmon extended his hand and said, "Proud to know you, Bao."

Mr. Shen said, "Now that you are identified, do you wish to come with us to the consulate? You would be safe there, and you could be examined by our own doctors."

Twist: "Maybe we ought to go slow with that. He is safe here. . . ."

Shay said, "No, he isn't. He needs medical care. As soon as he can get it. Remember what we read about Fenfang's condition. . . ."

Documents stolen from Singular reported that the experimental subjects developed seizures and then died within weeks or a few months of their procedures. Fenfang almost certainly knew it, and Bao, she thought, probably suspected.

Twist nodded, then said, "Whatever Bao wishes to do."

Bao said, "I wish to go with them. I am Chinese. That is my country."

"Thank you," Mr. Shen said to Bao. Then to Twist: "I will recommend that we speak to your government at the very highest levels. If everything you say is true, to treat a Chinese military officer in this way is unforgivable. Somebody will pay a large price."

Odin said, "What about Fenfang? Will you find out who she is now, too? And notify her family?"

"Yes," Mr. Shen said.

14

Earl Denyers was suffering through an episode of what his less generous colleagues referred to as a flop sweat, though the CIA building felt unnaturally cold after his short walk across the parking lot.

There were too many moving parts, he thought—too many people on the loose, too little control, too many bureaucrats hovering between cooperation and covering their own asses. His guy at the FBI was on the edge of panic. His guy at the NSA wouldn't even talk to him.

On top of it all, Singular's main security guy had vanished. Denyers had no idea what had happened to Sync. His car had been found at a small municipal airstrip. Sync had a pilot's license but wasn't shown as the owner of a plane. The guy at the fixed-base operator where the car was found denied any knowledge of Sync or his plane—but he would, if he were a friend of Sync's.

Even with Sync gone, they'd managed to temporarily chill out the law enforcement community in the San Francisco area about the ship with the experimental subjects. They didn't control the San Francisco FBI office, though, and the agent in charge was questioning why D.C. agents were suddenly showing up on his turf, talking about national security.

Then the Chinese guy went missing from the hospital. Denyers didn't know for sure, but he figured the goddamn kids were behind it. With Harmon on the loose, they now had professional help.

And now the Chinese foreign ministry was calling. . . .

Denyers locked himself in his office and went out on a top security line to a cell phone so secret that he'd bought it himself, with cash, at a Walmart, while wearing a hoodie and ball cap.

"Gotta talk to you," he said.

"Critical?"

"Yes."

"Two o'clock, usual place."

At one minute to two, Denyers walked through the pillared portico of Lawton Jeffers's country club, straight across the lobby, and past the kitchen to a small side room, where the vice president of the United States sat eating a chicken sandwich with a glass of beer. He was wearing golf clothes: a pink polo shirt and pleated khaki pants.

Denyers took off his baseball cap and ran his hand through his sparse hair, and Jeffers asked, "How are the hair implants doing?"

"All right, if I didn't keep trying to pull them out," Denyers said. He took his bug detector out of his briefcase, laid it on the table, looked at it for a moment, then shut it down and put it away.

Lawton Jeffers stopped chewing long enough to say, "You know what your machine wouldn't detect? Somebody with his ear pressed to a glass on the other side of the wall."

"Before we met here the first time, I had the wall checked," Denyers said.

"You're shittin' me," said the vice president, amused despite himself.

"No, I'm not," Denyers said. "It's fire-rated concrete block. If anybody wanted to bug the place, which I doubt, they'd have to do it from the inside. Which they haven't."

"What's critical?" Jeffers asked. "I want to hit a few golf balls before I leave, so make it quick."

"Charlotte's been lying to us. When those kids hit her house, they got a lot more than she said they did, including some top-secret documents from the Intelligence Committee," Denyers said. "Worse than that, they got a lot of paper on Singular."

"How'd you find that out?"

"We bugged her," Denyers said. "She's been talking to a lawyer. She's trying to recover, get back on her feet, but she's not going to make it. We're already getting questions about her involvement."

"Is my name in there? In the papers?"

"We don't know. Though I tend to doubt it. Singular's down and it ain't coming back. We sterilized all the computers at the research sites and the headquarters. Janes has been moved offshore. We sealed off a lot of trouble when the jet went down, but the problem is, Charlotte's implicated in everything. It's gonna come out. That she's involved. If anybody ever goes out to the New Mexico site . . . We can't have people poking around out there, looking for bodies."

Jeffers thought about it for a moment, then said, "You don't think Charlotte will keep her mouth shut?"

"Of course she won't. Once this gets totally out of control, and it will, the FBI will be on her like flies on dog shit. And for her, there'll be only one way out."

"A deal." Jeffers was a lawyer and a former federal prosecutor.

"Exactly," Denyers said. "And the only way she could make that work is to offer up somebody even bigger."

Jeffers said, "Goddammit." He was definitely bigger.

"Yeah. She could throw me in, as a bonus. And Royce, and there goes the money."

"Can your guy handle it?" Jeffers asked.

"Yes," Denyers said. "She's got some security now, but they're ex-Singular guys that Sync put in. That can be handled."

"What are you thinking about?"

"Suicide. I got a guy who could write the note, on her own paper, with her own pen. Cancer, Singular, lost top-secret documents, her career crumbling. She decides to end it."

Jeffers sighed and scratched his neck, then pushed himself away from the table and stood up. "I'm gonna go hit some golf balls."

"What do you think?"

Jeffers scratched his neck again. "Charlotte Dash's service to America was entirely selfless. We need more women like her. And we need to do more, devote more money, to curing this curse of breast cancer, which cuts down so many American women. . . ."

"I'm touched," Denyers said. "I'm sure her friends will be impressed when the vice president shows up to give the eulogy."

They looked at each other for a moment, and it occurred to Denyers that he'd always considered the vice president a friend. Now he realized that Jeffers didn't really have friends. He had associates. Denyers asked, "How about the other thing?"

"I don't want to talk about the other thing. If something should happen, I want to be surprised," Jeffers said.

Denyers ran his hand through his thin hair one last time and put his ball cap back on.

The vice president said, "Mmm. I got a new TaylorMade driver, gets me another five yards."

"I'll call you," Denyers said.

15

The group was up late that night, sitting in Twist's studio, arguing about a run to New Mexico. Nobody was against it, exactly, but they had already lost two in the fight against Singular, two more had been tortured, and one had been torn up by attack dogs.

Twist summed it up: "Going to New Mexico would be the biggest risk we've taken. There's nothing out there, where the ranch is. They could kill all of us, put us in the ground, and nobody would ever know."

There was a long pause as they sat surrounded by Twist's newly mounted aluminum painting supports, which Shay had coated with white primer. Twist had opened the windows while she was doing the priming, and the studio was suffused with the thin, oily odor of traffic on the 101.

Emily said, "If the Chinese diplomats do what they said they might, if they get in contact with the State Department, and maybe even the president . . ."

Cade: "That could take forever. You know how a bureaucracy

works. But Singular can shut down and move everything up in the cloud and offshore in days. If there's anything left in the U.S. to find, it'll be there—but not for long."

"That's right," Shay said. "If we're going to New Mexico, I think we have to start now. Tonight."

"Not tonight," Twist said. "We've got more work to do, maps to find, approaches to figure out. I say we start tomorrow morning, head for Phoenix—that's only six hours from here."

Harmon, who'd been sitting quietly, listening, said, "I'll tell you right up front, if we're going to do this, we'll need to take guns." He looked at Twist. "I know you hate them, but that's the way it is. If they've still got the pros working for them, we'll be outgunned and maybe even outsmarted before we get there. The other side will know the terrain; they may well be running patrols. They may have starlight scopes and night-vision goggles. . . ."

"After what happened with the ship, I thought Singular's security guys were bailing out," Cruz said.

"Some, but probably not all of them. We can't be sure," Harmon said.

Shay said, "We can't even be sure if the people guarding the ranch—if they *are* guarding the ranch—know about the ship and what happened there."

"I think they probably do," Cruz said. "If they're SEALs or former Delta guys, they'd have a lot of loyalty to each other. More to each other than to Singular. If Singular were falling apart, I think they'd pass the word along."

Harmon nodded. "You're right. Even Sync and I still think that way."

They thought about it, then Cade said, "I'd love to sneak onto that ranch, but I have to tell you, my ribs are still hurting."

"We all know that," Twist said. "You and Odin are the intelligence arm."

"Three vehicles," Harmon said, staring at the ceiling, thinking out loud. "Two recon teams, close enough to support each other but far enough apart that they can't jump both of us at the same time. Twist and Odin drive, me and Danny are on one team, Cruz, Shay, and X on the other. X could be important, if we're operating in the dark." The dog, lying nearby, had stood up at the mention of his name, and Shay waved him to her side as Harmon continued. "We'd want Cade close by, in a hotel with good Wi-Fi, ready to roll if one of the other cars has a problem. Emily here in L.A. as a final backstop to call in the cavalry if it all goes wrong.

"I can get some night-vision equipment from a guy in Gila Bend, which is almost on the way, but it'll cost. . . ."

"I can handle that," Twist said.

"We've got the walkie-talkies for when you're scouting around," Cade said. "It looks to me like there are big pieces of territory out there with no cell service at all."

They all contributed more ideas, refined the plan until it seemed solid. It was past midnight when Twist said, "Anything else before we sleep?"

Shay raised a hand. "Harmon's truck has a big orange circle on the roof. We might want to paint that out."

"You know where the paint is," Twist said. "See everyone in the parking lot at ten."

Shay was up at seven, out in the cool morning air with a can of black Car Art paint. She crawled up on the roof of Harmon's truck and painted out the orange circle. Harmon came out as she was finishing the job and said, "Well, that's about a five-thousand-dollar repaint job, when this is over."

She put the cap on the can and tossed it to him. "Wrong. You wash it off with soap and water."

Harmon looked at the can and said, "Huh. Never knew about this stuff."

Shay slipped down from the car and asked, "What do you think?"

"About New Mexico? I don't know; we'll have to wait until we get there. Lots of possibilities."

"Do we really need two teams? Maybe it'd be better if it was just you and me and X," Shay said. "Danny and Cruz as backup to come in and get us if we need it."

"Better to have two teams on the ground," Harmon said. "Then one can support the other—come in unexpectedly. I want you with the other team because . . . I know you. Cruz seems like a good guy, but he's not a killer. If we need a really quick action . . ."

"And I am? A killer?"

"You are what you are, sweetheart. If the shit gets heavy, I want somebody on the other team I can count on."

At ten-thirty, only a half hour past Twist's deadline, the group was on the road, headed out of L.A.

16

When Shay stepped out of the Jeep in Lordsburg, New Mexico, she felt like she'd fallen into hell. Again. A temperature sign outside a local business said it was ninety-nine degrees, and heat waves shimmered off the sidewalks, creating mini-mirages.

"Better than Phoenix, anyway," she said to Cruz. Phoenix had been a hundred and seven. They'd spent an hour there, buying backpacking gear, water, and a carryall vest for X, before moving closer to the ranch. Shay took a fabric bowl out of one of the vest's pockets, unfolded it on the sidewalk, and poured X a drink.

They were staying at another Twist motel special: all cash, no questions.

Twist came out of the motel office, blinking in the sunlight, unclipped his sunglasses from the V of his shirt, and put them on. "We're good. I'm told they have maximum air-conditioning and good Wi-Fi."

"Did you hear from Harmon?" Shay asked.

"Yeah. He'll be here in an hour. He got the night-vision goggles."
He looked around the half-empty parking lot. "Let's get inside."

They all piled into room 22, which had two beds, one chair, a flat-screen TV, a window air conditioner permanently set to high, and a sign that said GET YOUR WI-FI PASSWORD AT THE FRONT DESK. The room, Shay thought, smelled like wet rags.

"I gotta go back to the office for the Wi-Fi code?" Twist groaned. "My brain's already fried."

Odin shook his head. "Hotel Wi-Fi security is virtually useless."

Twist often used photographs as references for his paintings and had a large-scale, high-resolution photo printer in his studio. Cade and Odin had printed out full-color satellite photos of the ranch and the surrounding area for everyone. Odin got on his laptop and two minutes later was on the hotel's Wi-Fi system. The first thing he looked up was the weather for Silver City. "Cooler than here. Mid- to high eighties," he said. "Not too bad. Fairly cool at night, in the sixties. No rain."

Shay spent the next hour working on the daypacks that she, Cruz, Danny, and X would carry. In the human packs, there would be flashlights, one set of binoculars and one zoom-lens camera for each team, a short climbing rope, notebooks and pens, walkie-talkies, some energy bars, and four one-liter bottles of water. She stuck a half roll of toilet paper in each pack, squashed down to make it flat. X would carry his own food and water, plus a first-aid kit.

They would all be wearing boots, jeans, long-sleeved shirts, and baseball caps. They would pack head nets and gloves to fend off mosquitoes, should any show up, and would carry bandannas in case they needed masks.

Cruz and Shay would carry pistols. Danny refused to carry a gun, but Harmon would carry both a pistol and a .223 rifle.

Harmon showed up right on time, with four black-market Kevlar helmets, with binocular night-vision scopes mounted on each, and a handheld GPS. "I hope you've got a use for the night-vision rigs in L.A.," he told Twist, "because they cost as much as a new truck."

"Can always sell them on the street. Probably make a profit," Cruz said. "You know, to burglars and so on."

"That'd make me feel good," Twist said.

"You worried again?" Harmon asked.

"I'm always worried," Twist said.

They would leave the motel for Dash's ranch at eight o'clock. The ranch was roughly a half hour away, and they wanted it to be fully dark when they arrived. The two teams would be dropped off on a highway that paralleled one edge of the property.

"We're recommending that approach because you'll be moving downhill most of the way, rather than on the flat that you'd get if you came up from the river side," Cade said, drawing his finger across one of the map photos. "You should have a better view of what you're getting into. And it means we won't have to take the trucks off-road, which would be conspicuous at night, if there's anybody out there watching."

"The downside," Odin said, "is that you'll be almost a mile out from the ranch buildings when we drop you off. It's a rough walk, coming down that mountain. It'll be slow going."

Harmon said, "We shouldn't go in where the road runs closest to the ranch—if they're watching, that's where they'll be, so we'll start farther out. We won't last two full days in the desert—we can't carry enough water. If we go in tonight, we'll have to get out by tomorrow night, probably right after dark."

"One really good thing is," Odin said, tapping the satellite photo, "all these black dots you see are piñon trees. It's not really what you'd think of as a forest, but the fact is, you won't be able to see, or be seen, more than forty or fifty yards away."

Harmon nodded. "I once got pretty turned around in some piñons. Cloudy day, couldn't see the sun, took six hours to make a half-hour walk."

Cade and Odin worked out the GPS readings for the revised drop-off point.

"We're gonna have to stop to unload; we need to put some black tape over the trucks' interior lights so they won't light up when we open the doors." Harmon tucked extra flashlight batteries in his pack, then continued. "Oh, before I forget: no deodorant or anything with a perfume to it. If guys are hunting for us in the dark, they'll be sweating themselves, and they won't smell our sweat, but they *will* smell Old Spice."

"Good point," Odin said. "Can't believe you worked it all out."

"I didn't—credit goes to Special Forces and the guys who trained me," Harmon said. "We got operators risking their necks all the time, all over the world." He chewed on his lip for another moment, the whole group watching him. Then he said, "We're too close to the ranch right here for my taste. If they have reason to come looking for us, they'll probably look first in Silver City. That's closer to them and probably what they're oriented toward when they go shopping and so on. That'll buy us some time."

"You hope," Shay said.

"Yeah, I hope. Not that we got much choice. There's not much out here; no urban areas to hide in."

• • •

When they had the maps in their heads, they went to their various rooms to nap: it would be a long night.

At seven o'clock, they were up again, dressed in dark clothing. Harmon took Shay aside and had her cycle through her pistol, a last-minute check to make sure it was working perfectly.

At eight, they loaded into two vehicles—Twist driving the Range Rover with Harmon and Danny, and Odin driving the Mercedes with Shay, Cruz, and X—and started north toward the ranch. Five miles out of town, at a dirt trail pinpointed with Harmon's GPS, they turned off the highway, drove over a low ridge, and stopped. Harmon demonstrated the night-vision gear, and they spent a while working with it. Shay found that when she moved her head too quickly, she became a little nauseated; she learned to move her head and eyes slowly, like searchlights scanning across a landscape. When everybody had adapted, they headed back to the highway.

Fifteen miles up the road, Harmon called the other vehicle by walkie-talkie. "Five minutes. Get geared up. Trucks stop for two seconds, and then we've got to be off the road, with the trucks moving out. Make sure the tape's still stuck on the interior lights, and, Odin, don't use your brakes to stop behind me—stay far enough back that you can coast to a stop. We don't want your taillights flaring."

"So damn sneaky," Odin muttered. "Remind me to hack into Special Forces and download me some spy guides."

Harmon counted down, his voice carrying a slight buzz over the walkie-talkie speakers. "One minute. Twenty seconds. Ten seconds . . . Start coasting, Odin."

Odin turned his head to Shay, in the passenger seat, and said, "Nail them, and don't get killed."

Shay nodded, and she, Cruz, and X slipped out. Cruz pushed the door shut with a barely audible *click,* and the truck moved on.

Shay and Cruz and the dog darted twenty feet off the road, Cruz stumbling into an eight-foot-tall cholla cactus straight off, despite the night-vision lenses. He let out a silent scream as a pad of thorns lanced deep into his left palm. The pain wasn't commensurate with the bite force of Dash's trained attack dogs, but . . . it was close enough. He fumbled for his bandanna, and a bilingual string of curse words ran through his head as he yanked out eight or nine spines.

"Over here!" Shay whispered sharply, unaware of his troubles.

They crouched in the sandy dirt, turning their heads like searchlights, and waited. The night was cool and felt very dry, the air scented by piñon pines. A minute later, Harmon and Danny appeared, moving slowly along the edge of the highway; in the night-vision lenses, they were green-and-black outlines, and Shay could see the long shape of the black rifle in Harmon's hands. Shay waved, and the pair angled toward them.

"Okay," Harmon said quietly. "Danny and I'll go diagonally. You guys go straight in, several hundred yards, and then angle over toward the house lights. Stay in touch. Make sure you're alone before you click us. One click means you want to talk. Two clicks back means talk; a whole bunch of clicks means don't talk, that somebody's too close."

"We're gonna find the prisoners," Shay said. "I can feel it."

"Don't know," Harmon said. "But if you do, click. No approach until we talk. And X . . . keep him close. One bad bark and none of us are leaving the Land of Enchantment. Ever."

17

In ninth-grade English, Shay had been given a choice of poems to memorize, and she'd chosen Robert Frost's "Stopping by Woods on a Snowy Evening" because the last verse touched something in her:

The woods are lovely, dark, and deep,
But I have promises to keep,
And miles to go before I sleep,
And miles to go before I sleep.

At the time, the poem reassured her that whatever her problems—and she had more than a few, as a foster kid—she had miles to go in her life and promises to keep.

Now, walking into woods that were dark and deep and possibly even lovely, if she could have seen anything other than the black outlines of the trees in the starlight, she thought it was all coming true. Frost might not have recognized the arid desert landscape, but more than ever, Shay felt she had promises to keep and miles to go . . . before what she hoped would be a literal sleep and not a bitter, final one.

Cruz was leading the way, moving slowly, X, a pale shadow in the night-vision scopes, either by his knee or a few feet ahead, nose probing the night air. Fifteen minutes and a couple hundred yards down the slope, Cruz stopped and put up a hand. "Got lights."

Far off to their right, at about a forty-five-degree angle, a single light hung above the low trees. The light amplification in the night-vision goggles made it look like a too-close star.

"Keep going down," Shay whispered. "When it's straight off to the right, we should stop and sit for a while. And listen."

"You all right?"

"Yes. I'm fine." She touched the pistol on her hip and the knife at the small of her back, made a minute adjustment to the goggles. They were heavy and wanted to pull her face down.

Cruz and X moved on. Shay waited until they were five yards ahead of her and then followed. The sky above them was like something seen in a planetarium, the huge, starry arc of the Milky Way hanging overhead, barely diminished by the light of a new moon rising in the east.

Cruz did a tap dance, then said, too loudly, "Jeez."

Shay whispered, "What?"

"Branch. I stepped on it, and it moved, and I thought it was a rattler."

"Gotta be quieter."

They moved on, still going slowly. In the next few minutes, they picked up another light and then, suddenly, a whole cluster of them straight ahead. "We were looking at pole lights, maybe on a driveway," Cruz said quietly. "That might be a house we're looking at now."

• • •

The ground had flattened out and softened, but the piñons remained thick. While the trees provided concealment, they also kept Shay and Cruz from seeing what was up ahead.

A walkie-talkie clicked at her. She whispered at Cruz to stop, then clicked back twice. Harmon said, "There are other people out here. Be careful. A guy just went by, and he had a gun."

Shay felt the hair rise on the back of her neck. "Okay."

Cruz whispered, "Listen again."

They listened for five minutes but heard nothing. X was nosing around but never came to an alert stance, and Cruz moved out again, Shay following. They crossed a narrow arroyo, and then another, deeper, and climbed the far bank to find themselves only a hundred yards from a sprawling log house that showed lights in several windows and the flashing-blue-light signature of a television screen. There were two SUVs parked outside.

"Too close," Shay said. She knelt, Cruz beside her. X looked back at them, went a few feet farther on, then came back to wait by Shay. "Just listen again," Shay said.

They sat and listened for what seemed like a long time but probably wasn't much more than ten minutes. They hadn't seen another human since they'd left Harmon and Danny, and though it was fully dark, it wasn't that late.

"Let's move again," Shay said. "That way."

She pointed toward one of the pole lights that Cruz thought might mark a driveway. That route would get them closer to the cluster of buildings but no closer to the log house.

Cruz moved off, X beside him, Shay trailing. They'd gone a hundred yards, nearly to the pole, when headlights broke through the trees above them and a pickup rolled down what did turn out to be the driveway, crunching over the gravel. They crouched behind a piñon until the vehicle passed, then scuttled closer to the driveway. From there, they could see the pickup stop outside a small barn-shaped building, and a garage door lifted up.

The barn faced a building made to look like an old-fashioned farmhouse. A woman in jeans and a Western shirt came out onto the porch and stood under a light until a man carrying a grocery sack came out of the miniature barn. The garage door rolled down behind him, and the woman called, "Benny's on the phone! Got a real early flight coming in."

They heard the man ask, "Dash?" and the woman say, "No, she's later. . . ." But they couldn't hear the rest of it until the man said, ". . . assholes from Washington . . . ," and then the door closed and that was all.

Shay: "Did he say Washington?"

"I think so," Cruz whispered.

"We need to be here when the plane comes. We need to see who's on it. We need to get pictures."

"We should talk to Harmon now," Cruz said. "Let's get farther away from here."

Before they could move, Shay heard gravel crunching ahead of them. X spun toward it, silently pointing. Shay put her hand on Cruz's arm to stop him and hooked a finger beneath X's collar. A few seconds later, they heard another crunch, then another, the sounds resolving into footsteps. A man ambled down the driveway, a rifle over his shoulder. He didn't look at them, didn't seem particularly alert at all, but continued to the farmhouse, took a chair on the porch, and lit a cigarette. A very gentle breeze carried the smell of the burning tobacco toward them. They waited, and the man finished his cigarette, picked up the rifle, and walked slowly back up the driveway.

When his footsteps faded, Cruz whispered, "I wonder if he just walks up and down, patrolling, or does he have a guard shack? Might be the same guy that Danny and Harmon saw. . . ."

"We gotta call, let them know he's coming up."

They walked back the way they came, deeper into the trees again, then Shay got on the walkie-talkie and clicked the transmit button one time. Ten seconds later, she got two clicks back. "Where are you guys?"

"By the largest house," Harmon said.

"We're by the bottom of the driveway by the farmhouse-looking place. Listen, a guy just came down the driveway with a gun, like a rifle. He seems to be walking up and down. . . . He's heading back toward you now. Is he the same guy you saw?"

"Could be. We saw our guy coming *up* the driveway. . . . Haven't seen anybody since."

"We need to talk," Shay said.

"We'll come to you," Harmon said. "Which side of the driveway are you on?"

"We didn't cross it—we're by the bottom pole light, back in the trees."

"Ten minutes," Harmon said.

Ten minutes later, X, who'd been lying down, suddenly stood and peered into the darkness. Shay put a hand on his back and said, "No bark."

X remained on guard until they heard Harmon say softly, "You there?"

Even with the night-vision glasses, they couldn't see anyone. Cruz: "Over here."

A few seconds later, they saw Harmon and Danny move out from behind a piñon, and Shay waved, and they ran, bent over, then sank to the ground next to her. Harmon said, "If there's a guy on the driveway, we better move farther away."

Shay led them through the trees, fifty yards away from the driveway. They found a tight circle of piñons and crouched in the center of it and listened for the man with the rifle. Nothing. Shay asked, "You get to the airstrip?"

"Not yet. We're still poking around the main house and a couple outbuildings. Why'd you call us in?"

She told them about the log house and the garage and the farmhouse at the bottom of the drive and the overheard conversation. "Sounds like some people might be coming early from Washington. Dash, too, but later. I think we need to see who it is. Get some pictures."

"On the satellite views, the ground around the airstrip looked wide open," Harmon said. "We'll have to scout out a place to hide and still get pictures."

They talked about it and concluded that since Harmon and Danny had already worked the far side of the driveway, where the main house was, they should go back and continue the reconnaissance there. In the meantime, Shay, Cruz, and X would retrace their steps along the flatland, then make a wide circle around the far side of the ranch buildings to the landing strip and find a place where they could settle down and watch.

"The driveway guard didn't seem particularly careful: we heard him coming from pretty far away," Cruz said. "But you gotta be careful crossing the drive."

"Was he wearing night-vision gear?" Harmon asked. "The guy we saw wasn't."

"No. Not unless it was hidden in his cowboy hat," Shay said.

Harmon and Danny disappeared into the night, headed back across the driveway. Shay, Cruz, and X slipped deeper into the piñons, headed toward the landing strip. The night-vision gear was becoming more familiar, and they moved easily over the landscape but tried not to look directly at bright building lights, which would flare up on the imaging screens.

They'd gone the length of a football field when they saw more lights ahead and came to a brick building. The building had a row of small, high windows spaced at eight-foot intervals all down its length, only dimly lit, and a poorly lit parking lot in front with one SUV in it.

"Look at the windows. Bars," Cruz whispered.

"Wonder if that's to keep intruders out or prisoners in?" Shay asked.

"Who's here to keep out?" Cruz said.

The piñons had been cut well back from the building, but they could see knee-high brush all around it—brush that could act effectively as a burglar alarm. The bars were intriguing, but they decided to push around the building and continue on toward the airstrip.

A short way out, they saw another building that also had small windows, but without the bars, and this one was definitely occupied.

They could hear music and different men speaking, in both English and Spanish, and then, around the front of the building, out of their sight, a door slammed. A man crunched across the gravel driveway and got in a truck they couldn't yet see, and then head-lights came on and a pickup drove in the direction of the farm-house, where they'd learned about the incoming flights.

"Bunkhouse," Cruz breathed.

"Ranch hands or Singular security?"

"Don't know. Sounded like more Spanish than English, so . . . could be just regular ranch hands."

"How many, do you think?"

"Eight windows, eight rooms . . . maybe eight more on the other side . . . so . . . maybe sixteen?"

"There's got to be bathrooms. . . ."

"Okay, so maybe twelve, with the end windows in the bathrooms. They don't have separate bathrooms in bunkhouses."

They circled away again and saw a long, plain building with at least six vehicle bays. Three of the double-wide garage doors were open; one slot was empty, but in the others they could see the front end of an RV and what looked like an oversized horse trailer.

"RV—that's how they were moving the prisoners," Shay said. "I bet they're in the building with the barred windows. . . ."

"Gonna have to watch it in the daylight," Cruz said, "when peo-ple are coming and going."

"Why the horse trailer? Have you seen any horses?" Shay asked.

"No. Maybe it's just cover—what's supposed to be here."

"Hmm."

They made a cut through another stand of piñons and, twenty min-utes later, came out a hundred yards or so from the landing strip. All the trees had been cleared within thirty yards on both sides of the strip. Far down to their right, they could see a small building close to the tarmac. They sat and listened for a while.

"We'd be better off on the other side," Cruz said.

"So let's walk around it," Shay said. "See what else we can see."

Walking the length of the strip took more than an hour. When they finally reached the end of it, they could barely see the lights from the ranch buildings. At the tail end of the strip, down toward the river, they found a burn pit. X made several approaches to it but flinched away, as though his nose was offended. A tall pile of cut wood sat next to it, apparently to keep the trash fires burning.

They started back toward the ranch houses, now completely invisible in the dark. From the angle of their approach, they could see that the airstrip building had a ramp beside it.

Shay: "If that's where the planes park, then we should find a place up there"—she pointed uphill to an area between the strip and the cluster of ranch buildings—"to set up. Get in one of the deep tree clusters."

"If somebody walks through there . . ."

"But why would they walk through?"

"I don't know *why* they would, but if they *did,* they'd see us," Cruz said. "And they'd be between us and the highway."

"So we hide Harmon and Danny farther up the hill, deeper in the trees, where they can see down and sideways. If they see somebody heading toward us, they call and we take off."

"I don't know," Cruz said. "It might be pretty exposed in the daylight."

Shay took her cell phone from her pocket, pushed it down inside the front of her jacket so the light wouldn't show, and checked the time. Two o'clock. "Let's get the guys and work it out."

They were now on the same side of the driveway as Harmon and

Danny, but it took fifteen minutes to hook up, and not without a bit of chasing around. The trees were dense enough that in the dark they couldn't see through them at all, and the sandy soil killed the sound of footsteps.

When they came together, Harmon said, "We're three or four hundred yards from the driveway, so we're well out of sight of the guard . . . as long as he stays on the drive."

Shay and Cruz told the other two about the bunkhouse, about the building with the barred windows, about the garage with the RV and horse trailer, about the landing strip's parking ramp, and about Cruz's concern that somebody could stumble on them if they simply plopped down under a tree near the airstrip.

Harmon said, "I agree with Shay: we need to set up and get photos of anyone getting off the airplanes. It'd also be good if we could see what's going on around that building with the barred windows—who comes and goes."

Danny added, "The two big houses are mostly dark, so we don't know whether anyone is staying there. We got up close to them, didn't hear a thing. All we can see is some glow from what look like a few night-lights."

"Or alarm panels," Harmon said.

"Is there anyplace where we can set up and watch for people who might be coming and going—take their pictures?" Shay asked.

"One gap between trees," Danny said. "Looks right down to the parking area, but if they see us, we're screwed. We'd really be close to the house."

"If we can take pictures of people getting out of the planes, maybe we don't need to shoot them by the house," Cruz said.

Harmon nodded, then said he wanted to get a look at the sprawling log house with the SUVS, the building with the barred windows, and the bunkhouse. "Better if I go alone—quieter that way, and I've done this before. So. You guys see if you can find a good place to hide with a view of the airstrip. And I like the idea of two of us, or even three of us, watching from higher up the hill. Maybe you could find some potential spots. I'll try to get back by three o'clock."

When Harmon was gone, Shay, Cruz, Danny, and X moved back through the trees and finally found a spot where four piñons had grown close together and a shallow pit had formed in the middle of them. If they were down in the pit, they couldn't be seen by anybody scanning the ground level.

"We're a little far from the plane parking ramp," Danny said.

"We've got a zoom lens on the camera," Shay said.

"Yeah, well, you'd be surprised at how little zoom you really get," Danny said. "Still, this looks like the best there is."

After agreeing that they could use the pit for cover, they clicked Harmon and told him approximately where he might find them. Then they moved back up the hill and found more places where watchers could hide. By spreading three people across the hillside, they would be able to watch the photographer's back without being seen themselves.

That done, they all walked to the pit to wait. At three, Harmon still hadn't returned. Shay and Cruz were huddled together with X, all of them dozing, while Danny sat up on watch. Suddenly X was up, nosing Shay, and Shay's eyes popped open. X growled, and Shay touched his back. He went silent, and then they heard Harmon say in a low voice, "Don't let that mutt bark at me."

When he was down in the pit with them, he said, "That log house—I think that's where the security guys hang out. The gun guys. There are three SUVs total: two there and one near the building with the bars. I'm thinking there are three teams of two, two guys per SUV, and they're guarding the barred building in three shifts. That's six guys with guns. It's possible that a couple more came with the RV, so there could be eight or nine. The log house looks like it could probably sleep eight.

"I think the bunkhouse is for the regular ranch hands, though it's hard to tell how *regular* they might be. There's a horse trailer, but no horses I can see. And a ranch hand with a gun can kill you as dead as a SEAL, if he shoots you.

"The place with the barred windows—I got my ear right up against it and heard somebody moaning. Didn't quit—it was exactly like on the ship," Harmon said.

He concluded: "Bottom line: there are a lot of bad guys here and a bunch of them are going to be well trained and most of them will have guns. Altogether, ex-military and ranch hands, could be twenty of them."

"Want a gun now, Danny?" Shay asked.

"No. I still don't. But I would like to run away about now," Danny said.

Shay patted his arm and turned back to Harmon. "So what do you think?" she asked him.

"I think we hide as best we can, take some pictures tomorrow morning, then try to sneak away. We need to talk to Twist and the others, see what they think. But I gotta tell you guys, this looks tough. Don't know how we can get the prisoners out of here without getting killed. But we've got all night to think on it. . . ."

18

They'd scouted out the ranch buildings and the airstrip, and from what they'd seen on the satellite photos, there wasn't much else around, so they walked up the hill, away from the ranch buildings and the airstrip, and huddled in a heavy stand of piñons, trying to get some sleep before daylight.

X settled behind Shay's head, like a warm, furry pillow.

When Shay felt X stir, and opened her eyes, a thin dawn light was creeping across the desert. It'd be a while before they'd see the sun, but they wouldn't need the night-vision glasses anymore.

Harmon was next to her, sitting upright, sound asleep. She nudged him, and his eyes popped open. She tipped her head at X, who was now standing up, focused on the ranch buildings.

"I'll take a look," Shay whispered.

Harmon nodded and yawned, and Shay eased across the slope, trailed by X. A garage door rolled up. She couldn't see it, only heard it. An engine fired, a thick, rough noise unlike a car or a motorcycle, and began moving.

She hurried back to the group, now all awake, and said, "Something's coming this way."

"That's a problem," Danny said.

Harmon walked down the slope a few yards to listen, then said, "Not exactly toward us. He's angling down below us, maybe headed to the airstrip."

"Picking up somebody from the plane?" Cruz suggested.

"Could be, but it's still pretty dim out here. No lights on the airstrip."

The sound of the engine still seemed to be getting closer. When it passed them, two hundred yards down the slope, running along the edge of the airstrip, they caught a glimpse of a green utility-style vehicle, like a small pickup, with two seats in the front. It was driven by a man in a cowboy hat. There was a black bag in the back of the vehicle, and Shay said, "Burning trash. There's a trash-burning place at the end of the airstrip. We passed it last night."

Harmon said quickly, "Cruz, you go right up the slope from here, fifty yards or so, and face the driveway. Danny, you stay right here, watch down the slope. Shay and I are gonna run. You see anybody coming, click us."

Cruz started to object, but Harmon said, "No! Don't have time to argue. Shay, get your pack—we'll need the binoculars and the camera. Let's go. . . ."

Danny: "What's happening, man?"

Harmon had his rifle over his shoulder and was looking down the slope. "Garbage bags are round. That one looked flat."

"Yeah?"

"It looked like a body bag," Harmon said. To Shay: "C'mon, c'mon. . . ."

• • •

To avoid being seen, they had to keep a screen of piñons between themselves and the man in the vehicle, but they also needed to move fast. When they were fully covered, they ran. When there were gaps in the trees, they watched for a few seconds and then moved on, dodging between trees, always looking around for other movement, other eyes.

After four or five minutes of this, Harmon jerked an arm up, calling a halt. Shay, breathing hard, said, "I gotta get in better shape."

"Not today," Harmon said. "Let's slow it down. There's not much between us now. We want to get where we've got a clear shot of him. Hang on to X."

The dog glanced up when he heard his name, then looked back toward the burn pit. Shay peered around the edge of a piñon, saw that the man was out of the vehicle, throwing logs off the pile of firewood.

"He's looking away from us: we can get closer."

Now it was tree-to-tree creeping. They were eighty yards out when they got a click on the walkie-talkie. Harmon double-clicked back, and Cruz said, "We don't think they're coming toward you, but there's some movement around the houses. Lots of guys getting up."

Harmon: "Got it. We're getting in close here. Keep watching."

Seventy yards out, X now fully alert, staying at Shay's knee. One last tree, and they had a clear line to the man. He was taking off a jean jacket. He tossed it on the passenger seat of the utility vehicle and went back to throwing logs.

The logs were all piñon, as thick as Harmon's upper arm and six or seven feet long. The man laid down a crisscross pattern, eight logs on the bottom, crossed by eight more on top, crossed by eight more on top of those, and then eight more.

As he did it, Shay watched with binoculars, and Harmon took photos with the digital camera. "He's a long way out—his head's about the size of a pin on the view screen," he whispered. "I hope we can identify him in the prints."

Shay: "There's a dial on the back. You can enlarge the image on the screen, see what it'll look like when it's enlarged."

Harmon looked down at the camera, messed with the dial for a moment, then said, "Okay . . . Not bad. Not bad."

When the man had a pile of logs about waist-high, he horsed the black bag out of the utility vehicle and onto the pile of logs, Harmon taking pictures as he did. Then he went back to the firewood, piling more layers over the bag.

Shay muttered, "Are you sure . . . ?"

"It's not a garbage bag. I've seen all kinds of body bags, and that was a body bag, and there's a body in it."

"Aw, jeez, what am I doing here?"

Harmon looked at her. "Don't freak out on me."

"All right, but I'm gonna freak out later," Shay said.

"I'll freak out with you," Harmon said.

The pile of logs grew, then the man, wiping his forehead on his shirtsleeve, went to the utility vehicle and took out a can of gasoline. Walking around the pile of logs, he poured gasoline over it, the odor seeping across the ground to Shay, Harmon, and X.

That done, he put the can back in the vehicle, took a pack of cigarettes out of his pocket, walked maybe fifteen feet from the pile, lit the cigarette, took a couple of long drags, then snapped it into the logs. The pile exploded in flames ten, fifteen feet high.

The man walked to the utility vehicle and backed it away from the fire, out of the heat, then took a magazine off the passenger seat, got out, propped himself against the vehicle's hood, and began flipping through the magazine.

"They're burning the experimental subjects," Shay said. "The subjects are dying, and they're cremating them."

"That's what I'd say, too," Harmon said. "C'mon. We won't get anything more here—let's head back."

The day was getting brighter: not a cloud in the sky, and no shade outside the small spots thrown by the trees. They backed away from the fire and the man monitoring it. They were a hundred yards out when X pricked up his ears and turned back toward the fire, working his nose.

Then Shay smelled it and wiped her hand across her nose.

Harmon looked at her and said, "Yeah. That's what it smells like. Barbecue."

"That's awful," she said.

"Keep moving."

The odor of the fire moved faster than they did. When they moved the last few yards across the hillside to where Danny was hidden, he asked, "Is that what I think it is?"

"Yeah," Harmon said. "We need to stay here, see what they do with the ashes. If they scrape them into the river, it'll be a problem. If they leave them there . . . Bodies are hard to get rid of. You can usually find some sign of them, even after cremation. Find one little piece of bone, and a lab can prove it's human."

"Twist will cruise the place at eight o'clock," Shay said. "We ought to get the camera's memory card out to him so Odin or Cade can park the pictures in the cloud."

Shay went up the hill with X, found Cruz, brought him back down, told him about the fire. Cruz turned as grim as Danny had. "Anything that happens to these people, they deserve. *Anything.*"

Shay had the sense that things were moving now, that the pace would pick up. She was wrong.

They sat in the trees for another hour and nothing happened. They ate energy bars and drank water and nothing happened. Nobody went to the airstrip. They heard trucks and SUVs going up and down the driveway, but there was nothing they could do about that. Someplace off toward the ranch complex, somebody started a weed cutter. In the other direction, the smoke from the fire gradually diminished. The man who'd built it stayed where he was, watching, reading his magazine.

Then, a little after seven o'clock, an SUV rolled past on the airstrip and stopped directly below them, next to the building. A minute later, they heard a plane.

The plane, a red and silver twin prop, flew parallel to the runway, a few hundred feet up, and tipped toward it, giving the pilot a better look, then continued past the end of the strip and out of sight.

"Making his approach turn," Harmon said.

The sound of the engine dwindled to nearly nothing, then, a minute later, began getting louder. When they saw the plane again, it was no more than a hundred feet up, a half mile or so south of the strip. It touched down easily, swept past the ramp, pivoted on the turning pad at the end of the strip, and returned to the parking area.

A set of steps dropped down from a side door, and a passenger clambered out. He looked like an accountant on holiday: a pudgy man dressed in a blue golf shirt, jeans, and a gold-colored ball cap carrying a briefcase. He stopped to say something to the pilot.

"Wonder who he is," Shay said. "Doesn't look that important."

"What does important look like?" Danny asked. He was using the binoculars. "Notice that his jeans have a crease."

"What does that mean?" Harmon asked.

"It means he has a maid," Danny said. "You're not supposed to iron jeans, but maids do it anyway. He's important enough to have a maid."

Harmon looked at Danny as if reappraising him.

"What?" Danny asked.

"That's smart," Harmon said. "That's a good observation."

Down below, the pudgy man got into the SUV, and it headed back toward the big houses. They listened for a couple of minutes, until they heard the car doors slam.

"Twist will be coming in forty-five minutes," Harmon said. "We should head up to the highway, where we can flag him and get him the memory card."

The words had just left his mouth when they heard the sound of another plane approaching and the SUV starting up again. The second plane was smaller than the first, a single-engine prop, a Cessna, Harmon said, one of the most common small planes in the air. It followed the same procedure as the first, flying the length of the strip, turning, landing, parking by the airstrip building.

This time they didn't wonder about the identity of the person who got out.

"Thorne," Harmon growled.

"He's a pilot?" Cruz asked.

"Unless the plane flew itself," Harmon said. "But yeah, lots of us are. It's sort of a thing."

"You're a pilot?" Shay asked.

"Not a very good one," Harmon said. "I can get from here to there, but you might not want to fly through a thunderstorm with me."

"Could you fly those planes?" Shay asked.

"Not the twin engine, but I learned on a Cessna, and I rent one from time to time, when I'm looking for archaeological sites."

"Cool," said Danny. "I'm gonna learn to do that, if I get out of this." Then: "I wonder what was in the box."

Thorne had pulled a rectangular cardboard box perhaps six feet long, eighteen inches wide, and six inches thick from the cargo hold of the plane. He reached back in and extracted a black nylon suitcase. He loaded both into the waiting SUV and headed out.

Nothing happened for fifteen minutes, and finally Cruz and Danny went up the hill, walking diagonally away from the ranch to the highway, where Twist should be passing at eight o'clock, taking the memory card from Harmon's camera with them.

Then car doors slammed, and moments later, the SUV drove past on the airstrip, headed toward the burn pit. Harmon and Shay slipped farther down the hill until they could see through some trees. The SUV had stopped at a fence post near the end of the strip, and Thorne and the pudgy guy in the gold ball cap got out.

"What are they doing?" Harmon asked.

Shay was looking through the binoculars. "Can't tell yet; they're doing something to the fence post. . . ." Then: "They put up a stop sign."

"What?"

"A red stop sign," Shay said.

Harmon said, "Give me the glasses." She handed them to him, and he looked, handed them back. "A stop sign. What the hell?"

The men got back in the SUV. The vehicle went past the airstrip building and kept going—nearly to the other end of the strip—and Thorne got out and looked back toward the stop sign with what looked like oversized binoculars.

Harmon said, "That's a pair of binoculars with a laser range finder. But the stop sign's too far away to be a rifle target."

Thorne got back in the car, drove a little farther, got back out, and ranged the sign again. Rinse and repeat: Thorne and the other man made three more stops before pulling the SUV to the side of the runway. They popped the back doors and unloaded a table, two chairs, and some sacks.

"Beanbags. They're setting up a shooting range," Harmon said.

Then they took out a black nylon rifle case—"Bet that's what was in the cardboard carton"—and the black nylon pack. They took the rifle out of the case, and Harmon said, "That's a regular rifle, but it's a weird scope. I need to get closer and take some pictures."

"Daylight. You'll be exposed."

"I can handle that, and we need the photos. You stay here. When they shoot, watch that stop sign—see if they actually hit it. The bullet's going to take, hell, a full second and a half or two seconds to get to the target."

"Careful," Shay said.

Harmon took a bottle of water, an energy bar, the camera, and a walkie-talkie, leaving his rifle and pack with Shay. "I might have to run," he said. "If I do, I'll try to make it five miles down the highway and I'll be there at seven tonight. When you get close, I'll click you."

"Just come back," Shay said.

Harmon disappeared in the trees, and Shay and X moved thirty feet to another clump of trees, one with better shade, where they could lie flat and still see both the men and the stop sign through the binoculars.

The pair had emptied out the pack and set up what looked like a laptop. They began plugging wires into the rifle scope, she thought, although she was too far away to actually see wires.

A couple of minutes after that, the man in the cap went back to the SUV and returned with two more bags. From one, he took what looked like a telescope, and from the other, a tripod, which he set up a few feet to the right of the table. He dragged one of the chairs over and sat down, adjusted the tripod height, and then said something to Thorne.

Thorne had settled down behind the table. He picked up the rifle, put the forestock on the beanbags, looked through the scope, then reached over and typed something on the laptop.

He looked through the scope again, for a long time, and Shay tensed, waiting for the shot. But then Thorne lifted his head away from the eyepiece and took his hand away from the trigger, and Shay felt herself relax just a notch.

And the rifle fired.

The shot was so unexpected and so loud that she flinched, but she twisted in time to put the binoculars on the stop sign—and see the sign jump at the impact of the bullet.

He fired a second shot a half minute later, just as Danny and Cruz returned.

"What's up?" Cruz whispered.

"Target practice," Shay said as the guys settled in. "Harmon's trying to get close enough to take pictures."

Thorne fired the gun ten times, and each time, his finger was off the trigger when the gun fired. He hit the target all ten times, with the other man watching through the telescope and apparently calling the point of impact. After each call, Thorne would type on the laptop for a few seconds.

When they were done, they talked for a bit, then packed up the equipment and drove back to the ranch complex.

Shay, Danny, Cruz, and X went back to the pit in the middle of the clump of piñons, drank water, ate energy bars, and waited.

Harmon showed up twenty minutes later, and the first thing he asked was, "Did he hit the sign?"

"Every time," Shay said.

Harmon, who'd spent half his life on a shooting range, said, "That's impossible. The distance is too long."

Shay shrugged. "That's what I saw. Every time he fired a shot, the sign jumped."

Harmon took a gulp of water, splashed some in his hand, and rubbed it on the back of his neck. "Listen, I want to send everyone back with Twist. I don't know what else we could see here that'd be more damaging than what we've already seen. And we need to have live witnesses for it to mean anything."

"What are you going to do?" Shay asked.

"I need to wait until it gets dark again and then step off that distance on the rifle range. It's easier for one guy to hide."

"Why do you need to know the exact distance?" Cruz asked.

"Because that's a very weird gun. Heavy caliber, probably a TAC-338 sniper rifle, and some kind of computer rig that lets them get some unbelievable accuracy out of it. But they were so careful in measuring the distance, I've got to think that they're going to be shooting at a very specific distance. Very specific. It'd be helpful to know what that distance is."

"You think, what? They're . . ." Shay let the question die.

Harmon said, "Yeah. The only use for that gun is a long-range assassination. We need to find out who they're planning to shoot."

Shay said, "I can think of one person who knows way too much, who they might want to get rid of. Senator Dash."

Cruz said, "Remember when we were watching her house from that mountain in Santa Fe? I wonder how far it is from that mountain to her driveway."

"Why wouldn't they just kill her here?" Danny asked.

Shay locked eyes with Harmon and ventured a theory: "Because they'd want to kill her in a place, and in a way, where they could blame it on somebody else. Like a former army guy who's familiar with long-range shooting and who's hooked up with some crazies."

They all looked at Harmon, who said, "Awww . . . shit." And a few seconds later, "You're right."

Harmon argued that Shay, Cruz, Danny, and X should all go back into Lordsburg, but Shay wouldn't go. "It's not me you need; it's X. He's gone on alert every time somebody was coming, and before we knew it. You need his special eye and his ears and his nose, and I don't think he'll leave me."

After some argument, they decided that Cruz and Danny would go back, which left Cruz seriously annoyed. Shay took him aside and said, "Cruz, you're not here to take care of me. And anyway, having you here wouldn't reduce the danger; it'd add to it."

"Don't buy it," Cruz said. "If they see you, you might need an extra person to fight."

"If they find us, it's not going to be a fight with our little pistols— it'll be Harmon with his rifle and us running away."

Cruz eventually gave up. "But I still think I should stay."

"Gonna be really unhappy if you skip the ride," Shay said.

Cruz grumbled, "I'm going."

Shay and Harmon sat and drank water from time to time, and Harmon poured a full bottle into the bowl X carried in his vest pocket. X lapped it up, and Harmon gave the dog the other half of his. At one, they heard another plane, and the SUV rolled down to the airstrip.

This plane was a full twinjet, whining up to the parking ramp. Senator Dash got out, got inside the SUV, and the vehicle headed toward the big house. Harmon took more pictures.

"What we really need to do is find a way to bug the buildings," Shay said.

"Have to find a good bug first, and that's not so easy to do. And they probably have the best anti-bugging gear on the planet, which would give us away."

"I'm just saying," Shay grumbled. "In a perfect world."

"I'll tell you what would be good, though," Harmon said. "To get pictures of those people going up and down the steps from the prisoner building. But it would be really risky. We'd be right in the high-traffic area."

"Then let's not do it," Shay said.

Harmon looked at her and said, "I didn't expect that. You're always pretty gung ho."

"But not stupid," Shay said.

While they waited for more action, they heard trucks bouncing up and down the driveway and utility vehicles moving around, apparently doing routine ranch maintenance. They'd been up most of the night, and so they dozed, as did the dog. At four, the SUV drove down to the airstrip again, so they moved to the pit, where they watched as the man in the ball cap and Dash went to their separate planes. Before they parted, they stood talking for a moment, and Harmon took a series of photographs.

When the two were in their planes, he checked the photos on the camera's screen. "Good. Got them together, their faces. It'd help if we could identify that guy."

Other than routine ranch activity, nothing more happened until Thorne came out at six o'clock and flew away.

At seven, they began their move on the airstrip. When Harmon thought it was dark enough, they began walking from the shooting point down the long ribbon of still-warm asphalt. Harmon had Shay hold his shirtsleeve as he walked, head down. "Just keep me going straight," he said. "I need to watch my feet."

"You're trying to walk yards?"

"No, I'm trying to walk my exact regular flatland stride, which is thirty-four inches. Now don't talk to me anymore. I have to count."

So they walked down the airstrip, striding along, X trotting beside them, until they got to the stop sign. Harmon said, "Twenty-three forty-eight. Two thousand three hundred and forty-eight strides. Remember that."

They could barely see the stop sign against the sky, but Harmon put his hand up and rubbed it across the sign and then said, "Jesus."

"What?"

"They shot a seven-inch group at two thousand three hundred and forty-eight strides. If we hadn't seen it, I'd never believe it."

Shay did some quick math, then said, "Call it twenty-two hundred yards. What's that? A mile and a quarter?"

Harmon asked, "You do that in your head?"

"Yes, but it's not exact. It's close, though. So, a mile and a quarter—that's almost impossible?"

"People have been sniped from farther than that, but not much, and that's pretty much luck. Ten rounds in seven inches . . . that's . . . that's . . ."

"Scary."

"Yeah."

They were waiting when Twist came by at ten o'clock. They loaded up and headed north, then found a turnaround and drove back south toward Lordsburg. Nothing much doing on the road.

Twist said, "Well, that was long. Was it worth it?"

They told him about the shooting distance and the hit rate, and he said, "That's, uh, alarming. We'll be pulling the shades at the hotel."

"Oh, yeah," Harmon said. He turned to Shay, who was in the back with X. "You didn't think of that, kid."

Shay shook her head. "No. But I don't think they'd waste that gun on us."

Harmon agreed. "They're after bigger game."

"So, hell, let the sun shine in," Twist said.

"Uh-uh," said Harmon. "We crawl around the room like babies and pull the damn shades."

19

Back in Lordsburg, everybody gathered in Twist's room.

"Well," Harmon said. "We found what we were looking for, but I don't know what to do with it. The piñon forest is thick enough that we can move around without being seen. We can get close to everything, but close doesn't help."

"We've got to do *something*," Shay said.

Danny raised a finger. "I'll tell you what we need to do, but as a professional doper, I'll deny it if you ever tell anybody I said this: we need to find somebody high enough in the FBI to authorize a raid on that place and tell them what we know. . . ."

"Who's going to raid a ranch owned by a U.S. senator?" Shay asked skeptically.

"They'd do it if they thought our story was real," Danny argued.

Shay said, "But after Dash's press conference, we're back to being crazy animal rights radicals."

Twist said, "This thing has gotten away from us. There must be twenty guys in there. With guns. What are we supposed to do?"

"Something," Odin said. "Harmon and Shay saw them burning a body. Those people are dying."

They argued about it into the night, went to bed late, though they were all exhausted. The next morning, the decision was made for them.

Twist, Shay, Harmon, and Odin were in Twist's room when Twist's phone rang. Twist looked at the screen and said, "It's Lou."

"She wasn't supposed to call," Odin said.

"Unless it was an emergency," Twist said. He punched the answer button and listened, then said, "Tell the kids to chill—the feds can look at anything they want. No interference."

He listened for another moment, swore, then said, "Okay, tell him I'll be back tomorrow morning and will talk to him then. Tell Emily to lie low. Get everybody to behave, and let them in."

He hung up and said to the group, "The FBI just showed up at the hotel. Six agents. The kids blocked them, and they threatened to come back with more people and bust everybody. They've got a search warrant for my studio, so I told Lou to let them through—there's nothing there."

"Unless they're the bad guys and they dump a bag of cocaine in your closet," Odin said.

Twist said, "Yeah, well, if they did that, I could fight it pretty effectively. People know my attitude toward hard drugs. I got *cops* who'd testify for me.

"Anyway, there's more. They've got a photo of Danny, and they're asking if anyone's seen him."

"What? How?" Shay sputtered.

"He must have been spotted at the hospital when we boosted Eight," Harmon surmised. "Shit."

Danny said the same thing when they got the rest of the group together to fill them in.

"Shit, man. When I said I thought we should talk to the feds, I meant *you* should talk to the feds. I can't be talking to the feds. . . ."

"I know," said Twist. "I dragged you into this, and you've put yourself on the line to help . . . and now I think you should go home."

"What?" Odin was shocked.

But the rest of them thought about it and nodded.

"Wait," said Danny. "I can't just leave now. . . ."

"Yes," Shay said as she put an arm around him, "you can. It's okay. You need to keep yourself safe. The rest of us might need to hide when this is over, and we'll be knocking on your door again."

Danny was quiet a long time. Then he sighed. "Oh, man . . ."

"I've got to go home, too," Twist said. "I can't leave the kids to face the feds alone. And if they have a picture of Danny, then I worry they'll be on to Emily next. . . ."

Harmon: "All right. I suggest we split up. Danny goes home. Some of us go back to L.A. with Twist, some stay here to keep an eye on the ranch."

Twist peered at him for a bit, then said, "I wouldn't want you to attack the ranch, you and whoever stays. You'd get killed."

Harmon: "I wouldn't go along with anything I thought was foolish."

"That's not exactly a promise," Twist said.

"None of us can exactly make a promise," Shay said. "We don't know what's going to happen when you get back to the hotel. What if you all wind up in jail?"

"Lou said the lead fed told her that he didn't have an arrest warrant—only a search warrant. . . . Might be an agent in the group I can confide in. Maybe they'll be on our side. . . ."

Shay said, "Then Harmon's idea makes sense. Half of us to L.A., the other half stay on and watch the ranch."

Twist nodded. "Don't think I've got much choice. Let's haul butt."

Harmon, Shay, Odin, and Cruz stood in the parking lot and watched Twist and Cade pull out in the Range Rover, and Danny in the Jeep. Emily would drive Danny's Volvo out of L.A. and meet up with them to make the swap.

When they were gone, Odin said, "Okay, that leaves just us crazies here. I say we hit the ranch tonight."

Harmon: "I won't do anything that'll get us all killed. I will *not*."

"I'm with you," Cruz said.

"Odin's the crazy one," Shay said. "I'll hold him down, if it comes to that."

"I resemble those remarks," Odin said. "Let's go get breakfast and get serious about what's next."

Returning to the ranch in the daylight would be a risk, but Odin argued for it as they huddled in a booth at the back of a local café. "That's when everything is going on. Besides, they have no idea that we're around—they'll be as slack as they were the last couple of days."

Harmon said, "Only one way I'm going for it. Me and one other person—"

"Me," Odin said.

Harmon continued, "Me and one other person get dropped off way down the highway—like, two miles down. Then we hike back. We know where everything on the ranch is, so we watch the airstrip to pick up on people coming and going. We take some more pictures. And we watch that building where they've got the experimental subjects. See what the guard routine is like."

"And Cruz and I just sit here?" Shay asked.

"You'll probably think of something to do," Odin said.

"Hey!"

"Sorry. Anyway, I'd go with Harmon's idea," Odin said. "I want to figure out a way to help those people, if Twist can't do something with the feds."

Shay looked at the time on her cell phone. "They'll be back in L.A. by six or seven. We should know today what's going on there."

"If they don't bust everybody," Cruz said.

She looked around the table. "So, what're we doing?"

"Back to the ranch," Odin said.

Harmon and Odin bailed out by the side of the highway, and Shay drove on in Harmon's Mercedes with Cruz and X, headed toward Silver City. They'd look around town for a while, then cruise the ranch again in the late afternoon, and again after dark.

Odin and Harmon moved off the shoulder of the road and into the trees, where Odin nearly walked into a rattlesnake. The snake was thoroughly camouflaged, and Odin would have stepped on it if Harmon hadn't grabbed his arm and blurted, "Whoa."

The snake didn't move, and they detoured around it. Harmon said, "That's a Mojave. I didn't know they were around here. Those are bad ones, so keep an eye out. Where there's one, there'll be more."

They walked slowly and carefully back toward the ranch, with Harmon coaching Odin about pace, concealment, and listening for others. An hour after they were dropped off, they were above the airstrip but saw no planes.

Harmon left Odin in the pit they'd found over the airstrip and then went to hide himself near the building with bars on the windows to see if he could get a feel for the guard situation there. There seemed to be a shift change at noon, with two guys in and two guys out, but then nothing more, so he went back to Odin, who'd seen even less activity.

It was midafternoon when they heard the sound of a plane.

As the others had done, the incoming plane flew along the length of the airstrip, made a turn at the far end, and put down. At the parking ramp, a thin, gray-haired man climbed out of the pilot seat. He was carrying a suitcase-sized bag, and from the way he strained to carry it, it had to be heavy. One of the ranch SUVs pulled up, and the driver helped the man lay the bag inside.

Harmon took pictures of the plane and said, "With the tail number, you can track down the owner and probably the pilot, if they're different. At least, my computer guys could have."

"Yeah," Odin said, "Cade and I did that. Dash's plane is her own. The pudgy guy and Thorne both came in on planes owned by private companies. We're still digging to see if we can tie those companies to one of our players."

Harmon nodded.

After a moment, Odin asked, "You've never said much about what you did with Singular. Just 'intelligence.' You have anything to do with me getting waterboarded?"

"No, I didn't," Harmon said. He kept his voice down and added, "Torture doesn't work. It seems like a simple answer for a big problem. Which it would be, if it worked. But it doesn't."

"So your problem with it is pragmatic, not ethical," Odin said.

"Well . . . if you said, 'Would you waterboard Mr. X if it'd stop the 9/11 attacks?' I'd say, 'Hell, yes.' But waterboarding Mr. X wouldn't stop the 9/11 attacks. Might make you feel like you're getting revenge or teaching somebody a lesson . . . but even that doesn't work. What was your lesson from getting waterboarded?"

Odin said, "I didn't get a lesson. Or maybe, 'Don't get caught.' "

"Exactly. It didn't change your mind, just made you meaner. Or more determined. From what I understand, you gave up nothing, and you're not even some combat-ready Ranger or radical Muslim fighter. Same thing when Thorne beat up Cade. Didn't work. Didn't get anything."

They sat silently for quite a long time, then Harmon broke the silence by asking, "Did the waterboarding hurt?"

"Not so much physically—I barfed a lot," Odin said. "But it makes you crazy. You feel like you're going insane. If you did it to somebody long enough, they probably *would* go insane. Then, you know, I have the feeling that it'd kill you, if they did it long enough. Not any one episode, but you feel like your body is breaking down. It's supposed to be mostly a psychological thing, but I don't think you could take it forever—your body would just give up and die."

Harmon shook his head. "Don't know if I could handle it."

More silence, then Odin said, "Shay said you've been shot. Is that right?"

"Yeah, a couple of times," Harmon said.

"That's gotta hurt."

"Yup. Do you get snow in your part of Oregon?"

"Yeah, but it never amounts to much," Odin said.

"Well, getting shot feels like being hit in the face with a really icy snowball, maybe with a rock in it. It hurts and stings and goes numb, kind of all at once. If you've been hit bad, you go into shock . . . bleed a lot. At least, I did."

"Where'd you get hit?"

"Got hit in the triceps, and the same slug went through and

grooved my back, and got hit another time in the hip. That's a polite word for butt. I got hit once by shrapnel from an IED, but that was mostly a lot of cuts. I was standing behind a truck when that went off and was hit mainly from the knees down. That hurt like hell. But you know, you get hit, the army gives you some time off."

"Good of them," Odin said. "Why'd you do it for so long? Why are you doing this?"

A little more silence, then Harmon said, "Because it's interesting. You know, why bother to go through life if you can't do interesting shit? Even that crazy animal rights stuff you do. At least it's interesting. Better than sitting around waiting to die."

"Absolutely," Odin said.

Another hour passed, then the gray-haired man was driven back to his airplane. Harmon took more pictures of him boarding—he wasn't carrying the black case this time—and the plane taxied and took off. A few minutes later, a utility vehicle fired up and drove past them toward the end of the airstrip, a man in a cowboy hat at the wheel. A black bag overhung the cargo bed of the vehicle.

Harmon said, "Oh Jesus, another one."

"What?"

"That's a body bag," Harmon said. "We need pictures. Stay close to me, stay quiet."

They scuttled across the slope, stopping to listen, looking for signs that other people might be around, and saw nothing at all. When they were back where Harmon and Shay had been when they saw the first body burned, Harmon whispered, "Stay low. Lie flat. If the guy looks in this direction, don't look directly at him. . . . People can feel eyes."

The man with the body never looked at them. Instead, he built another piñon bier, dragged the body onto it, doused it all with gasoline, and set it on fire. They could smell the burning flesh, and Harmon took pictures; in an hour, the flames were dropping, and the man probed them with a rake. Satisfied that the body was gone, he tossed the rake in the utility vehicle and headed back toward the ranch.

Odin asked, "Did the guy in the plane kill somebody?"

"I wondered the same thing," Harmon said.

"We've got to do something about this," Odin said. "You saw them getting rid of a body yesterday and another one today. There aren't that many of them. And we don't know how many they've already killed."

Harmon scratched the side of his head and said, after a few seconds, "I don't know."

"If we don't do something, they'll get rid of all of them, and then there won't even be any evidence."

"There'll be evidence," Harmon said. "When you burn a body like that, you get rid of ninety-nine percent of it, but a good forensic team will find the other one percent. Teeth, hard pieces of bone. That kind of stuff. What I'm afraid of is that if we raid them, and if we don't manage to pull that off, they'll bring a tractor out here with a blade and push that ash and dirt into the river. Then it would truly be gone.

"Come on. Get your shit together. Shay and Cruz will be coming through in a half hour or so. Maybe between all of us, we can figure something out."

Odin nodded, his expression fierce. "No more burned bodies," he said. "One way or the other, no more burned bodies."

Cruz picked them up at the side of the road just after four o'clock. Shay was in the passenger seat, wearing a straw cowboy hat she'd bought in Silver City.

"Another body burned," Odin said as he and Harmon got in the backseat. X was there, too, and he settled between them.

"Ah, no," Shay said.

Harmon turned around to pull out a fabric rifle case that he kept in the back, put his rifle in it, and tucked the case away under a cooler and their packs.

As they passed the turnoff to the ranch, they saw a man with a rifle on his shoulder step back away from the road into the piñons. "Hope he didn't see us on the earlier passes," Shay said.

"This is only the third pass for the Benz, and unless he's the only guy out there, we oughta be okay," Harmon said.

They'd gone another ten miles when a white Chevy Tahoe came up behind them and flared its red roof flashers.

"Now what?" Shay asked.

"Cruz, keep your hands in sight, on the steering wheel," Harmon said. "Odin, when Cruz rolls down his window, you roll yours down, too, like you want to hear what's going on."

Cruz took the Benz to the dirt shoulder, shifted into park. The truck pulled off behind them, and a moment later, two men in olive-green uniforms got out. One waited behind the Benz, the other walked up to the driver's-side window. He was wearing a pistol on his hip and kept his hand on it.

As he came up to the window, Cruz asked, "What'd I do?"

The man said, with a Hispanic accent, "Border Patrol. Everybody here an American?"

"Yeah, we all are," Cruz said.

The patrolman looked into the truck at Shay, Odin, Harmon, and the dog, then looked back at Cruz and asked, "You got a driver's license, paisano?"

"Yeah." Cruz fumbled out his wallet, extracted his license, and passed it to the patrolman, who looked at the picture, looked at Cruz, then handed it back. "Los Angeles, huh?"

"Yeah, we're all from California," Cruz said.

Shay said, "Odin and I aren't—we're really from Oregon, but we're living in Los Angeles right now, going to school." Odin gave the guy a placid wave.

The patrolman said, "What are you folks doing here? You're a long way from nowhere."

Harmon jumped in: "I teach archaeology. We were up at Gila looking at some Mimbres sites. These three are students. We're headed to Lordsburg for the night, then it's back to L.A. tomorrow."

The patrolman said, "Well, okay, then. Have a good trip."

As he stepped away, Cruz asked, "How come you're so far from the border?"

"We patrol all the main routes north. We could see a lot of heads in this truck, and we always stop a truck with a lot of heads."

Cruz said, "Huh. Well, take it easy."

"You too," the patrolman said.

Cruz eased off the shoulder, and the flashers on the unmarked truck died. As they pulled away, Odin asked, "You think they were really Border Patrol?"

"Seemed right to me," Cruz said. "I've been stopped before."

Shay said, "It's possible that they're real Border Patrol and that they also talk to the people at the ranch. You know, some extra eyes."

"You're very suspicious," Harmon said. "I like that in a young woman."

But they were feeling shaky about it. A minute later, the truck caught them again and passed, the patrolman on the passenger side giving them a wave. Shay said, "If they see us up here tomorrow, they'll be asking more questions."

"It's a complication," Harmon agreed.

Shay asked Harmon, "There's a trailer hitch on this truck, right?"

"Sure."

"I don't know much about trailer hitches, but I know there are different hitch sizes. . . ."

"I've got three different hitch balls stored in the back," Harmon said. "Why would you need a trailer?"

"I got an idea," Shay said.

Cruz: "That's not necessarily good."

• • •

Twist, Cade, Danny, and Emily met up near Joshua Tree, and Danny was full of parting advice before he made his way home.

"Look, you don't have to incriminate yourselves. You don't have to answer a single question. But you can give them information—and if they insist on knowing how you got it, then demand immunity for giving it to them."

"You're talking like a lawyer," Twist said.

Danny said, "I've had to get advice from lawyers once or twice. That's what they told me."

"Slight difference between a half ounce of weed and mass murder," Twist said. "These guys might insist a little harder."

"If they know enough to ask about it, they'll know you didn't do it," Danny said.

Cade: "Maybe we ought to have a lawyer with us."

"The only lawyer I've ever hired specializes in artists' rights," Twist said. "Why don't we see what they want to know and then decide whether we need a lawyer."

"Exactly the kind of decision that will come back to bite you on the butt," Danny said.

"We'll see," Twist said. "We'll see what the FBI has to say."

The agent's name was Brian Barin. He was eating dinner when Twist called.

"We need to talk to you," Barin said.

"Well, I'm here," Twist said. "When do you want to talk? And should I have a lawyer?"

"That's your call. We're trying to get information on the incident up in San Francisco in which a young woman was killed and a group of illegal aliens were detained. We believe you can help us with that, given your television interview. At this point, we have no intention of arresting you."

"At this point," Twist said.

"Yes. At this point."

"And you want to do this when?"

"Tonight. Right now. I'm in Los Feliz. I can be there in a half hour or so. I have another agent on standby; he'll be coming with me."

"Make it an hour," Twist said. "I need to call some people."

"An hour it is. Thank you for calling me."

Twist thought about it for fifteen seconds, then called the lawyer who knew about artists' rights, who said he had no idea how to deal with the FBI but knew a woman who did.

"How do I get in touch with her in a hurry?" Twist said.

"I pass the cell phone across the table," the lawyer said. "She's my old lady. And I'll tell you, she ain't cheap."

The lawyer's wife turned out to be about thirty-five, with long blond hair and a briefcase the size of a Volkswagen. Her name was Lynne Tanner, and she got to the hotel about twenty minutes after Twist's call and took a digital recorder out of the briefcase.

"I charge two hundred dollars an hour until we go to trial, when it goes to five hundred an hour," Tanner said. "I rarely lose cases that go to trial, but sometimes I do, because there's no hope, and we're just maneuvering for a lower level of conviction than the DA was willing to give us in a deal," she told Twist as she looked for a place to plug in the recorder. "I need you to brief me on what the feds want, and when they get here, I need you to answer only the questions that I say you can answer. Can you do that?"

"I can try," Twist said. "See, this isn't a typical case. . . ."

"Tell me," she said. She glanced at her watch. "We've got fifteen minutes. We can stall them for a while if we need to, but not forever. Talk fast."

Twist pushed his hands through his hair. "Where to begin . . ."

Shay had the idea, had fleshed it out with help from Odin, against the doubts of Harmon and Cruz. Cruz wanted to wait until they found out whether Twist had been arrested—but Shay said that by the time they found out, it might be too late.

"If Dash's people get one little hint that we're out here, it'll be too late," Shay said. "They murdered those two people they burned. They'll have no choice but to get rid of the other prisoners if they get spooked."

"I feel bad for saying this . . . ," Cruz started.

"What?" Shay asked.

"Well, the prisoners are pretty much doomed, right? After what Singular's done to them. Will it help to rescue them?"

Odin started to object, but Harmon cut him off. "It's a fair point. Is the risk worth the gain?"

Shay tried to be practical: "It'd keep the news about Singular rolling. The TV stations need good video, and they'd get it if we produced another group of messed-up people. Plus, it'd tie the whole thing to Dash beyond any doubt. . . ."

But Odin wasn't having it. "It's not about 'good video,' or even about getting Dash. It's about doing the only right thing." He looked at Harmon. "Would you go get them if they were prisoners of war? Or some of your army pals, injured and behind enemy lines? Would it matter then that they might be dying already?"

Everyone went quiet for a few moments, and then Harmon nodded at Odin and said, "This plan requires a car. Where are we going to get a used car, that we can afford, right now?"

"I already found one," Odin said. "Craigslist. There's a thousand-dollar car for sale, listed today."

"A thousand-dollar car is a piece of junk," Cruz said. "It might not even make it to the ranch."

"We can assess that when we see the car," Odin said. "If we had to, we could get some ropes and tow it."

They all looked at each other, then Shay nodded. "This is gonna work."

The thousand-dollar car was owned by a man named Roger Rodriguez, who lived on a dirt road a mile outside of Lordsburg and was waiting at the front door of his trailer home when Harmon and Cruz arrived.

The car was a 1998 Saturn SC2, which Rodriguez said, "Runs okay, but it's gonna need some work pretty soon, I won't lie about it."

The work, he said, would include major overhauls of the engine, transmission, and rear end, and new tires. The left-side door was coming off and was being held in place with ropes. "I thought maybe somebody would use it for knocking around on a ranch. You know, take the doors off, throw them in a ditch. Work good for that, if you put some new rubber on it. Fix up the tranny."

"We live thirty miles from here. Is it gonna make thirty miles?" Cruz asked.

"Oh, sure . . ." Rodriguez thought about it. "Probably."

A half hour after getting their first look at the car, Cruz eased into the driver's seat and followed Harmon out the dirt road and back to the motel.

When they walked in, Shay said, "I tried to call Twist again and he answered, but the feds were still there. I asked."

"Let's get our gear together, our packs," Harmon said. "We're gonna need flashlights, water, and bolt cutters, in case they're chained to the beds. . . ."

"Our guns," Cruz said.

"Yes."

Shay called to X and connected him to her laptop through the Thunderbolt port behind his ear. X was one of their best weapons—best to be sure he was fully powered up.

Twist, Cade, Tanner, and the feds were sitting in a circle of chairs in Twist's studio, like in a session with a shrink.

Twist looked at his lawyer, who said, "If you have information about this, and you answer the question now, there's no going back. Do not make any assertions of any kind about your personal involvement or where the information comes from. If Agent Barin wishes to take you before a grand jury to get that information, he will have to provide you with immunity."

Twist nodded and said to the two agents, "We learned from our . . . contacts . . . that Senator Dash is providing a place for these operations on her ranch in New Mexico. One of our sources says that the employees have burned the bodies of experimental subjects who died at the ranch. They burn them in a pit off the end of a jet runway."

The two feds looked at each other, and the junior agent, Joel Cantor, gave his head a shake. "This is all very hard to believe."

Cade was getting seriously irritated: "Have you even bothered to *look* at the X-rays done on Fenfang or those subjects you took off the ship? What do *you* think is going on with those wires stuck down in their brains? Did you go on that ship? It was a prison ship, right? Deny it was a prison ship and I'm walking out of here. . . ."

"Not until we say so," said Cantor.

"Bullshit," said Cade. "If you deny that the ship was a prison ship, if you deny those wires down in those peoples' brains, then you must be working for Dash, and I am out of here, because the last time Dash's people got their hands on me—"

The lawyer said, "Cade!"

Cade stopped, but Barin said, "I want to hear that."

The lawyer said, "He'll talk to the grand jury."

Barin said to her, "Let's you and I step into a corner for one minute."

Tanner nodded, and they walked across the studio to a far corner, which had a bunch of unprepped canvases stacked against a wall. They huddled together, then Tanner called, "Cade? Twist? Come here for a moment. Agent Cantor, you stay there."

When they'd gathered in the corner, Tanner said to Cade, "Agent Barin wants to hear what happened the last time Singular got its hands on you. Your story begins the moment you arrived at their building in Sacramento and ends when you escaped. You give him no details—just the outline. He will decide whether you need to talk to a grand jury and promises nothing said here will be used for anything other than his own information."

Cade nodded. "Basically," he began, "they kidnapped me, threw me in a van, and took me to Sacramento. There was a guy there named Thorne. He's the same guy who waterboarded Odin Remby—"

Barin: "What!"

Tanner: "No, no, no . . . only your story."

Cade told him about being beaten up and the escape. Showed him the yellowing bruises over his broken ribs, told him where he'd gone to an emergency room for repairs. "That can all be checked," he said. "They did X-rays and prescribed some very restful controlled substances."

Barin stared at Cade for a moment, then said, "Let's go back."

Back at the circle of chairs, Barin sat down and said to Cantor, "He gave me some more checkable data points."

"We're getting quite a few of those," Cantor said. "We've got to kick this upstairs. Real quick."

"*If* they check out," Barin said to Cantor. "I'm going to put you on a plane and send you up north to talk to some people in an emergency room."

Twist said, "With all the stuff you already have—the experimental subjects in San Francisco, Fenfang's body—have you busted anyone from Singular? Somebody's killing them, you know. Their CEO and top lawyer went down in a plane in the mountains. . . ."

"We know about that."

"There's a guy in Eugene, Oregon, named Janes, he's a scientist . . . ," Cade began.

The two agents glanced at each other, then Barin said, "He seems to be missing."

"Ah, shit," Twist said. "He'll be in a fresh grave somewhere."

"We're not sure of that," Barin said. "He took quite a bit of stuff with him and cleaned out his bank accounts. The ones we know about, anyway."

Cantor asked, "Do you know about a guy named Stephen N. Creighton? They called him Sync?"

"Yes, we've seen on TV," Twist said. "Is he missing, too?"

"Can't seem to find him," Barin said. "There are other people that were in the know, a guy named Harmon and that guy Cade mentioned, Thorne. . . . You haven't seen him since then?"

Cade shook his head. "No. If I see him again, I plan to run over him with a truck."

Barin looked at his watch, then said, "We've got to go. We want you all to stick around town. If you talk to any of the other fugitives, anyone from Singular, the Rembys, any of their friends, we want to know about it. Instantly."

"Right," Cade said. "We'll call instantly."

Barin picked up the tone in his voice, gave him a long look, then shook his head. "You don't know how deep you're in this," he said.

Twist: "You're wrong. We do know. But *you* don't know how deep *you're* in this. You seem like a sincere enough guy, and I will tell you—all of this is coming out. This is going to be the biggest scandal since . . . well, I can't think of anything bigger. Everything law enforcement does is gonna be examined for years to come. We're on the right side: when it all comes out, nobody will touch us. But you guys . . . I'm telling you, Agent Barin, you guys are now more in the line of fire than we are. So act fast and act wisely."

Barin grunted and picked up his briefcase and said, "We'll see."

21

Cruz, Shay, and X were outside the motel, and Cruz bumped Shay up against Harmon's Mercedes with his hips and said, his face close to hers, "Sometimes you scare me."

"All the way through this, it's been on us—and it's still on us," Shay said.

Inside, Odin and Harmon were looking at a laptop screen, measuring distances at the ranch, checking out a short, narrow bridge over an arroyo.

Harmon stuck his head out. "If we're going to do this, let's do it. Cruz, did you put the gas can in the car?"

"Yeah, it's in there."

"Then let's go."

Odin drove the Saturn, Cruz drove the Mercedes with Harmon in the passenger seat. Shay sat in the back, and X sat in the cargo space, looking out the rear window. As they drove, Shay tied his leash to a loop on the floor so he couldn't follow her out of the car. As she did it, he stared her in the eyes and barked at her once, a clear objection to the leash, and she said, "Shush. This is only for a short time."

Odin drove the battered Saturn slowly, never faster than forty miles an hour, not because he was being careful, but because he didn't want the engine to blow. The driver's-side window had a hole in it, and he could smell burning oil as he went along, and the car shuddered and shook on worn-out shocks.

They took the highway north out of Lordsburg, headlights searching out the dark road. Coyotes crossed in front of them a couple of times, and some kind of small animal that Odin didn't recognize. They passed the entrance to the ranch, continued north for a mile and a half to a narrow bridge over an arroyo. Odin pulled to the side of the road, and Cruz did a U-turn in the Mercedes and pulled up beside him.

Odin got out of the car and asked, "Do I turn it off? The battery's pretty weak."

"Still better to turn it off," Harmon said. "If you can't get it started again, we'll push it."

"I should be going with you," Odin said.

"We talked about it," Shay said. "All the right people are doing all the right things. Do what *you* need to do."

"Please, please . . . don't get hurt."

Cruz pulled away from the battered car, leaving Odin in the night, and Harmon said, "All the windows down."

Shay was in the passenger seat, Harmon in the backseat, where he could shift from one side to the other. The cool night air flowed over them as they dropped all four windows.

"We need to take it slow," Harmon said to Cruz. "If the guard's there, we've got to let him stop us and then we take him. We can't have him loose and alert out behind us."

"What if we don't see anyone?" Cruz asked.

"Then we go on in," Shay said.

The turnoff to the ranch came up, and Harmon said, "Here we go. Turn signal."

Cruz hit the turn signal and slowed: Harmon told them that the turn signal suggested somebody who was both innocent and careful, and might give them an edge if the guard was on his toes. The entrance to the driveway was guarded by some pines, taller than the desert piñons, with bare trunks. They arched overhead, creating a tunnel-like effect: it was totally dark beneath them.

And the guard was there, in a flannel shirt and jacket, smoking a cigarette, ten feet off the road. As the Mercedes made the turn, they caught him in the headlights, and he stepped to the side of the driveway and held up a hand. He had a rifle in the other hand. He was on Shay's side, and she felt Harmon moving over behind her.

Cruz braked, and the car rolled slowly up to the guard, who leaned toward Shay's window and opened his mouth to say something, but Harmon spoke first: "You make one peep and I'll shoot you in the head."

The guard looked at Harmon and mostly saw the large hole at the muzzle of Harmon's pistol. He glanced back at Shay and saw the hole at the end of her pistol's muzzle.

"Are you . . . those guys?"

"Yeah. We're those guys," Harmon said.

He pushed open the car door with his knee, made a quick move with the pistol to clear the window frame, and stepped out next to the guard. "I'm going to tell you what we're going to do. We're going to tape up your feet and hands. I want you to drop your rifle, then sit on the ground. . . ."

"You don't know what you're doing, man," the guard said. He was a hard-looking Hispanic, speaking Texas-accented English.

"We've been watching you for a long time," Harmon said. "So we *do* know what we're doing. Now, the young lady in the front seat, she's going to hold that pistol on you from her spot, and I'm going to hold mine on you from my spot, and our friend the driver is going to tape you up. I should mention that the young lady is the one who shot Thorne. She *likes* shooting people."

The guard looked again at Shay, who said, "I really do."

The guard dropped his rifle, and Harmon kicked it away from him. Cruz got out of the driver's seat with a roll of silver duct tape. Two minutes later, he'd taped up the guard's feet and hands, with extra wraps around his knees, and more around his body, pinning his elbows to his sides. Three final wraps went around his head and mouth.

Then Cruz and Harmon picked him up and put him in the cargo area of the truck, crowding X into a corner.

Harmon said, "Don't piss off the dog or he'll rip your face off."

The dog bared his teeth at the bound man, who went very still. Shay got on the walkie-talkie and called Odin, who was on the very edge of the walkie-talkie's range: "We're in."

Harmon picked up the guard's rifle and heaved it into the brush.

They rolled down the hill, and halfway down, Shay and Harmon pulled on their equipment packs and slipped out of the car and into the trees. Cruz took the truck on. He passed the gatehouse and garage at the bottom of the hill, moving slowly but not hesitating, and then drove on through the cluster of buildings to the garage where they'd seen the horse trailer. He turned in a tight circle, then backed up to the garage door where the trailer had been.

It was closed. He got on the walkie-talkie: "The horse trailer door is down, but the one next to it is open. I'm going inside to see if the trailer's still there. So stay cool."

Harmon clicked once on the transmit button: a yes.

Shay and Harmon had moved down the hill almost as quickly as Cruz but had jogged off to their left, away from the drive, around the gatehouse and toward the building with the barred windows.

When Cruz called, they sat down behind a piñon: getting the horse trailer was critical. If Cruz couldn't get it, they were done.

Cruz got out of the Mercedes and walked over to the garage, around the nose of the pickup in the second bay. There was enough light from the Mercedes's headlights to see that the horse trailer was still in the third bay, but when he tried to lift the door, it clanked against some kind of lock.

The light was too dim to see where the locking mechanism was, and he felt around in the dark for it, couldn't find it. Finally, he stepped back over to the bay with the pickup to look at that door . . . and realized that it had an electric lifting mechanism, with an electric switch on the wall. He went back to the horse trailer bay, found the switch, and flicked it. The door started up.

And the light came on, illuminating Cruz and everything around him.

Nothing to do but continue hitching up the trailer. Harmon had guessed that the trailer would take a two-and-five-sixteenths-inch ball, which they'd already put on the hitch at the back of the Mercedes.

Cruz returned to the truck, got in, and backed it toward the horse trailer, until he thought the trailer's hitch was overlapping the ball on the truck. He got back out, found he was a foot short, got in the truck, and backed it up that much more.

The garage light went out.

Cruz got out of the truck again, picked up the hitch on the trailer, pulled it over to center it on the ball, and let it drop. The ball was the correct size. The hitch fell into place snugly, and he screwed the safety bolt tight.

He got on the walkie-talkie: "Hitched up. Good to go."

That done, he opened the back of the truck, pulled out the taped-up guard, lugged him into the garage, and left him on the floor in the middle of a darkened bay. X whimpered at him from the back of the vehicle, worried about the leash, his electronic blue eye a spark in the dark, and Cruz whispered, "Quiet, boy."

The automatic headlights in the truck had gone out, so he went around to the driver's side, climbed in, and simply sat there, engine off, waiting. Nothing was moving on the ranch, as far as he could see. And then he spotted Harmon moving in a crouch across the driveway to the porch outside the building with the barred windows. He couldn't see Shay yet. She'd be waiting in the background until Harmon tried the door. . . .

"*Madre de Dios . . . ,*" Cruz muttered.

From where he was sitting in the truck, Cruz saw a man step out onto the porch at the gatehouse at the bottom of the hill—the gate-keeper, as Harmon had called him. The man looked down toward Cruz in the Mercedes and then started toward him. He was a hundred yards away. Because of a line of piñons along the driveway, the man couldn't see the building with the barred windows, or Harmon, but he would be able to in the next minute or so.

Cruz got on his walkie-talkie and hit the transmit button several times, their "panic" call, and saw Harmon straighten up, still not on the porch. Cruz said, "Man from gatehouse coming down driveway. He'll see Harmon in a minute."

Harmon turned and faded back into the trees, and a few seconds later, Cruz saw him in the trees, again in a stalking crouch, moving toward the driveway.

The man from the gatehouse was striding along now, focused on the Mercedes; he had a flashlight in one hand. As he was about to move into the open, he suddenly stopped.

Harmon said quietly but sharply, "Freeze, asshole, or I will shoot you in the head. Let me see your hands, let me see your hands. . . ."

The man stopped, lifted his hands chest-high, and said, "Don't shoot, don't shoot. . . ."

Harmon stepped out of the trees, reached out with his free hand, grabbed the man by the collar, and said, "Walk backward, I'll pull you along."

"Who are you?"

"Shut up," Harmon said. He got the man back in the trees and said, "Sit. Put your legs out in front of you."

Shay materialized beside them. "Somebody'll be looking for him."

"You're *them,*" the man said, bug eyes on the teenager.

"Tape him," Harmon said. "Gotta go quick now."

Shay started taping him up. When his hands and feet were bound, Harmon patted him down, found a Glock pistol and two spare magazines of 9 mm ammo in a holster at the man's right side and a key ring on a pull cable.

"This should help," Harmon said. They'd planned to pound on the door of the building with the barred windows, feigning panic, hoping that somebody inside would simply push open the door to see what was happening. But a key was much better.

Shay finished taping up the prisoner, and they left him lying on the ground, looking like a badly cocooned caterpillar.

Running now—up on the porch of the building with the barred windows, pushing on the front door. Locked. Penlight in his mouth, Harmon knelt, shined it on the lock, ran through the keys, found several that looked right, and began slipping them into the lock, trying them, pulling them out. He hit it on the fourth key.

"You push the door," he whispered. "I'll lead."

Shay nodded. Harmon asked, "Ready?"

Shay nodded again and pushed the door open. Harmon slipped through, and Shay followed. They were in an antechamber with another locked door on the other side.

Harmon muttered, "Shit," and started running keys again. The lock turned with a different key.

"Ready?"

Shay pushed the door, and Harmon went through—in the next second shouting, "Down. Down. I'll kill you, man, I'll kill you. . . ."

Shay followed him through, gun in hand, pointing, like Harmon had shown her. There were two men frozen by the sight of the pistols. Both were tough-looking, muscular. One was sitting at a computer; the other was in an easy chair with a stack of magazines. Shay could see a pistol on the man at the computer; but it was pinned by the arm of his office chair.

The computer guy said, "Hey, Harmon. You won't shoot me."

"Gonna shoot you, Jeff. Try not to kill you, but you're a long ride from a doctor."

Harmon said to Shay, "These guys will both have more than one gun, so don't get close enough where they can grab you. Start taping up their feet."

Shay moved up until she was standing by Jeff's legs, but Jeff was talking to Harmon: "You shoot me, there'll be thirty guys here in a minute."

Shay pulled the knife out of her waistband with her left hand and asked, "How about if I stick you?"

Jeff ignored her. He said, "You got one chance, Harmon. Get—"

He didn't finish the sentence because Shay stuck him: took the knife and drove it into his thigh, then jerked it back out. Jeff gasped, and dark purple blood bubbled out of his leg. "You bitch," he groaned.

"Got your attention?" Shay asked. "Next time I stick it in your belly button."

Harmon was looking at the other man now and said, "Do not move that hand again. . . ."

Shay threw four wraps of tape around Jeff's feet. Blood had soaked his entire right thigh. Shay backed away and said, "Facedown on the floor. Put your hands behind your back."

"You—"

"I told you," she said, and turned the knife in her hand, holding it like a rapier aimed at his stomach, and he flinched away, believing her now.

"On the floor!" she said.

Jeff unfolded onto the floor.

When Jeff gave up, the resistance went out of the second man as well.

Three minutes later, they were both taped up, a puddle of blood forming under Jeff's leg.

Shay walked down the room to a second set of doors and pushed through. Behind them was a hospital ward, smelling of alcohol and floor cleaner, with six prisoners scattered between a dozen army-style beds. They were all lying on their backs, covered with sheets and army blankets. One looked at her—but the other prisoners didn't move. There was another door on the far side. Following the muzzle of her pistol, Shay pushed through and found a fully equipped operating suite, but no more guards.

"We're clear!" she called to Harmon. "Tell Cruz."

Five seconds later, Harmon answered: "He's on the way."

There were four men and two women; five of the prisoners were Asian, with one white man. They were all awake, but only three seemed really aware, while the other three continued to stare at nothing. All of them had the same wired-up scalps that Fenfang had had, and all were chained to their beds. Shay took the bolt cutters out of her pack and cut them free, and then the white man said in English, "Don't hurt me, don't hurt . . ."

"Who are you? Who are you?" Shay asked.

"Bob Morris . . ." He might once have been a heavy man but now was shrunken, with folds of loose skin on the sides of his face, and yellow-and-blue bruises around his eyes. Fresh pink surgical scars were slashed across his scalp.

"Morris? From St. Louis?"

There was a spark in his eye. "Yes. Bob Morris from St. Louis. Don't hurt me. . . ."

"We're here to help," Shay said.

Harmon snapped at her: "Save it. Get the mattresses. We gotta move. . . ."

Harmon picked up one of the Asian men and, cradling him in his arms, carried him to the antechamber. As he was doing that, Shay began pulling mattresses from the beds and carrying them to the front door.

Jeff said, "Harmon, for Christ's sake . . ."

"Shut up."

A moment later, Cruz was there, looking tense. "A light just went on in the bunkhouse."

"Gotta hurry," Harmon said. "Somebody's getting curious."

When all of the prisoners had been freed and collected in the antechamber, Harmon said to Shay as he pointed at a wastebasket, "Jam the door open and start throwing the mattresses. Cruz and I'll get the prisoners into the trailer."

Shay jammed the door, then grabbed two of the mattresses and dragged them to the trailer, parked just outside, and threw them in, one on top of the other: they'd decided to make them two-deep, if possible, to give the prisoners the best possible padding from road vibration.

Harmon was right behind her with one of the prisoners, one of the females, who suddenly stank of urine. Harmon ignored it and kicked the mattresses until they were tight against a sidewall, then laid the prisoner on it. Cruz was already there with the other female prisoner, who was groaning against his chest, and put her on the same stack of mattresses.

Shay got back with two more mattresses and put them down, and Harmon brought Morris out, and Morris said, "Bob Morris, Bob Morris," and she went back for more mattresses.

Cruz was settling the fourth prisoner. Shay couldn't fit the last two mattress in the trailer lengthwise, had to put them in sideways, and had just done that when she saw a woman walking down the driveway, apparently from the gatehouse, and she called quietly, "Woman coming down the driveway."

Harmon ran back for the last prisoner while Cruz loaded the fifth one, jumped out of the trailer, and ran around to the driver's seat.

Up the driveway, the woman had stopped, then suddenly began screaming: "Hey! Hey! They're here, they're here. Help! Help! Help!"

Harmon loaded in the mumbling man in his arms and said to Shay, "Get my rifle. I'll stay back here in the trailer."

As Cruz fired up the truck, Shay got Harmon's black rifle from the back and ran it to the trailer, then Harmon pulled the gate-style doors shut and said, "Throw the latch, right there, throw the latch."

Shay threw the external latch and ran back to the passenger side of the truck, jumped in, and said, "Go!"

Up the driveway, the woman was still screaming, and off to her right, Shay could see lights go on in what they thought were the guards' quarters and, farther away, in the ranch hands' bunkhouse.

"They're coming," she said.

"Woman's got a gun, got a gun!" Cruz shouted, and Shay looked up the driveway to where the woman had taken a gunner's stance, both hands on a pistol, pointing it at them. There was a muzzle flash, although Shay didn't hear any sound and didn't hear anything hit the truck.

Shay pulled her pistol as Cruz gunned the truck toward the only way out, right toward the woman. Shay stuck her weapon out the window, aimed more or less in the direction of the woman, and pulled the trigger as fast as she could, and the woman turned and ran sideways off the road, fell, scrambled farther off the road. As they went by, Shay fired her last shots well over the woman's head, and then they were up the driveway, slowing for the turn onto the highway.

Shay had no idea how far down the highway they'd gotten when Cruz, looking into the wing mirror, said, "Headlights turning onto the highway."

Just as he said it, they heard the sharp crack of Harmon's rifle from the back. "Keeping them off," Cruz said.

Shay was on the walkie-talkie to Odin. "We're coming fast. We've got somebody behind us."

Odin came back: "Car's started."

Thirty seconds later, Cruz said, "There's the bridge. They're getting closer. With this trailer . . . can't go fast."

Cruz rolled over the bridge and then braked, and Shay jumped out. Odin drove the old Saturn onto the bridge, turning it sideways, blocking the road. Shay could smell the gas pouring out of the five-gallon can onto the backseat. Odin jumped out and, when he was clear, pulled a matchbook from his pocket, lit a single match, used it to set off the others, and, as Shay shouted, "Hurry! Hurry!" and Harmon's rifle barked in the background, threw the matchbook through the window. The car exploded in flames, and Shay and Odin ran back to the truck. Odin fell just as he got there, and Shay shouted again, "Get up—hurry!"

Odin tried to get up, raised a bloody hand. "I think I'm shot. In the leg."

Shay grabbed her brother by the wrist and got him standing, heard more gunfire from Harmon in the trailer, and helped Odin hop on one foot until she could push him into the back of the Mercedes.

When he was in, she crawled over him and shouted at Cruz, "Go! Go!"

22

Cruz pushed the truck as hard as he could while still keeping the trailer on the ground—the highway was not the best. In the back, Shay was freaking out, walking on a thin edge of self-control as she helped Odin pull down his bloody jeans and found his left leg a mass of blood, with more blood seeping out of wounds on both the front and back of his leg.

"Oh my God," she cried. "No, no, no . . ."

"How is he?" Cruz shouted. "How bad?"

"Bad, bad—we gotta stop and I gotta trade places with Harmon, he knows about this stuff. . . ."

Odin: "Hurts . . . but it's not broken."

Cruz stopped and Shay hopped out and Harmon shouted, "Why are we stopping? What happened?"

She pulled the latch on the back gate of the trailer and said, "Odin got shot in the leg. You gotta help him. Go help him. I'll stay back here with these people."

"Ah, Jesus . . . Take my rifle. If you use it, make sure you know who you're shooting at."

Harmon hopped out, Shay took his place, and Harmon threw the closing latch, and a second later, she heard the car door slam and they started rolling again.

Three of the people on the mattresses were simply slack and silent. Not dead, but blank-eyed and unmoving. The other three were aware of her; one was moaning. Only Morris spoke English, and he was no longer talking.

The ride in the trailer was gritty but not terrible, and the mattresses softened the bumps.

There was no one behind them that she could see, so Shay busied herself with simply keeping the ex-prisoners flat on the mattresses and talking softly and reassuringly, even though they wouldn't know what she was saying. Given the way they were taken from the barred building, she thought they'd know a rescue was being attempted.

Or she had to hope that they did.

Harmon used his brightest flash to look at Odin's wound. "Okay," he said, "you're not going to bleed to death, but you're going to hurt, and you could get pretty badly infected if it's not treated. You got some fabric from your jeans in the wound; it has to be cleaned out. We really need to get you to a hospital, but it would be best if we took you all the way through to my friends' place at First Mesa and then over to the Indian clinic. That could be six hours from now, pulling this trailer, even going straight through."

"I can make it," Odin said through gritted teeth. "Can you do anything for the infection problem? I don't want to lose the leg."

"Yeah. I can fix you fairly well. Not hospital quality, but pretty well. I can put some pressure bandages on the wounds—the slug went straight through—and give you a couple of antibiotics and some pain tabs in my aid kit. When we get around the corner on the truck route, we'll stop again and move you into the trailer, where you can stretch out on the mattresses. You'll sleep most of the way, and we'll get you to a doc at the Indian clinic."

"Sounds . . . okay. But you know how you told me getting shot feels like a snowball with a rock in it?" Odin asked. His face was a dead-white oval in the truck's overhead light.

"Yeah?"

"What a crock of shit. I've been hit with a snowball; this doesn't feel like a snowball."

Harmon grinned and said to Cruz from the backseat, "Gonna want to pick up a little more speed—the people in the trailer are comfortable enough."

In the distance, they could see the nighttime glow of Silver City. Cruz said, "Bypass coming up pretty quick."

Harmon was digging through his aid kit. "First things first," he said. "Let's stop the bleeding."

When they pulled to the side of the road a second time, Shay was worried that something even worse had happened, but Harmon jogged around to the back of the trailer, unlatched the gate, and said, "We're moving Odin here so he can stretch out."

"How is he? And where are we?"

"He'll be okay, but we need to get him to a hospital sooner or later. He's gonna need some work. We're getting close to the main highway north. Once we're on it, we don't want to stop. Let's get Odin back here. . . ."

The transfer took only a minute, Harmon and Cruz making a cradle of their arms and gently moving Odin into the trailer. Odin stretched out next to Morris, who looked at him but made no sound.

Harmon said to Shay, "You go on up front with Cruz. The two of you look pretty innocent. God help us." He laughed and shook his head.

"What?"

"Never mind. Anyway, lock me in," he said.

Before leaving Odin, Shay knelt beside him and said, "You'll be okay."

"Harmon gave me some dope." Odin gasped then: "It hurts, but not so bad as it did."

Shay touched the man next to Odin. "This is Robert G. Morris from St. Louis. You remember the video we saw, the man with the mind transfer. . . ."

Odin looked at Morris and said, "Oh my God. It's really him?"

"It is. And you helped save him. Now sleep."

A minute later, they rolled on into the starlit night, the long highway pointing toward Arizona. Cruz placed a hand on Shay's leg and said, "I just . . . I just . . ."

"What?"

"I don't know."

"Yeah," she said softly, and rubbed his hand. "Me neither."

Twist called at one o'clock in the morning and asked, "You still watching the ranch?"

Shay said, "No. We raided the place, grabbed the prisoners, and now we're running north in Arizona."

"What!"

"Yeah. We saw a second body hauled out to the burn pit, and we were worried that the FBI might arrest you and then figure out where we were. So we raided the place and we got out okay. . . ."

She gave him the details, and he said, "Harmon's got some interesting friends. First Mesa, huh? We'll meet you. If we drive all night, we can be there in the morning."

"You gotta get Cade to track down Robert G. Morris's relatives in St. Louis. If we can get them to identify him . . . it'll be another nail in Singular's coffin."

"We can do that. Tell Odin to hang tough. We'll see you tomorrow."

Harmon stood in the back, rifle at his side, watching cars coming up behind them. None seemed to pay any attention to the horse trailer—they were common in that part of the country, and most cars had only a single driver.

Odin was asleep, with a heavy dose of painkillers. Robert Morris spoke aloud a few times, mostly gibberish. The others were silent, and eventually all of them were asleep.

Harmon gazed at these ruined people, these violated people, and thought about his work for Singular and everything that happened afterward.

The help he'd given them, Shay and Odin, didn't make up for what he'd done for Singular. He'd known that something smelled wrong; he'd known that a company working on prosthetics really didn't need heavy security agents like Sync, or gunmen like Thorne, but he'd turned his face away from that reality.

He looked at the wounded bodies around him and wondered if it could ever be put right.

• • •

At dawn, they began the drive up the remote tabletop mountain that was part of the Hopi Reservation. Harmon had moved up front to guide them in, and Shay's jaw had literally dropped at the strange beauty on the horizon: three caprock mesas rising out of the high desert like some sort of lunar landscape. She'd let X off the leash, and he stood on the seat next to her, watching out the window with what looked to her like doggy awe.

"My friends' ancestors have lived on these mesas for more than a thousand years," Harmon said. A dozen villages were sprinkled along the cliffsides and on up to the flat tops, with a couple of the mesas considered too sacred for visitors to enter without a Native guide. They were passing a scattering of small, weather-beaten houses along Highway 264 when Harmon said, "Up there . . . It's the blue house."

Cruz took the truck off the highway and down a dirt road and pulled up to a small blue rambler-style house with three old cars parked in the yard. A stocky man with a braid, wearing jeans and a plaid shirt, stuck his head out a screen door as Harmon and Shay got out of the truck.

"Harmon! Man!" He turned back and called through the open door, "Dorrie—Harmon's here!" and the two exchanged a shoulder hug, and Harmon said to Shay, "This is Cheveyo, my old army pal."

As they shook hands, a woman came to the door in a terry-cloth nightgown and cried, "Harmon!" and came out and gave Harmon a kiss on the cheek and asked, "Why didn't you call?"

"Got a big problem, Dorrie, and we need help," Harmon said. "Come look."

They walked to the back of the horse trailer, and Harmon opened the gate. The couple looked in at the bodies on the mattresses. Odin's bandaged leg looked a lot like he'd been shot. Cheveyo said, "Jesus! Harmon! What is this?"

"We need to get these people to a hospital where we won't get busted by the cops as soon as we walk in. There's a story that goes with this, and when you hear it, you'll be on our side. What was done to these people . . . it's awful. It's the worst thing you ever heard of."

A young woman curled on her side was weeping, and Dorrie leaned into the trailer, looking past Odin, and said to her, calmly, "You're safe now, sweetie. No one's going to hurt you. We'll get you to some medical people right away." The woman tilted her head toward Dorrie's voice, but she didn't seem to actually see Dorrie or know that Dorrie had pulled a Kleenex from her robe and was holding it out to her. Still, as Dorrie continued speaking to her in a soothing voice, the woman stopped crying.

Cheveyo took Harmon by the elbow and said with a grimace, "Okay. You ride with us to the health center; you tell your friends to follow us. You can tell the story on the way."

"We've really got to stay away from the cops for the time being," Harmon said.

"Not a problem," Cheveyo said.

The people at the health center were less happy to see them.

"What are we supposed to do? They're not Native people, and we don't have the facilities here to treat them anyway," the doctor on duty said. "The guy who's been shot, he needs to get up to Tuba City or somewhere. . . ."

Cheveyo said, "Hey, Doc—we need to make sure the shot guy *can* get to Tuba City, and then we'll take him. Just take a look, huh? That's not costing you anything. And the rest of them—"

Harmon interrupted: "For the rest of them, call the FBI. They have jurisdiction here on the reservation, right? So call them. Tell them this is the same bunch of people that they found in San Francisco, experimental subjects from Singular Corporation. There's an agent named Barin from Los Angeles—the local FBI agents should talk to him about this. . . . All you need to do is watch these people until help arrives."

There was more arguing and arm waving, which was finally settled by Shay, who said, "You want to load all these poor people back in a horse trailer? That's not going to look good. That's gonna look criminal."

So the doc took a look at Odin's leg, recleaned the wounds and redid the bandages, and said, "He needs to get to a surgical unit somewhere. Your best bet is Flagstaff. That's two and a half hours by car, but he'd get the right care there."

Harmon said to Shay, "That's where the feds would fly into, probably. So . . . that's probably not a bad idea for Odin. He can talk to the feds while we hide out here. . . . Better than dealing with the local sheriff's office."

"That sounds like a plan," Odin said. "I could use a couple more pills, though."

They left the experimental subjects and the horse trailer at the health center and drove south to Flagstaff, and on the way, they talked about exactly how they'd manage Odin's arrival at the hospital and everything that would come afterward.

And they talked to Twist, who at that moment was north of Phoenix, on the way into Flagstaff. He gave them the phone number for Agent Barin. "I can't tell you how reliable the guy is, but I don't think he's involved with Singular. Do you think they'll hold Odin? Arrest him?"

"We don't have much choice," Harmon said. "He's got to be hospitalized, and anytime there's a gunshot wound, the cops get called. . . . Barin's probably preferable to the locals."

"Yeah," Twist said.

"When will you get to Flagstaff?" Harmon asked.

Cade answered: "About an hour."

Shay said, "Harmon's friend says we can hide out with his aunt up on the Hopi Reservation. It's out in the countryside, so nobody will find us. We'll have time to get some sleep and figure out our next move."

"We'll meet you there," Twist said. "Good luck."

At the Flagstaff Medical Center, they parked outside the emergency room doors. Shay went inside, spotted a wheelchair, and pushed it outside. Harmon and Cruz helped Odin into it, and Shay pushed it inside, where an admissions clerk looked up from a computer and said, "Can we help you?"

Shay said, "He's got a gunshot wound in the leg. He needs to be taken care of."

The clerk said, "Stay right here—let me grab a doctor."

He disappeared, and Shay kissed Odin on the forehead and said, "You're on your own, brother. Take care of yourself. Be smart. We'll see you when we can."

"I love you, too—now go," Odin said.

She hurried out, climbed into the back of the truck with X, and they rolled back to the street.

"Anybody chasing us?" Cruz asked.

Harmon and Shay turned to look. "Not yet."

"Might have a camera there; they could get our plates," Cruz said. "We better get back to Hopi."

As they headed out of Flagstaff, Shay called Twist to tell him that Odin had been delivered to the hospital, and then, as they got to the edge of town, she called Barin. The FBI agent answered on the second ring with a terse "Barin."

"Agent Barin, this is Shay Remby."

"Ms. Remby, thank you for calling. Where are you?"

"We just dropped my brother at the Flagstaff Medical Center. He was shot in the leg last night while we were rescuing six more experimental subjects from Senator Dash's ranch in New Mexico, between Lordsburg and Silver City. The six subjects are now at the health center at First Mesa, Arizona, but to tell the truth, they aren't in great shape. They need major medical treatment, and they need it right now. One of them is an American missionary who was kidnapped in North Korea. His name is Robert G. Morris, and he's from St. Louis. He is still somewhat . . . talkative."

"Ms. Remby, we need to talk to you, as well as your brother, and anyone else involved in this situation. . . ."

"You can talk to my brother in Flagstaff. He'll tell you how they've been burning bodies at Senator Dash's ranch. You need to get a team in there fast, before they destroy all the evidence—"

"Ms. Remby—" Barin tried to interrupt.

But Shay just said, "You've got miles to go before you sleep, Agent Barin. Get moving."

She clicked off, pulled the battery out of the cell phone, and dropped them in the truck's center console.

23

The sun was just going down when Varek Royce flew into Albu-querque in his private Boeing 747M, a combination passenger and freight aircraft that was too large to land at Santa Fe's quaint airport. The passenger section had been reworked into an office suite and a private apartment with a compact bedroom and full handicapped bathroom. The rear of the jet was a garage with a specially equipped Mercedes-Benz Sprinter van.

When the plane taxied to a stop, Royce rolled his power wheel-chair into the garage and up the van's ramp. A moment later, the belly door on the 747 began to retract, and another ramp projected out to the ground. Royce's driver asked, "Are you locked in, sir?"

"Yes. Go." He slipped on his sunglasses. "There will be two men waiting for us at the bottom of the ramp."

"Yes, I see them."

• • •

The van stopped to pick up the two men. As they climbed aboard, Royce nodded and said, "Thorne. Earl."

Thorne and Denyers, each carrying a briefcase, took seats at the van's conference table; the van's door closed, and they were on their way. Denyers took out a bug detector, put it on the table, and turned it on. Royce said, "There are some microphones in here, Earl, although they're all turned off."

Denyers, looking at a small LCD on the side of the bug detector, nodded. "Three of them. Okay."

"So this is being recorded?" Thorne asked.

Denyers threw a switch on the side of the detector. "Not anymore," he said.

"They were turned off," Royce said again.

"No reason to take chances," Denyers said. "I wouldn't want anyone else to hear this."

"How bad is it?" Royce asked.

Denyers said, "It's about as bad as it could get. Those goddamn kids hit Dash's ranch last night. Harmon was with them; he must've planned it out, because it was like a military operation. . . ."

He told them about the raid, the escape, the burning car on the bridge. "Then, as everybody was about to turn around and get back to the ranch to shut it down, who should show up but two guys with the Border Patrol."

"The Border Patrol?"

"Yeah. We have nobody with the Border Patrol. Anyway, about half the ranch hands are illegals, and some of them were there at the bridge. The Border Patrol guys wanted everybody's IDs, and five of the hands had no papers, couldn't even speak much English. . . . They busted them."

"Jesus. The ranch security guys couldn't do . . . anything?"

"No. And the Border Patrol said they'd be making an 'audit' at the ranch this morning. Most everybody took off, so we haven't been able to sterilize the place. . . ."

"Gotta stop the bleeding," Royce said.

"That's why we're here," Denyers said.

Royce made a snorting noise, then flipped a switch that controlled his exoskeleton and suddenly raised his spine up straighter. "What are we going to do about the project?"

"Moving what we can," Denyers said. "We've got all the computer files but none of the equipment."

"We can buy the equipment anytime," Royce said. "The files were the important thing. Where are they?"

"They're safe," Thorne said.

"That's not what I asked," Royce snapped.

"That's what you get, until I'm in the clear," Thorne snapped back.

Denyers jumped in: "We're moving everything we can to the Honduras site."

"Probably should have gone there to begin with," Royce said. He looked out through the bulletproof window; the van had slowed to make the turn onto I-25 North toward Santa Fe. "What's happening with Charlotte?"

"After last night, she's coming unglued," Denyers said. "She can't see a way out. We've got a source in the FBI who tells us that agents we don't control are heading for Arizona, where the experimental subjects are being held at an Indian hospital. He didn't know which one. We do know that Harmon had contacts on all the reservations down there."

Royce fulminated. "We've gotten beat up by a bunch of goddamn children. . . ."

Thorne snapped again: "I've gotten tired of saying this—they aren't children. We've got people their age fighting in Afghanistan. I've been shot by one of them, the same one who stabbed Jeff Sanders last night. If I ever get a clean shot, I'll kill her."

Royce peered at him for a minute, then said, "Huh. Kicked you in the balls, too, didn't she?"

Thorne glared at the billionaire cripple and mentally tipped him over. Royce knew what he was thinking and flashed a grin, then shut it down just as quickly. He turned to Denyers and asked, "What are you going to do about Dash's security?"

"They work for me," Thorne said. "They do what I tell them."

The trip north to Santa Fe took the best part of an hour, night falling along the way, and the climb up the mountain to Dash's house took another ten minutes. From high on the hill, they could see most of Santa Fe, a wash of twinkling, multicolored lights. They were met in Dash's driveway by two security guards, who nodded at Thorne, who asked, "Where's Ben?"

"He's set up on the back porch, up on the second floor, with night-vision gear. He can see the whole back end of the house from there, and most of the side yards."

"Okay. And the dog?"

"Put away, as requested."

"Good; Mr. Royce is allergic. We won't be long."

One of the guards said to Thorne, "Uh, sir . . . Senator Dash has been a little cranky with us today. She's had a few."

"More than a few," said the other one.

"Good to know, thanks," Thorne said.

The front of the house was covered by a stone porch with a discreet handicapped ramp off to one side. Royce spotted the ramp and led the way up. Dash met them at the door. She was holding a drink and smelled of alcohol. "About time," she said. "You know about the ranch."

"Yeah, we do, and we know about the papers those kids took out of here, too," Royce said. He led the way into the house. "What we need to know now is, What did they get? Whose names were mentioned in the papers?"

"Nobody's," Dash said. She was wearing her wig, which was crushed on one side, as though she'd been sleeping in it. "The Singular papers were all about my account, and some introductory stuff about the procedure. They didn't even say who the doctor was. . . . It's probably the same stuff you saw, Varek."

"You're sure."

"Yes, of course. The dangerous stuff was the intel papers, but those are on national intelligence, not on Singular. Really wouldn't want the Russians to get them, or the Chinese, but it's nothing personal about any of us."

"Let's go sit for a minute," Royce said. "I'm on my way to Miami. I don't have long, and I'm too tired to be looking up at you all the time."

"We need to settle what we're doing next," Dash said. "It's getting harder and harder to deny. . . ."

She led the way into the living room. She dropped into one of the chairs, and Denyers, digging in his briefcase, walked behind her. As he came around her chair, he said, "Charlotte?"

When she looked at him, he sprayed her in the face with a small aerosol canister. She gasped once and then nearly toppled over. He walked away and said, "Nobody breathe deeply . . . just for another ten seconds."

After fifteen seconds, Denyers said, "We should be safe."

"But what if we're not?" Royce asked.

"It's degraded enough that you wouldn't get more than a headache. But Charlotte got a full shot of it; she'll be down for an hour. . . . Let's get this done."

The house had an elevator, and they took her up to the second floor, where the master bedroom was. Royce watched as Thorne and Denyers, both wearing plastic gloves, efficiently pulled her clothing off, then got her into a pair of oversized pajamas.

They put her in bed and propped her up on some pillows. Denyers took a medical lavage apparatus out of his briefcase. It consisted of a rubber bulb with a soft rubber tube extending down from it. He went into the bathroom, turned on a tap, filled a glass. He brought the glass back to the bedroom, took a small brown bottle from his briefcase, and poured it into the glass. Then he put the rubber tube into the glass and sucked the liquid up into it.

That done, he and Thorne carefully pried open Dash's mouth and put the tube down her throat, past her windpipe. Denyers squeezed the bulb. "That'll do it," he said.

He carefully rolled the glass through both of Dash's hands, then left it on the bedside table with the brown bottle.

Royce had watched the proceedings with interest. "What is that stuff?" he asked.

"Prescription painkiller for her husband. You're supposed to put three drops under your tongue. She got about two hundred drops, all at once. It's five years old, well documented, from a local pharmacy. . . ." He went back to his briefcase, packed away the lavage equipment, took out a flat envelope, and carefully slipped out a piece of paper.

"Suicide note," he said. He pressed random parts of it against

Dash's still-warm fingers, then propped it against the bedside lamp.

"Huh," Royce said. "Is she gone yet?"

"A few minutes," Thorne said. He went into the bathroom, came back with a washcloth, and wiped off Dash's face.

"The mist doesn't leave a residue," Denyers said.

"I'm fussy," Thorne said. He took the washcloth back into the bathroom, rinsed it, and left it to dry on the edge of the bathtub. "That should do it."

They went back down to the living room and waited.

Small talk.

Ten minutes passed, then Thorne excused himself, took the stairs to the second floor.

He was back a moment later. "It's done. Let's go."

At the door, before they went out, Denyers said to Royce, "You shoot, right? Skeet, or trap, or something like that?"

"Yes. Why?"

"Because I want you to be telling me a skeet-shooting story as we go past the security guys. Something that they'll remember. Stop right in the middle of the driveway and show how you swing on a clay, you know, from a wheelchair. If one of them says something about it, or asks a question, stop to chat."

"I see, I see," Royce said. "We're fixing in their minds the fact that we were talking about trivia when we left. Laughing, even."

"Maybe stay away from laughing," Thorne said. "No offense, but you don't laugh so good."

They talked skeet on the porch, and Thorne took a moment to chat with the guards—"You're right, she's really whacked. She says she's going to bed"—and they got back in the van to leave for their return flights. Thorne would be dropped at Santa Fe's airport, where he'd flown himself in, and Denyers would catch a commercial flight out of Albuquerque.

On the way, Denyers said, "I talked to Jeffers last week. He won't discuss that other thing at all. He wants it to be a . . . psychological surprise, he says."

"Mmm, there would be some value to that," Royce conceded. "For him, anyway. Not so much for me. If it happens, there'd be substantial turmoil in the markets for some time. Anytime there's turmoil, there's money to be made."

"For you," Denyers said. "But for us, it's the same old government salary."

"Until you pull the trigger," Royce said. "Then . . . well. You will be quite well fixed."

24

Twist and Cade showed up looking dusty and beat.

Cruz and Harmon were sound asleep on plastic air mattresses on the living room floor of a house owned by Cheveyo's aunt, whose name was Marti.

Shay had been turning restlessly on a mattress next to Cruz, feeling sweaty and slippery against the plastic. X was sitting on a wooden bench, looking out the back window: Marti had a female German shepherd named Chickee, who was in heat. X was definitely interested, and Chickee was definitely interested right back.

Shay heard Twist's Range Rover pull into Marti's side yard and rolled to her feet. But Cruz and Harmon slept on, like dead men.

Shay gave Twist a squeeze, stood on tiptoe to give Cade a peck on the cheek, and said, "We've been told that the FBI is at the medical center, looking at the experimental subjects. . . ." Then, "I wish we had a better name for them. *Experimental subjects* sounds like lab rats."

Cade said, "But *zombies* . . ."

"Yeah, we're not calling them zombies," Twist said. "Though some of them seem to be."

"We need some sleep," Cade said.

"Harmon and Cruz are sleeping inside. We've got air mattresses for everyone. The lady who owns the house has a bunch of grand-children, and she has air mattresses for when they visit."

"Enough for all of us?"

"Yeah. She went to work, but she'll be back around five o'clock. She's going to stop and get some dinner."

"Does she know . . . ," Twist began.

"Most of it," Shay said. "She's on our side."

"Let's get our stuff," Cade said. He yawned, hard, and added, "We can talk when everybody's awake."

"Did you manage to track down Robert G. Morris's relatives in St. Louis?" Shay asked Cade.

"Yes," Cade said. "I've got a phone number, but we haven't called it yet."

"I'll do it," Shay said. "It's not right that he's here and they don't even know about it."

Morris, Cade had learned, had been married, with two young children. He'd found a cell phone number for Morris's wife, An-gela, in an AT&T database.

Shay made the call, and Angela Morris picked up on the third ring.

"Mrs. Morris? . . . No, I'm not selling anything. . . . Uh, I've been working with a group of people investigating a company in San Francisco called Singular. There's no easy way to say this—I'm sorry—but we think that your husband Robert may have been vic-timized. . . . No, no, please, this is *not* a crank call. . . ."

Angela Morris was skeptical, perhaps angry, but also hopeful in some measure, Shay decided when they ended the call. "It's about fifty-fifty that she believed me," Shay told Twist and Cade. "I gave her the numbers for the medical center and Agent Barin, and I think she'll call, at least to check. I can't imagine how she's gonna react when she actually sees what they did to her husband."

"If she'll even recognize him," Twist said.

For the rest of the afternoon, they alternately napped and talked, watched television and probed the Internet, hoping to find indications that Singular was being taken down. They didn't find much: nothing on television, a couple of brief stories from California and New Mexico hinting that some things were happening.

Marti showed up at five-thirty with enough food for an army, and Cheveyo and his wife, Dorrie, arrived soon after.

As they ate chicken, tossing scraps to X, Harmon gave Twist and Cade a summary of what had happened at the ranch, and Twist told them about his visit with Agent Barin. "I don't think the FBI is all that interested in us," Twist said. "They've got a finger up, and they're beginning to figure out which way the wind is blowing."

"Either that, or they think they can find us anytime they need to," Cruz said.

Cade was looking at an iPad they'd borrowed from one of the girls in the hotel—it'd been given to her by her mother—so they could get online without the searches being traced to them. He checked Odin's name and found nothing. If he'd been arrested at the hospital, the arrest had not yet been made public.

Marti was dishing out seconds when Cade said, "Here's something."

Twist: "What?"

"Thorne's in Santa Fe. Or, at least, the airplane he's been flying is."

"Going to see Dash," Twist said.

Shay: "Still plotting . . ."

Cade said, "Is there anything *we* should be plotting?"

They talked about it and decided to call all the Arizona news media they could reach and tell them about the experimental subjects at the medical center.

"If they're still at the medical center," Cheveyo said. "Let me check. I've got a cousin who works there."

They all sat and looked at him while he talked to his cousin. After he hung up, he said, "They're going to move them tomorrow. A bunch of feds showed up just before Vernon finished his shift. They're getting some ambulances up here from Flagstaff tomorrow, and then . . . this is what Vernon heard anyway . . . they'll fly them out of Flagstaff to Los Angeles."

Cade said, "Okay, Singular's shut down in San Francisco and Sacramento and Eugene, and the feds are all over those places. Hopefully, with all that Odin's telling them, they'll be at the ranch soon. And we've broken this whole thing into the public eye as much as we can. We'll let the media know about the experimental subjects here, get another hit from that. . . ."

Shay said, "Now that they're down, I'd like to find a way to kick them, one last time. Just to make sure. Sync told Harmon that Thorne was sending all Singular's data to the cloud. . . . That sounds like they'll be starting up again, somewhere else."

"Not likely in this country," Twist said. "Not where we could do anything to stop them."

"What about all the people who were providing the money for this?" Shay asked. "Will they just walk away?"

"If they're consolidating in North Korea, there's not much we can do about it," Cade said.

Shay said, "But who are *they* anymore? We know about Thorne. And Dash. And Janes. We know the vice president's involved somehow. But who else flew to the ranch? Can we identify them?"

Cade said, "Some. I tracked down the tail numbers on the airplanes we saw. One is owned by a Dr. Ian Wyeth; he's a neurosurgeon from St. Louis. One's a dead end—owned by a private company that hardly seems to exist. The one Thorne's been flying is also owned by a private company, but that one's more legit. It's a subsidiary of a subsidiary of a company owned by Varek Royce."

"Whoa," said Twist.

"Why? Who's that?" asked Cruz.

"Software giant," said Twist. "You know—the guy in the wheelchair."

"Yeah," Cade continued. "From what I can tell, he's got a whole fleet of airplanes, along with thirty billion dollars or so."

"Why's he in a wheelchair?" Cruz asked.

"He's got Lou Gehrig's disease—ALS," Cade said. "It'll slowly paralyze him until it gets to his lungs, and then he'll smother. There's no cure. As I understand it."

"Sounds like someone who'd be interested in keeping the program going," Shay said.

Cruz said, "So we give those names to the FBI, with all the evidence we've got."

Shay sighed. "Is that all?"

Cade was still working the iPad. "Okay. I've got the websites and the tip lines for all the major TV stations in Phoenix, Scottsdale, and Tucson, and also the newspapers and the TV station in Flagstaff. I'm thinking a press release . . . if you want to give me a little help here."

• • •

Shay and Marti did the dishes, Marti washing, Shay drying. The men didn't assist.

"The equality thing hasn't gotten very far," Shay said as she put a cup in the cupboard.

"You know how they do this to us?" Marti asked. "It's because they can stand living in a trash heap longer than we can. My ex-husband, he'd lay on the couch until the empty beer cans built up around his neck. And he had, like, thirty pairs of underwear—that way, he said, he only had to do laundry once a month."

"I think you're onto something," Shay said. "You should write a book."

Marti peered into the living room, where Cruz was talking to Harmon. "Well, your man seems nice enough."

"Not exactly my man," Shay said. "I'm not sure I'm old enough to have a man."

"How old are you?"

"Going on seventeen."

"That'd be old enough around here," Marti said. "Not that it always works out so well."

"Yeah . . ."

"Still," Marti said with a grin, "he's not bad. Even if he's not exactly your man."

They spent the evening getting the press releases out and updating Mindkill with the latest information. Still feeling a little beaten up from the previous long night and day, they were all asleep on Marti's living room floor by midnight.

Sometime around dawn, Shay woke briefly when she heard Marti moving around. An hour later, her eyes popped open; she was aware that something was not quite right. She sat up and looked around: all of the men were still asleep.

But X was missing.

She heard somebody moving in the kitchen and found Marti drinking orange juice and reading the paper. Marti whispered, "You all get up so late. I'm getting ready for work."

"Where's X?"

A possibly guilty look crossed over Marti's face. "He wanted to go out in the backyard. . . ."

"But isn't . . ."

"Mmm-hmmm. X would be a good daddy."

"Oh, jeez, I don't know," Shay said anxiously.

She went to the back door. X was waiting, his tongue hanging out and with what Shay would have sworn was a smile on his doggy face. Chickee was lying down in a corner of the yard looking fairly relaxed as well.

"Good morning, buster," Shay said. "You want to come in?"

X walked past her into the kitchen, where he sat and peered at Marti. "Just like all men," Marti said. "If they don't go to sleep, they want something to eat."

Shay made some oatmeal and put down a bowl of leftover chicken for X. As Marti was gathering up her work stuff, Cheveyo showed up, slamming the door on his truck and jogging across the yard. Marti said, "Uh-oh. Chev don't jog. Something's up."

She opened the door, and her nephew came in, out of breath, and looked at Shay. "You watching the news?"

"I just got up," Shay said. "What happened?"

"Your friend Senator Dash. She killed herself."

25

Shay froze, hardly able to respond. "What? What?"

"It sounds like she overdosed on something," Cheveyo said. "They're not giving out details, but the chief of police in Santa Fe said she took her own life. He didn't say it like they usually do, that it 'appears' that she took her own life. He just came right out and said it."

"We gotta . . . ," she began, but she had no idea what to do.

She turned and walked into the living room.

Twist had been laughing at something Harmon said, but when he looked at her face, his smile vanished. "What happened?"

Shay said, "Dash is dead. She supposedly killed herself. At her house in Santa Fe."

Harmon looked at Cade and said, "You said that Thorne's plane was in Santa Fe."

Cade nodded. "Yes."

"So they killed her," Twist said. He turned a circle around the living room, thumping the floor with his cane.

Shay asked, "Is this the result of our raid on the ranch? Are we responsible for this?"

"Do you care?" Cruz said.

Cade said, "I'm going to sound like an asshole for saying this, but this could be a good thing. They'll have to do an autopsy, and they'll find the electronic leads in her head. It's another nail . . ." He didn't have to add "in her coffin."

"I'm going to call Barin and talk to him," Twist said.

They all looked at him, and Harmon said, "Yes. Put it on speaker. We all need to listen in."

Twist placed the call. Instead of "Hello," Barin said, "I told you to stay in L.A. What are you doing in Arizona?"

Twist didn't answer that. "You've heard about Senator Dash, of course."

"Yes. The Santa Fe police say it's a suicide."

"It was murder," Twist said. "You know that guy we told you about? Thorne? The gunman for Singular? The guy who tortured Cade Holt and Odin Remby?"

"I remember the name," Barin said.

"He's a pilot. Cade, give Agent Barin his plane's tail number. . . ."

Cade read the tail number off his computer file, and Twist said, "His plane was in Santa Fe yesterday."

There was a long moment of silence, then: "We can check that."

"Also, when your guys look at Dash's body, have them take a close look at her head. You'll find those ports we were talking about—or the holes from them, anyway. The ones she said didn't exist."

More silence.

Shay asked, "Are you at Dash's ranch?"

"I can't really talk about the investigation," Barin said.

"Jesus, man," Twist said. "They've probably already pushed the ashes into the river."

Barin said, "We're pursuing several aspects of . . . Senator Dash's relationship to Singular."

Harmon spoke up: "In other words, you're covering the ranch."

Silence, but no denial.

"Have you talked to Odin?" Shay asked. "Is he okay?"

"We're speaking with him," Barin said. "He's cooperating with us."

Cade made a throat-slicing gesture with his finger, so Twist said, "We'll leave you to the investigation. Check you later."

Barin said, "Did you give my phone number to Angela—"

Twist clicked off the phone, and Cade pulled the battery. "He was trying to keep you talking. The feds are probably on the way, and we're sitting here like a bunch of mushrooms."

"How close can they get?" Cruz asked.

Cade shrugged. "I don't know how they'd be tracking us, but he knew right away that we were in Arizona."

"The least we can do is move the cars behind the house so they can't see them from the road," Harmon said. "If they've got agents up at the medical center, they could just have them go look around."

"Better hurry," Shay said. "It's a real small town."

They hid the cars, and no feds showed up, although Cheveyo said there were several unfamiliar SUVs in town. "That would be them," Harmon said.

At ten o'clock, Cheveyo's cousin called from the medical center and said that four ambulances had just departed for Flagstaff, taking the experimental subjects with them, including Robert G. Morris.

And, he said, Morris's family went with them, in their own car.

Shay got Angela Morris on the phone and said, "This is Shay Remby. I spoke to you yesterday."

"Yes, Shay. Thank you so much for calling. I called that FBI agent, Agent Barin, and then we caught a plane to Phoenix and drove all night. . . ."

"I have to ask . . . was that your husband? We were never quite sure."

"Yes, but not all of him! Not all of him!" Morris said. "I don't know what they did to him. . . ."

"I'm so sorry, so sorry. They're doing that to a lot of people," Shay said. "Are you on the way to the Flagstaff hospital, or are they moving them somewhere else?"

"We're all going to a hospital in San Francisco," Morris said. "They've got a plane waiting in Flagstaff to take them."

"If a TV station was waiting outside the airport, would you talk to them?" Shay asked.

Angela Morris hesitated and then said, "They've asked us not to contact the media. But we don't know exactly who we can trust. The FBI agents were really . . . standoffish. They didn't even want to let me talk to Robert."

"Angela, the more public this becomes, the less they'll be able to cover up," Shay said. "There are some high government officials involved in this, and some very, very rich people."

"Well . . . we'll talk about it, anyway. Between ourselves. I'm here with Robert's parents. But, Shay, whatever happens, thank you. For helping Robert. For finding me."

"I worry that we didn't do enough—that nobody did. There are more people like him, and like the others, and many more who've died," Shay said. "Angela, they'll keep doing this if they're not caught. Please talk to the television people."

She said, "I . . . the FBI . . ." Then, after some muffled talk in the background, she said, "We don't owe the FBI. We owe you. If the TV people are there, I'll talk to them."

Cade sent a news tip to the Flagstaff TV station: all they could do.

Cade said, "There's not much more to do from here—not if the feds are going to the ranch, and the . . . experiments . . . have been moved."

Harmon cleared his throat and said, "How far do we trust the FBI to break this open. All of it?"

"They'll do what they have to, but there are so many important people here—politicians, political contributors, those kinds of people—it'll be hard going," Twist said.

Shay asked, "Harmon, what are you thinking?"

"I'm thinking that Singular's still operating at a pretty powerful level, if they've murdered Dash and think they can get away with it."

"Well, we know the vice president's involved . . . ," Cruz said.

Harmon rubbed his temples, staring down at the floor between his shoes.

Shay got impatient and said, "What? What's bugging you?"

Harmon looked up. "They didn't shoot Dash."

"No, they probably poisoned her or something. So . . . ?"

"So who are they shooting at twenty-two hundred yards?"

Shay said, "Oh," and pressed her fingers to her lips.

Harmon said, "I don't even like to think this, to suggest this, but I don't see how they can get out of this mess unless somebody shuts down the investigation at the very top. The vice president isn't quite at the very top, but if something were to happen to the president . . ."

"What?" Twist said. "That's . . . that's . . ."

"Nuts," Harmon said. "I know."

"Perfect one-word description of Thorne," Cade said.

"Did we get pictures of that gun? Should we send them to Barin?" asked Twist. "I don't think I've mentioned the vice president—we could send that photo we found in Janes's files. The one with the heads of Singular, the North Koreans, and Lawton Jeffers . . ."

"I can pull all that together," said Cade. "He might believe us."

"What else?" Shay said. "What else can we do?"

Harmon was staring at the floor again. "I know about a guy Singular was trying to recruit. . . . His name is Gerald Armie. Another billionaire. I was there when he was first told about the Singular project—well, I wasn't exactly there, I was eavesdropping. I later heard that they were still talking to him . . . he was dragging his feet. But I have to believe he knows more names. Somebody had to recruit him, somebody had to vouch for Singular. But it seemed like he might have been resisting."

"He's a thread that could be pulled," Shay said.

"Yeah. If we think we should do that," Harmon said. "The whole idea of an assassination . . . Anyway, Armie's got resources. He's got all the resources that Varek Royce has. And that could be useful, too, if he was on our side."

"Then we should talk to him," Shay said. "We should keep attacking."

"He lives somewhere in Oklahoma," Harmon said. "I don't know exactly where—or even if he's there now."

Twist looked at Cade. "Can you find that out?"

It took Cade an hour. In two minutes, he'd learned that Armie lived in a suburb of Oklahoma City, that he ran a chain of supermarkets covering most of the central states, that he was sixty-two years old, and that he was halfway up the *Forbes* list of the richest four hundred people in the U.S.

Figuring out where he'd be was harder, but Cade eventually found an online item on the *Oklahoman*'s site saying that he, his wife, and their daughter would attend a charity ball . . . in two days.

"Can we get to Oklahoma City in two days?" Shay asked.

"Yeah. It's probably a thousand miles, but it wouldn't be a problem driving it," Harmon said.

"This whole fight with Singular has been like a moving geography lesson," Shay said. "I'd hardly ever been out of Oregon before it started. Now I can tell you the driving distances for almost anyplace in the West."

Cruz said, "So . . . are we going?"

Twist looked at them all. "This doesn't feel done yet."

They all nodded. They were going.

Harmon said good-bye to his friends, and they all thanked them profusely for the hospitality. X gave Chickee a snoot good-bye as they headed for the cars.

"I don't know if he was really ready for a committed relationship," Shay said to Chickee, and she led X to Twist's truck.

I-40 seemed to stretch on forever under the big bowl of the Southwestern sky, Twist singing out the Eagles' "Standing on a corner in Winslow, Arizona . . ." as they went through Winslow, then on and on and on through New Mexico and all the heat mirages on the highway until they got to Amarillo, Texas, which was basically a concrete gulch filled with fast-food joints and motels. They got a McDonald's dinner and found a motel on the east end of town.

The next day, they did it all again. The miles rolled by in a blur of small towns as they left Texas for Oklahoma and, finally, five hours out of Amarillo, rolled into Oklahoma City.

They found a Twist motel special with Internet not far from the site of that evening's charity ball. "I found some pictures from last year's event. All the men are wearing tuxedos, and the women are in gowns. . . . We might not be dressed right for this," Cade said.

"Probably be best to catch him outside, if we can," Harmon said. They were all together in Twist's room. "We won't be able to talk to him in a crowd anyway."

"What do the waitresses look like?" Shay asked. "I've still got my hotel outfit from San Francisco."

Harmon said, "Might have some blood spatter on it." Shay gave him a look, and he said, "Okay, maybe not."

Cade called up photos from the previous ball, but none of them showed waitresses.

Twist said, "So we play it by ear."

"Gotta do better than that," Harmon said. "We actually have to talk to the guy for a while. And to tell the truth, I don't want to strong-arm him. I'm seeing some possibility now that we could get out of this without going to prison, and I wouldn't want to screw up our chances."

"What do you have in mind?" Shay asked.

"We figure out how we can approach him at a place where we can actually sit down and talk."

"There'll be a lot of cops around that ball tonight," Cade said. "It's a pretty big deal. If he started yelling . . ."

Cruz: "Why don't we find out where he lives and go knock on his door?"

They all looked at him for a moment, and he shrugged. "We'd be alone with him. . . ."

"He'll have security," Twist said. "He's a billionaire."

"If he's got security at his house, he'll have it everywhere," Harmon said.

"What about his office?" Shay suggested.

Harmon shook his head. "He'll be surrounded by employees—we could get swarmed." He looked back at Cruz and said, "I'm thinking Cruz might be onto something. Can we get his address on the Web?"

Cade could, and he found a street view as well. "No gate across the driveway. We could drive right in."

Shay said, "What if I put on my hotel outfit and got a box with a ribbon on it—like a big chocolate box—and knocked on the door? I'm this nonthreatening teenager. . . ."

"Probably be answered by a maid," Twist said.

"But that gets us to the door," Harmon said. "How about this: Shay won't turn the box over. Instead, she gives the maid a high-end-looking envelope with a message that says something . . . that makes our pitch."

"That says if he doesn't come to the door in five minutes, we're leaving," Shay said.

"I'm liking this," Harmon said. "What would we say in the message? How would we know that he'd be at his house?"

"The ball starts at seven o'clock, and he's giving some kind of speech, so they probably won't be late, or too late, anyway," Cade said. "And they've got to get all dressed up in fancy clothes. . . . Which means he'll probably be home no later than six o'clock or so."

"Okay, okay, I'm seeing this," Twist said. He kicked back on the couch, then sat up and said, "This couch smells bad, like somebody . . . Never mind. Anyway, let's nail this down."

26

Armie lived in a rambling two- or three-story—it was hard to tell—red-brick home set on a broad expanse of grass with carefully plotted trees and shrubs and petunias.

"Pro tip," Harmon said to Shay the first time they cruised the place. "Flower beds can be used to hide security equipment."

There was no gate at the entrance, which would have been mandatory with a similar home in L.A. A multiple-car garage sat partly behind the house, but its size was obscured by more plantings along the curving driveway. The driveway was bordered on the house side by a two-foot brick wall, with another flower bed running along the top.

"Another tip," Harmon said as they passed the end of the driveway. "You see that low wall? Looks decorative, doesn't it? It also makes it impossible to get a car or a truck to the front of the house. You see walls like that in the Middle East. The place looks open, but suicide bombers can't get their trucks close to the target."

Shay said, "Hmm." And a second later, "Looks like four cars in the driveway. . . . Wonder if they have visitors. If they're having a pre-ball party, we could have a problem."

"Yeah."

They went on, and a minute or so later, Twist, Cade, and Cruz drove by. Twist called Harmon and Shay on the walkie-talkie and said, "Somebody's leaving. Young blond lady in a Lexus."

"How many cars in the driveway?"

"Three . . ."

They spent fifteen minutes driving around, checking possible escape routes and looking for police. They never saw a patrol car. "Doesn't mean they aren't there—it just means we didn't see one," Cade said.

"Oh, now we've got Mr. Optimist with us," Twist said.

"But he's right," Cruz said.

"You know what?" Cade said. "If we had a few firecrackers, with long fuses, and dropped them out behind the local police station just before Shay and Harmon went into Armie's house . . . I bet every cop car in the city would be pulled into the station. They'd think somebody was shooting at them."

"Nope. Not going to do that," Twist said. "I have an aversion to spending time in an Oklahoma penitentiary."

"Aw, come on, man, it'd be fun," Cade said.

"Nope."

Cade looked at Cruz, who said, "Nope."

"You guys are hopeless," Cade said.

• • •

Harmon and Shay were on the main drag when Harmon spotted a FedEx drop and told Shay to pull over. He got a couple of FedEx envelopes and said, "A minor improvement in the plan."

They met at a bagel shop, got sandwiches, and carried them to a nearby park, where they could let X out and talk over what they'd seen.

Cade pitched the firecracker idea to Harmon and Shay, who both said no.

"You don't want a bunch of scared cops running around with their guns out—too much chance somebody would get hurt," Harmon said.

Cade let it go, and Twist looked at his watch. "Getting close to six o'clock."

"Time to pull the pin," Harmon said.

Cruz asked, puzzled, "What pin?"

Harmon said, "Just an expression. There's a safety pin on a hand grenade. When you pull it . . ."

"Yeah, I see. You need a better expression," Cruz said.

They pulled the pin.

Harmon, Twist, and X would stay in the Mercedes while Shay went to the door. Cade and Cruz would circle the area, ready to call in any signs of trouble.

"Nervous?" Twist asked Shay as they got close to the mansion.

"Sure. A little," Shay said.

"Good," Harmon said.

There were no cars on the narrow street in front of the Armie mansion, and as they turned into the driveway, Twist said, "Only two cars now."

Harmon pulled forward until they were even with a short set of flagstone steps that went through the wall along the driveway to a sidewalk that led to the front door.

Harmon handed Shay the FedEx envelope, and she hopped out of the truck. She was wearing black pants, a black shirt, and high-heeled black boots. The outfit had passed for a chic hotel employee's in San Francisco. It was more ambiguous here. Fashion-forward delivery girl?

The front door was actually two doors, set into a wide, heavily decorated niche in the front wall. Metal doors, disguised as wood, with small, lightly mirrored windows, she noted. Somebody inside could see out; nobody outside could see in.

She rang the doorbell and waited. A minute later, she could hear footfalls from inside, and then a nice-looking, sandy-haired young man with big white teeth—a frat boy, Shay thought—opened the door, took her in, the red hair and the black outfit, and said, "Whoa. You ain't selling Girl Scout cookies. What's up?"

He'd made her smile, and she said, "I have a FedEx special express for a Mr. Gerald Armie. I'm supposed to wait to see if there's an immediate response."

The young man looked past her at the Mercedes in the driveway. "FedEx delivers in Benzes now?"

"I'm a contract worker, and I'm usually in a totally trashed Subaru, but it broke; I borrowed my father's car," Shay said.

"I hear you. Well, step inside. Uh, I'll run this up to Dad."

"I can only wait a couple of minutes—I've got seven more deliveries."

• • •

Gerald Armie was sitting in his dressing room, getting into his tux. His black patent-leather shoes were next.

"Goddamn shoes," he said as he pulled the first one on. "They make me look like a sissy."

"Yeah, you and every other shiny-shoed gazillionaire in Oklahoma," his son said. "You don't look like sissies, you look like . . . old guys crashing a prom."

"Thank you. You've been disinherited," Armie said.

"A FedEx delivery girl brought this"—he handed his father the envelope—"and said she was supposed to wait for an answer, but it's gotta be quick because she's got more deliveries. She said it's a special express, whatever that means."

"Never heard of it," Armie said. He put on the second shoe, took the envelope, said, "Feels empty," and pulled it open.

Inside, he found a single folded sheet of paper with a note:

My name is Shay Remby. I'm with the group that has brought down Singular. Senator Dash was murdered by a professional assassin still employed by the men behind Singular. We are uncertain of your status, but would like to discuss it with you. I will wait for two minutes, then I am gone.

Armie read it a second time, then said, "Hoyt, run downstairs and tell the girl that I'm on my way. I have a reply. And hurry, before she leaves."

Hoyt started to walk away, and Armie snapped, "Hurry. Hurry. Tell her I'm coming."

Hoyt disappeared, and Armie read the note again, sighed, and briefly considered the possibility of calling the police. But that might turn out to be a really, really bad idea, especially if this group had tied him to Singular, and if Dash had actually been murdered.

He sighed again, said, "Shit," then stood, picked up the black cummerbund that had been sitting next to him, and put it on. Then he walked over to a necktie drawer, pulled it all the way out, and removed the compact semi-automatic pistol that was nestled in the back. He checked to make sure the pistol's safety was engaged and then tucked it into the cummerbund at the small of his back and put on his jacket.

He walked down the hall to his wife's dressing room, where a hairdresser was putting the final touches on her updo, and said, "No hurry, Alice. Some business came up. . . ."

"Gerald . . ."

"Yeah, yeah, I know. I'll make it as quick as I can."

Another thirty seconds took him down the main staircase, then through a corner of the living room to the front door. Hoyt was there with a young woman in a severe black uniform and with flaming red hair. He thought, *She's just a little girl.*

"What do you want?" he asked.

"We'd like to talk to you for five minutes," she said. "We need to tell you some things and also ask you some questions."

Hoyt said, "Wait a minute. . . ."

"That's okay, Hoyt," Armie said. Then to Shay, "Who's *we?*"

"Two of my friends, who are still in the car. I hope you didn't call the police, because if you did, we could all be screwed. Including you."

"Who are these people?" Hoyt asked, stepping away from Shay.

Armie said to his son, "I want you to listen into this conversation, but keep your mouth shut." And to Shay: "I didn't call the police. Get your friends in here, and let's talk. I've been worried since I heard about Charlotte."

Harmon still had the car's engine running, in case they needed to leave in a hurry. "She should never have gone inside," he said.

Twist didn't disagree, but then the door opened and Shay waved them in.

"We're up," Twist said. "You're not carrying a gun, are you?"

Harmon said, "No."

"Good."

"But Shay is."

"What!"

"Less likely to be searched by any security personnel."

"You are a very bad influence," Twist said.

"And a hippie painter anarchist isn't?" Harmon asked as they walked up the sidewalk.

"Everybody should have a hippie painter anarchist in their lives," Twist said. "It's the guys in silvered aviators with guns that you've got to be wary of."

Gerald Armie was a square-built man of average height, with silver-white hair and a ruddy complexion. His son, standing behind him, was taller, thinner, and almost blond.

Armie said, "Gentlemen," which made both Twist and Harmon smile and caused Harmon to say, "Let's just go with *men*. We got a place to sit?"

Armie took them in and then asked Harmon, "You carrying a gun?"

Harmon held his arms out to the sides. "No, of course not. We're not here to hurt anyone."

Hoyt asked, "What the hell is going on?"

"Just listen," his father said. "Come this way."

They all went into the living room, to a rectangle of beige Italian couches, and sat down. Shay outlined their involvement with Singular and where things stood now.

When she was done, Harmon leaned forward and said, "I was there the day you came to San Francisco to talk to Cartwell, Stewart, and Sync. That's when I figured out they were killing people, and I started to edge away. I heard through the grapevine that you hadn't been fully recruited, as they say. That you were edging away yourself."

Hoyt stood up and said, "Killing people? Dad, what are they talking about?"

"Sit down, Hoyt, and just listen," Armie said, then turned back to Harmon. "They didn't tell me they were killing people. I had to figure that out. I couldn't see how they could deliver what they said they could without killing people. So—I never went through with it. They're still pushing me, though. I talked to one of the top people a few days ago."

Twist said, "No time to beat around the bush, Mr. Armie— Cartwell and Stewart and Senator Dash are all dead. They're trying to move the company—the research records and the critical personnel—to a new location, while leaving the impression that the company has been destroyed. They can't have any loose ends. And you might be one."

"You're telling me I need to buy some protection."

"The best you can afford, at least for a while," Harmon said. "I have some friends who could give that to you, if you need a recommendation. We're trying to track Thorne, who's their main killer. We know he flew into Santa Fe, but we don't know where he is now."

"So he could be coming here."

"He could be—but they've got lots of problems right now, and you're not the worst of them. Unless you know more than we think you do."

"I know some stuff," Armie said.

"Like what?" Shay asked.

He shrugged. "I was recruited by Varek Royce. You know him?"

"Yes," Harmon said.

"He was my original contact with Singular. They put you together with another rich guy, like they're recruiting you for the country club. He likes to talk about the way he set the whole thing up, because it was so complicated. He didn't give me any of the details on the research, but he hinted at some of the other players so I'd know I'd be covered against . . . government interference."

"I'm going to tell you something I probably shouldn't, but I'd like to hear what you have to say about it," Harmon said.

"Okay."

"We believe that the political protection goes all the way to the vice president."

Armie rolled his teeth across his lower lip, stared into the fireplace, then said, "Well, that scares the shit out of me."

"Why is that, Mr. Armie?" Twist asked.

Armie said, "Because Varek called me the day before yesterday, told me that some environmental crazies were making lots of noise about the company and the plane accident and so on. That would be you."

They nodded.

"Well, he said it would all be resolved in the next few days, that the FBI would be pulled off, that everything about the company would be as normal. I said I wasn't sure how that could happen, and he just said, 'Watch.'"

He continued: "I've been thinking about it ever since. You can't just stop an investigation like this, not after it becomes public. Not now, especially after Senator Dash . . . died . . . however that happened. And the Chinese are involved now—I saw it on a news feed this afternoon. So how do you stop that? The only thing I can think of is to have the president squash it—though it'd be ugly even then. But the vice president . . . he has no executive power. . . ."

Harmon said, "Tell him."

Armie asked Twist, "What?"

"We're running a little scared here. If the vice president should *become* president . . . ," Twist said, "the whole Singular story would be lost in the publicity that would follow an . . ."

"Assassination," Shay said.

"Whoa, whoa, whoa!" Hoyt said, and was on his feet again, looking wild-eyed at Shay. "What are you, some sort of terrorist? Dad, we gotta get these people out of here. . . ."

Armie stood up and said, once and for all, "Hoyt, SHUT THE HELL UP!"

Hoyt sat down. Armie held on to his forehead for a moment, as if it were throbbing, then wandered over to the fireplace and said, turning back, "I can't even begin to believe that something like that would be on order." But he didn't sound so sure.

Harmon shook his head and asked Armie: "If you really had to, who's the highest guy in the government you could get to? Who'd take your call?"

Armie said, "Well, I'm a lifelong conservative Republican, so nobody very high in this administration. I guess maybe the Speaker of the House could find a few minutes for me."

"If you could get to him, tell him what's going on here, ask him to talk to the head of the Secret Service . . ."

Armie was already shaking his head. "Can't do it. First of all, I don't know him that well, and he'd think I was a right-wing nut peddling a conspiracy theory. Then, if anything did happen, if there was just an attempt of some kind, I'd be implicated. I'm willing to help with anything reasonable, but I can't be the public face on this."

They all sat silently for a moment, then Twist asked, "What might 'anything reasonable' include?"

"What do you want?" Armie asked.

Harmon gave Armie the name of a company in Washington, D.C., that provided protection for high-risk government and corporate executives.

"Most of them are ex–Secret Service, and a lot of those guys worked on the presidential protection detail. They're very good, and they'll provide you references—people you know."

"So what do *you* want?" Armie asked.

Twist asked, "Does your company issue business credit cards?"

"Sure. Both Amex and Visa."

Twist said, "We need to travel fast, but we haven't been able to fly on our own credit cards. . . ."

"Not a problem. You want a plane, too?"

Ninety minutes after they'd paid their house call, Shay, Harmon, and Twist rolled up to the front of an ordinary-looking yellow-brick building in downtown Oklahoma City. Harmon got out of the Mercedes, met a security guard at the door, and was escorted inside.

When Twist took the truck around the block, they found that the building that was so simple-looking from the front actually occupied two full city blocks.

Ten minutes later, Harmon called and said, "I'm coming out."

They picked him up at the front door, and he said, "If Armie's lying to us, which I don't think he is, they might be able to track us with these things, but otherwise—no more Twist motels. We're checking into someplace decent and we're getting room service. We got an Amex black card. We could rent a *jet* if we needed one."

"Let me see," Shay said.

Harmon handed her the two cards, and she squinted at them in the overhead light. A black Amex and a Visa, issued in the name of . . . Dallas Harmon. She looked at Harmon and said, "Dallas? That's your first name? Dallas?"

"I don't use it much," Harmon said.

"What do your friends call you?" Twist asked. "Dally? Dal-a-reeno? Dal-issimo? The Daller?"

Harmon waited until Twist ran down, then said, "No."

"No nicknames at all?"

"My friends sometimes call me Harm, because of what I do to people who call me Dal-a-reeno."

"Ooh," said Shay.

They got three rooms at the Skirvin Hilton, which, Shay thought, was the best hotel she'd ever been in, with sheets that appeared to have been ironed, marble Jacuzzi baths, and twenty-four-hour room service. The desk clerk glanced at the black card, then the company name on it, and after that, there was no problem with anything. They were even happy to see X, or pretended to be.

In the elevator, Shay petted X on the head and said, "Room-service cheeseburgers."

There was no talk about it, but Cruz and Shay took a room together, with X. Cade and Harmon shared another, and Twist, who didn't share, was by himself. Shay and Cruz were in the shower, with a fragrant bar of hotel soap, when the doorbell buzzed and Cruz said, "Can't be room service. We put a DO NOT DISTURB sign out there."

The doorbell rang again, and then again, and again, and Cruz put a towel around his waist and found Twist outside the door. "You weren't answering either the phone or the walkie-talkie. . . ."

"We turned them off," Cruz said. "Because we didn't want to talk to anybody."

"Okay, but we need you down in my room, like, in one minute," Twist said.

"What happened?"

"Cade found something. One minute."

Five minutes later, after a thorough rinse, Cruz and Shay were in fresh clothes and in Twist's doorway, Cruz muttering in frustration, "Damn Cade is messin' with us, I just know it. . . ."

"I don't think so," Shay said, finger-combing her wet hair. "I don't think Twist would let him."

"Get in here; close the door," Twist said. Harmon and Cade were sprawled in chairs around a desk, Twist standing over them. Twist said to Cade, "Tell them."

Cade looked up from his laptop at Shay and Cruz—and all of them felt a bit of his heartache as he took them in—then looked back to his screen and said, "I lost Thorne for a while. So I started looking back through old flight plans to see where else he's been, see if there were any patterns or other sites we should know about. I found a trip into Mid-Way Regional Airport, which is near Waxahachie, Texas, which is south of Dallas–Fort Worth."

"Used to be a hell of a whorehouse in Waxahachie," Harmon said. Then, into the following silence, "That's what I heard, anyway. And I don't think that's why Thorne went there."

Cade said, "No. I don't think so. The name Waxahachie is so unusual that it stuck in my head from something I'd seen before, but it took a few minutes to get it back. It's where North Texas Ballistics is."

Shay: "And that is?"

"A custom gun company. I think that's where he got the super-gun. When I looked, I couldn't find anyone else making them. Not like you guys saw . . ."

"Okay," said Cruz. "Why is that urgent news?"

"Because I just found a new flight plan for Thorne—he's going there again."

"Getting another gun?" Twist said.

"The one they have is working pretty good," said Harmon.

They thought about that for a minute, then Shay asked, "How far is it down there?"

"Three and a half hours, more or less," Cade said. "I already looked it up."

"We could get there faster by driving than we could by trying to fly," Harmon said.

Shay looked at them all. "So you want to check out and go? I'm a little worn down, to tell the truth."

"We all are," Twist said. "We thought we'd get some sleep tonight, something decent to eat, and take off at seven o'clock tomorrow morning. We'd be there before noon."

"Good, let's do that," she said. "And hey, Cade, great work tonight."

"Yeah," he said into the screen. "Thanks."

Cruz gave her a nudge, and Harmon twiddled his fingers, and Twist said, "Get some sleep."

Shay and Cruz went back to their room and ordered room service. It was outrageously expensive, and Cruz scrawled an equally outrageous tip at the bottom of the bill, after which the room-service guy bowed his way out of the room.

Shay pulled the top off a silver tray and found the largest steak she'd ever seen.

"I'm thinking of becoming a vegetarian," she said. "Some other time."

They ate and talked about nothing and went to bed. Shay had been surprised to find that Cruz was gentle and not all that experienced. In the midst of so much ugliness, it was wonderful to be alone with him again—to focus on each other for a night and let their worries and fears slip away.

Before she slept, her thoughts turned to Odin. Where was he, what was he doing? Was he in the hospital still? In jail? And how would she find out?

She might have worried about it longer, but rest had been scarce, and she felt herself sinking, as though sleep itself had caught her by the hand and pulled her under.

• • •

At that same hour, Odin was in none of the places Shay imagined. He was asleep in a Holiday Inn. He'd spent the day at Dash's ranch with an FBI forensic team. The doctors at Flagstaff hadn't been happy about it, but they'd given him a wheelchair and released him under the supervision of the FBI.

The FBI was all new faces: the lead investigator was named Karl Barnstead, a tall, thin, red-faced man who wore a cowboy hat and boots and reminded Odin of Harmon.

Once at the ranch, Barnstead said, "Show us where this so-called cremation area is."

Odin pointed down the runway. "That way. Right at the end."

And so three Chevy Tahoes headed down there. Odin was relieved to see what appeared to be an undisturbed mound of ash.

An older, gray-haired man with a handlebar mustache got out of one of the Tahoes, followed by a middle-aged woman with maroon hair. They both looked at the ash, and the woman said, "Wood ash."

"Yeah. What they'd do is make a big pile of wood, put the body on it, stack more wood on top, and set it off with gasoline," Odin said.

The man sniffed. "I can smell some gas. Of course, this *is* a landing strip." He looked at Odin and said, "My name is Frank Cantone, and my colleague is Anne Wexler."

Wexler said, "Let me go get a probe."

She took out what looked like the shaft of an extra-long golf club without the head. She stuck it in the ash, moved it around a bit, and said, "We got about four feet."

Barnstead said, "Some of these places burn their garbage."

Cantone shook his head. "Not garbage. You can always smell that. Could be paper trash."

"Better make a cut," Wexler said.

Cantone looked up at the clear blue sky. "Yeah. We're gonna get hot."

They put on white suits that appeared to be made out of paper, or some kind of thin plastic, and breathing masks and pulled paper hoods over their heads. They made a cut through the ash using a narrow hoe, carefully scraping a thin, straight trench in the middle of the heap. Progress was slow, but Barnstead and Odin sat in the back of a Tahoe, where they could watch in air-conditioned semi-comfort.

After a half hour of work, both the forensic scientists stopped and put the hoe aside and knelt near the cut. Cantone reached into it, and they both huddled, and Barnstead got out of the Tahoe. Odin rolled down his window so he could hear, and Cantone said, "Piece of black plastic."

Barnstead asked, "Mean anything?"

Odin called, "Body bag. They didn't take the bodies out; they burned them in the bags."

"That would be consistent," Wexler said.

"Keep working," Barnstead said.

A fed from another one of the trucks carried some water bottles to the sweating forensic team, then came back to Barnstead's truck. "We got cold water and Coke. Want anything?"

"How come you got cold water and Coke?" Barnstead asked.

"I was a Boy Scout," the other agent said.

• • •

The wait grew longer, but then Cantone and Wexler came up with something black-and-white and perhaps a half inch long.

Barnstead got out of the truck again. "What?"

"That's what you call a piece of a spinous process," Wexler said. "It's a bone—once, not long ago, part of somebody's spine, now somewhat burned."

"Not long ago?"

"It's fresh."

"Told you!" Odin called from the truck.

When they took him to the Holiday Inn, late that evening, more than twenty pieces of human bone and a few teeth had been taken out of the ash heap, and they'd examined less than a tenth of it. None of the material was old, Cantone said, and though they'd need DNA work to determine how many bodies were involved, and DNA would be tough because of the burning, he was confident they would get some from the interior of the teeth. In the meantime, he had two different slivers of what he said were femurs—and they didn't match.

"Two different individuals, at least. From the way the finds are layered, I think we got a lot more than that."

Barnstead said, "I gotta make a call. *Really* got to make a call."

Before Odin went to sleep, he wondered where Shay and the others were. And what would happen to him: the investigators had been nice so far, and now that they had bodies, they seemed to believe him. What they might do, though, was unpredictable. They certainly had enough on him to put him in jail—for the Eugene raid that started it all, if nothing else.

He didn't worry about that, though. Instead, he thought about Fenfang . . . her powerful will, their first laugh, the way she kissed. . . .

It took a while, and his wounded leg ached, but he finally slept.

Of the interstate highways that Shay had driven, I-35 ranked near the bottom for scenery. On the other hand, it was efficient, taking them through the Dallas–Fort Worth glob fairly quickly.

They never got into the main part of Waxahachie. North Texas Ballistics was located in a business-industrial park along a frontage road north of town, behind a big Owens Corning plant. They missed the exit they needed, took a while turning around, and cruised North Texas Ballistics for the first time just after eleven o'clock.

The parking lot would accommodate perhaps twenty vehicles. The concrete-block building had a single glass door on the front and two high, unfriendly-looking windows; both the windows and the door were barred.

There were two SUVs in the parking lot.

"If one of those belongs to Thorne . . . I mean, I really don't want to take him on right now," Harmon said.

"It's pretty public," Shay said.

Harmon grinned and shook his head. "I was thinking I might *lose.*"

"Oh. Yeah."

"Don't really believe it, do you?"

"I'm going to live forever," Shay said.

Harmon sighed and put the walkie-talkie to his face and called the other car. "Let's find somewhere we can watch that door for a while," he said.

"Let's try them on one of the clean phones and see who answers," Twist called back.

"Go ahead and do that," Harmon said. "Let us know what happens."

Twist called back a minute later. "Rang twenty times—no answering service or recorder. Just kept ringing."

"Call them every five minutes," Harmon said.

"For how long?" Twist asked.

"Let's give it a couple of hours, anyway. See if Cade can run the plates on the cars in the lot."

A half hour later, Cade, who was looking at the iPad, said, "Thorne filed a flight plan for an airport near Phoenix two hours ago. Deer Valley Airport. It's just coming up in my database."

Twist, sitting beside him, said, "If he's gone, then let's go knock on the door."

They called Harmon, who talked to Shay and Cruz, and they agreed.

Shay and Harmon made the approach. Finding the door locked, they looked through the glass and saw a small lobby with a waist-high counter with a dish of jelly beans on it, two chairs, a coffee table in a corner, and a door that apparently led to the back of the building.

No doorbell, so Harmon rapped with a key, one of the sharpest and most annoying sounds in the world, as every hotel maid knew. Nobody came to the door. Shay cupped her hands around her eyes and peered through the glass and said, "But there are two cars here. . . ."

"Let's check the back."

There was a single door, made of steel, with a good lock, but no handle. Apparently meant to be opened only from the inside. They knocked on it for a while, with no response.

"I'm getting worried here," Harmon said.

Shay nodded.

Harmon said, "I need to get into my stuff."

They went back to the truck, and Cruz asked, "Nobody home?"

"Nobody answering, anyway," Harmon said. He pulled what little luggage they had—mostly clothes in duffel bags and backpacks—out of the back of the truck, lifted the tire cover, pulled the spare and then the floor cover out, and finally pried up a small trapdoor in the floor. Beneath it was a shallow box containing two fattish foot-long tubes wrapped in nylon cloths. He set them aside and pulled on a tab that lifted the floor of the box, revealing an odd-looking instrument with a pistol grip and a trigger and, instead of a barrel, a long loop of stiff wire.

"What is all this stuff?" Shay asked.

"The stuff they'd probably put us in jail for." He touched the tubes. "These are sound suppressors for the M15s. You screw on one of these things and a shot sounds not much louder than a hand clap."

"What's the gun thing?" she asked.

He held it in his hand and said, "Called a rake. It opens locks. Battery-operated."

"Where do you get this stuff?" Cruz asked.

"Actually, we're trained in it—the guys I used to work with. All that James Bond stuff—hot-wiring cars, picking locks, building atomic bombs out of trash cans and women's cosmetics. . . ."

He checked the area for watchers, then said to Cruz, "Pretend like you're changing a tire," he said. "I'm going to try this."

He went to the door, knocked a couple more times, looked around again, then pushed the wire into the lock and pulled the trigger while twisting the lock cylinder. There was a chattering sound, and in ten seconds or so, the lock suddenly rolled over, and he pulled the door out an inch.

He walked back to the others and said, "Door's open. Let's put this all back together before we go inside . . . in case we have to leave in a hurry."

Twist called: "What's going on?"

Shay answered him in a low voice, even though there didn't appear to be a soul around to hear: "Go out to the entrance road and watch for cops. We've got the door open; we're going in."

When they had the car back to normal, they walked up to the front door, X on a leash. As soon as Harmon pulled the door open, X snarled, showing his teeth, and took an odd stance, his back legs cocked for attack but his front legs and head pulled back, as though he were frightened.

"That's not good," Harmon said.

He took his handgun out of the lower pocket on his cargo pants and edged inside.

There was nothing to be seen in the lobby, but Harmon said, "Blood."

"Where?" Shay asked.

"I don't know, but I can smell it," he said. "X can, too."

Shay sniffed and picked up the odor. She slipped the compact 9 mm pistol out of the concealed-carry holster on her hip. Harmon said, "Cruz, don't touch anything—cover your hand with your sleeve and pull the door shut."

Cruz did that, and Harmon said, "Shay, we need to go through that door to the back, but we don't want to touch it. Get one of those brochures on the counter, and use it to cover your hand when you turn the doorknob. Stand off to the far side of the door and push it open with your foot. And be sure to put the brochure in your pocket when you've done that. We can't leave it behind."

Shay did as he said and kicked the door open. Harmon went through, his gun up in a two-handed shooting position. He said, "Oh boy."

Shay stepped in behind him. Two bodies were sprawled on the floor, both burly males with short hair, sharing a puddle of almost black blood; they both had holstered guns on their hips. They'd been shot in the head.

"Do not touch anything with your skin," Harmon said. "Don't spit or vomit. That DNA shit's gotten really good."

"Let's just get out of here," Cruz said from the doorway.

"I need to look around for a sec," Harmon said. "Cruz, you go back to the car and drive it out of here. Take X with you. Do not touch anything as you're doing it. Call Twist and Cade, tell them about this, tell them again about calling us if they see cops. Oh, pull the front door shut behind you. It'll lock automatically."

"If you're staying, I'd rather stay. . . ."

Harmon said, "I need you to get our car out of here. Look for cops and warn us. If we get caught here, we're going to jail for a while."

Cruz looked at Shay, who nodded and said, "Go."

When he was gone, Harmon said, "Don't step in the blood."

They were in a small room with a heavy wooden bench that was chest-high to Shay and had a scarred top and four high stools around it. On one wall was a pegboard with a lot of screwdrivers and screwdriver-like tools and a few expensive-looking wooden-handled wrenches and pliers. An alarm panel hung on another wall: Harmon looked at it and said, "The alarm's off."

Shay said, "Why would . . . ," thought about it, then said, "Of course. They turned it off when Thorne showed up, Thorne shot them, but he wouldn't know the code to turn the alarm back on, even if he wanted to."

Harmon nodded and edged toward another partly open door. He nudged it all the way open with an elbow, and they stepped into a much larger room with metalworking equipment that Shay didn't recognize and several more of the heavy benches with a variety of vises. Long, scary-looking rifles stood on special racks on two of the benches, both rifles on barrel-mounted tripods wired into Apple laptops. One wall had a barred storage area with racks that contained various gun components and parts, along with a stack of unopened laptop boxes.

At the far end of the room was a glass wall, behind which were three desks, each with a desktop computer, and some filing cabinets. Harmon went that way, and Shay followed. He found a server whose connection had been pulled out of the wall.

Harmon pointed at it. "Probably had a video capability that might have been running out to the Net. . . ." He scanned the ceiling and then said, "There."

Shay looked and saw a small, dark hole just where one wall joined the ceiling. The camera behind it would have been pointed at the door and would have covered most of the room. Harmon knelt in a corner beneath the camera and found a cable and said, "It was hard-wired, not wireless . . . and it ran into . . ."

He found a fist-sized box that in turn was connected to the now disconnected server. Another wire ran into the box, and he traced it to a ceiling-mounted camera in the large workroom.

"Thorne was cleaning up," Harmon said. He waved a hand at the filing cabinets: they were all open, and several of the drawers were empty. All the computers had been taken apart, and when they looked inside, Shay said, "No hard drives."

"He erased himself from their records," Harmon said, "and, by killing them, all their memories of him. Okay, there's nothing here. Let's get out. Don't touch—"

"Anything."

Going out, Harmon paused both in the smaller back room and in the lobby. "No cameras. The first time Thorne was here, he wouldn't have missed the cameras in the back, so this time he probably came in, walked into the second room with them, and killed them right there. Then he'd have put on a mask, gone into the back, and ripped out the server. So the cameras went out to a spooling memory bank on the Net, but all they'd have seen for a couple seconds was a guy in a mask."

"What about the first time he came here? There'd be a record of that."

"Maybe, but probably not," Harmon said. "These things usually spool a month, then start over. They don't just spool endlessly. If he got the gun two months ago, or three or four, that memory has probably been written over."

"Wonder if there was another gun? You know, a super-super-gun," Shay asked.

"No way to know for sure, but I don't think so," Harmon said. "If he's planning to do something like what we're thinking about, he'd want a gun he'd shot a lot. Not something new. With a shot like what we're talking about, even the slightest unfamiliarity could screw things up."

"We've been here too long," Shay said. "Gotta go."

"You're right."

Because Harmon wanted to get as far away from Waxahachie as they could, as fast as they could, they wound up going all the way back through Dallas on I-35 East until they saw signs for the University of North Texas. They got tacos from a food truck and sat on benches under some trees in front of a red-brick-and-stone building.

"Why do you want to go back to Oklahoma City?" Twist asked.

"Because we can get there in a hurry, like we've never left," Harmon said. "We'll talk to Armie again, if we can. He'll have seen us last night and then again today in midafternoon. We can't let ourselves be hooked into these murders. And if Armie was serious about a plane . . . we might need one. Depending on what Thorne does."

Shay said to Cade, "You gotta keep tracking him. Anything new?"

"Not yet," Cade said.

Twist asked Harmon, "On a scale of one to ten . . ."

"Eleven," Harmon said.

29

Thorne rode in a deep sleep and near silence from Scottsdale to Washington, D.C., in one of Varek Royce's jets. The rifle and its sound suppressor were contained in an aging Fender guitar case, covered with a variety of stickers from EarthQuaker Devices, MESA/Boogie, and other music equipment manufacturers, in case somebody didn't get the point.

He'd flown from Waxahachie to the Deer Valley Airport, then had ridden with his bags and the rifle in a limousine from Deer Valley to Scottsdale. The whole idea had been to break up his trail, in case it was ever investigated. The Gulfstream G280 jet had been waiting for him, and they took off just minutes after his arrival. The pilot and copilot had asked no questions but told him that a cold box lunch was available in a bin just behind the cockpit. Thorne hadn't bothered with it but asked if he could pull out a couple of blankets and sleep in the aisle.

Not necessary, he was told: the two seats closest to the forward bulkhead would fold flat, into reasonably comfortable beds. He had them set that up, and a minute after the plane's wheels left the ground, he was asleep.

He was very nearly exhausted. The past few days had been loaded with stress, and he'd had very little sleep; the anxiety of his new assignment had worn on him. He thought he had maybe an eighty to ninety percent chance of pulling it off. That was worth doing, but the call was a close one. At this point, he could still run. Plenty of jobs in Africa and the Middle East for "security consultants" who weren't too fussy about who got hurt, or why.

On the other hand, if he pulled off this mission, he could have almost anything he wanted. Almost anything—and right here in the good ol' U.S. of A. Varek had promised a major payday, he'd get a shot at some kind of high-level White House or CIA security role, if he wanted one, and he might even live forever. . . .

They flew into Manassas Regional Airport, a half hour or forty-five minutes south of Washington, in the early afternoon. Thorne carried his guitar case and gear bags to a waiting black limo with tinted windows and sat in the back without talking to the driver, who asked no questions but took him north. They never got to the capital, but pulled into an underground parking lot at an expensive-looking red-brick apartment building. There were a dozen other cars—Mercedes-Benzes, Jaguars, Porsches, one fiery red Ferrari—and three more black limousines. The driver stopped next to a bank of elevators. Thorne called the left-hand elevator and, once inside, took a key out of his pocket, stuck it in a lock below the floor buttons, turned it once to the left, and punched the 9 button.

The procedure locked out all other floors and prevented the elevator from stopping for any other calls.

At the ninth floor, he got out, looked both ways down an empty hallway, turned right, walked to a door marked 920, and went inside.

The room had been designed for confidential conferences, with a dozen chairs, a couple couches, a bar. Three people were waiting next to a wall of tinted windows: Royce, Earl Denyers from the CIA, and Lawton Jeffers, the vice president of the United States. Denyers had his anti-bugging machine sitting on a coffee table.

They all looked at him as he came in, and the vice president finally said, "So you're the guy."

"So far," Thorne said. He put the guitar case on the bar. "We've still got time to back out."

"The FBI was at the ranch yesterday with that Odin Remby kid," Denyers said. "They had a forensic team in there, and word is, they've identified parts of at least four bodies so far."

"And we can't stop the trouble with Dash? Make *her* the top dog at Singular?" Thorne asked.

Denyers shook his head. "See, there's the problem—how did the kid know exactly where the burn pit was? How did they manage to remove the experimental subjects? They must've had the place under surveillance, but for how long? You and I flew out of there, Royce was there, Dash was there, Ian Wyeth was there. If they have any brains at all, they'll have taken pictures. They'll have tail numbers of the planes. We have to stop the investigation right where it is or we're all finished."

"But the vice president wasn't there?" Thorne said, a question in his voice.

Royce smiled and said, "No, but the vice president probably figures if it comes right down to it, either me or Earl will roll over on him in exchange for immunity."

"That's what I figure," Jeffers said with dry humor. He rattled the ice cubes in the glass he was holding. "We got another shot of that Johnnie Walker?"

When it came to talking about what they were actually going to do, the vice president shied away until Denyers said, "Goddammit, Law, we're going to kill the president. You can't keep trying to sneak that off your plate. We're gonna kill him and you're in on it. We've got a plan that can pull it off, but if we don't, there's a good chance we'll all go to prison. So let's get that out there and figure out the last moves."

"Just have a hard time saying it," Jeffers said.

"You gotta say it, and you gotta think it. Now, have you scheduled a place you can be that's pretty far out? Not San Francisco or anywhere near New Mexico . . ."

"Yeah, there's a private fund-raiser down in Florida for the senior senator. He'll be delighted that I'm droping in—he's been begging me to, and I've told him I'll try. So I'll be in Palm Beach."

Denyers turned to Royce. "How about you?"

"I'll be in San Antonio, on business."

Denyers nodded. "And Thorne and I'll be on-site."

They talked about tactical details for a while, and Thorne gave them rehearsal notes—he'd been on the shooting platform twice, had timed his exit from the building.

"Nobody'll hear the shot," he said. "They may never find the shooting platform. If they do find it, I estimate best time possible to pinpointing the platform at two hours. By that time, I'll be eighty or ninety miles away. It should be a very clean op."

And then there was a long, long gap of silence.

• • •

Jeffers stood up and walked over to the Fender case. "A talented man—with everything else, you play the guitar. You mind if I look?"

"I don't mind you looking, but don't touch the weapon, and especially not the scope," Thorne said. Almost as an afterthought, he added, "Sir."

Jeffers threw the latches on the case and lifted the lid. He took in the rifle and said, "Looks like a regular old elk gun."

"If you look closely at the base of the scope, you'll see there's a USB 3.0 port," Thorne said.

Jeffers peered at the scope, then said, "I don't understand all this new computer shit."

He eased the lid shut, latched it, and said to the others, "I gotta run to the can."

He took his briefcase with him.

When he had gone, Royce looked pensively out the windows toward the Washington Monument. From where they were, in Virginia, they could see about half of it over the trees. Without looking at Thorne, he asked, "Can you give me some odds?"

Thorne nodded. "I'd say for everything included—the man dead, us getting away clean—it's eighty-five, ninety percent. The problem with an op like this is that all kinds of random shit can interfere. Curious cop, camera we don't know about, a Secret Service agent who's too smart . . . But basically, ninety percent. We'll never get more than that."

"Nine chances in ten," Royce said, and turned his wheelchair around to face the men. "I've never done a deal that I thought was less than eighty percent to work out—and I've never truly lost a big deal."

• • •

Lawton Jeffers sat on the toilet with his pants down around his ankles. He'd opened a small leather kit, which sat on top of the briefcase now, and had taken out a needle. He injected himself in the thigh with the cocktail of longevity hormones Dr. Wyeth prepared for all his clients, gasped once when the drug hit, and felt the flush of the growing high.

Then he leaned forward, put his arms on his thighs, his head down, said, "God help me."

He thought, a few minutes later, as he washed his hands and stared at himself in the bathroom mirror, that God probably wouldn't bother to help.

He went out into the main room, and Thorne stepped forward to pose the question for the last time: "Shall I move into position, Mr. Vice President?"

Jeffers stared at him, not speaking.

Denyers said, "If you say go, Law, you're president of the United States in forty-eight hours. And after that, you live forever."

Jeffers nodded and said to Thorne, "Yes. Go."

30

Back in Oklahoma City, back in their rooms, Harmon made a call to Armie, who said he was at his office and that they could come over. Shay, Twist, Harmon, Cruz, and X went. Cade stayed at the hotel, working the Internet, searching for Thorne. They didn't entirely trust Armie, so at Armie's office complex, Cruz and X stayed in the truck, circling, ready for an emergency pickup.

A security guard with a navy blue sport coat and khaki slacks met them at the building's front entrance, gave them ID tags, escorted them to Armie's office on the fourth floor, and said he'd wait to take them back out.

Armie had a billionaire's office, but a restrained one, not one from Hollywood, Dallas, or Manhattan. It was done in wood and subdued earth colors, and two assistants and three secretaries worked in small offices outside his private office. A receptionist sat at a large desk in front of the office doors. Most people would not have noticed that the small landscape painting on the entry wall was a real Monet. Twist did, and got so close that his nose was inside the frame.

The receptionist said, with a smile, "You must be Misters Twist and Harmon and Miss Remby." She didn't alert Armie to visitors by phone or intercom but by some more secret system, because a second later, Armie came out to meet them and said, "I hope nothing untoward has happened."

"That would be a vain hope," Twist said.

"Ah, shit. Come on back."

Harmon scanned Armie's private office and said, "I hope you're not recording this."

"I'm not," Armie said.

"That's good, because I'm going to tell you something that could cause you some problems. If the cops knew, and dropped a search warrant on you."

"Maybe you shouldn't tell me," Armie said.

"Up to you," Harmon said.

Armie looked at them all in turn, then said, "Tell me."

Harmon said, "We've learned from an absolutely reliable source—*absolutely reliable*—that Thorne went to Waxahachie, Texas, this morning, to the company that supplied him with the computer-assisted rifle he'll use in the assassination. If he's planning an assassination."

"I still find that hard to believe," Armie said. "Though I worry. A lot."

"Yeah. Well, Thorne killed two of the company's employees and emptied out their file cabinets and also took the hard drives out of their computers."

Armie went pale and was quiet as his mind worked through the news. Then: "He couldn't have witnesses. If you go that far—to murder innocent people—then the target's got to be large."

"Correct," Twist said.

Shay's phone rang and she looked at the screen. Cade. She said, "I need to take this," and walked away from the group to a corner of the office.

Armie watched her go and then asked, "Does that little girl have a gun on her hip?"

Twist said, "We're not babysitters. . . ."

Armie got back on topic: "You have to tell the feds about the rifle and the murders."

Twist said, "We've told them about the gun. We'll tell them about the murders when we're in motion again. We really don't want to be . . . sequestered."

"Got to tell them soon, nip this in the bud."

Shay overheard that as she came back from the corner and said, "The problem with the FBI is that they make a lot of phone calls and push stuff up the ladder and then back down the ladder, but by the time anything gets done, it's too late. They're like cleanup guys instead of preventers."

"Is *preventers* a word?" Twist asked.

Shay held up a hand and said, "I don't care," and then, "That was Cade. He thinks he's found Thorne."

Harmon: "He thinks?"

"Thorne flew into an airport that's north of downtown Phoenix. One of Varek Royce's jets left an airport on the east side of Phoenix two hours later. Cade said he could have taken a cab or a limo between the airports in that time—if, of course, he got on the second plane at all. He can't find a car rental or another plane rental from the first airport."

"Not that tight a connection," Twist said.

"Royce's plane filed a flight plan to an airport just south of Washington, D.C."

"Okay, that's tighter," Harmon said.

Armie: "You want a plane?"

Shay said, "Yes."

Armie walked over to his desk and pushed a hidden button and said, "Lynn, call the guys and tell them we need the Gulfstream outta here ASAP, going into Washington. Any airport's fine. . . ."

Shay said, "Manassas. Manassas Airport."

"Make that Manassas, Lynn." Armie turned to the three of them and said, "You want a hotel?"

"That'd be great," Twist said.

"How many rooms?"

"Three," Shay said.

Armie pushed the button again and said, "Lynn, we'll need three rooms at the Four Seasons in D.C., too."

He looked back to them and asked, "Anything else?"

They checked out of the Skirvin Hilton and called Barin as they drove to the airport. Twist did the talking. He started with, "How's it going, guy?"

"Mr. Twist, you're getting yourself in deeper and deeper."

"I'm counting on you to get me out," Twist said. "Do that, and we'll make you into a national hero."

"I don't really need to be a national hero. . . ."

"Of course you do," Twist said. "You hunger for it. I'm going to see that it gets done whether you like it or not. Here's what I'm telling you, and you should write this down, because it is super important and it's not something you want to forget."

"Mr. Twist—"

"It's just Twist. You got a pen?"

"Yes, but—"

"So, those pictures we sent you. Of the fancy rifle. The guy firing it is a former SEAL named Thorne who works for Singular, and he is going to attempt to assassinate the president sometime in the next few days."

"What!"

"He's already in Washington, D.C. The gun is a computer-assisted high-power large-caliber sniper rifle built by a company called North Texas Ballistics. We have it on exceptionally good and accurate authority that last night Thorne flew into an airport near Waxahachie, Texas, where North Texas Ballistics is located, and murdered the two employees . . ."

"What!"

". . . murdered the two employees, stripped the place of both paper and electronic records, and locked up behind himself. Let me give you the address of the place. . . ." Twist read off the address for North Texas Ballistics, then continued: "We suggest you send a forensic team over there and check for spooled video on an Internet security site. It'll probably show Thorne wearing a mask."

"Mr. Twist, you gotta—"

"I suggest you not send the Waxahachie cops over there—you don't want a bunch of flatfoots trampling all over the crime scene."

"Twist . . . Mr. Twist—"

"Now, the other photo we sent—that one's a gift from Dr. Janes. You'll have noticed that it shows Senator Dash, Micah Cartwell, and the vice president at a meeting with several North Korean officials. You'll recall that Dash and Cartwell are both dead now."

"You're killing me here, Twist. How do I know that's not a Photoshop invention?"

"Have we been wrong yet? You've got to think about that. Also, Thorne is being flown around by a rich guy named Varek Royce."

"The guy in the wheelchair?"

"He's the money. And that's about what we know. It's in your hands, big guy."

"Twist—"

Twist turned the phone off and yanked the battery. "I have little faith," he said, "that I just did anyone any good."

They left their vehicles at the airport. An hour later, they were on the way to Washington.

The Gulfstream jet felt like another luxurious hotel room, the way it was laid out, with beige leather seats the size of Barcaloungers, mahogany cocktail tables with built-in liquor cabinets, and, to everyone's surprise, a tufted pink silk sofa positioned along one side of the cabin.

Harmon kicked back in a recliner and said, "I could easily get used to this."

Twist: "Yeah. Go anywhere, anytime, bring your guns and dogs, get a couch."

Shay: "That's why Royce flew Thorne out of Phoenix last night: so he could bring the gun."

Cade: "My folks have one of those plane services. I've been on those rent-a-jets, but they're not like this. For one thing, they all smell funny."

Shay: "This is the first airplane I've been on since I was about six years old."

Cruz, peering out a window on takeoff: "This is the first time I've ever been."

They all looked at him, and he said, "Hey—I'm an Angeleno. Why would I want to go anywhere else?"

"Good point," Twist said.

• • •

Three hours after leaving Oklahoma City, they walked off the plane into a muggy evening in northern Virginia, found two SUVs waiting at Hertz. Twist and Cade took one, Harmon, Cruz, Shay, and X took the other, and they headed north into the gathering dusk.

Twenty minutes later, Shay said, "Oh my gosh, the Washington Monument."

The monument looked like a white spear sticking into the night sky. Cruz craned his neck to see, and Harmon said, "The Eiffel Tower, the Statue of Liberty, and the Washington Monument—nothing quite like them anywhere else."

"I'd like to climb up there someday," Shay said.

"On the inside or the outside?" Harmon asked.

"Outside, it'd be tough," Shay said. "You'd need a drill and a lot of bolts. . . ."

"And some stick-in-the-mud bureaucrat would probably get really, really pissed," Cruz said.

At the Four Seasons, the desk clerk took in X, frowned, said, "One moment, please," and went away. One moment later, a manager appeared, who asked, "Do you have reservations?"

"Should have been made by Gerald Armie's office out of Oklahoma City," Harmon said. He handed the man the black card.

The manager took it, smiled, and said, "Of course. Three rooms. We'll have a couple of Milk-Bones sent up. We have Purina Dog Chow on hand. Would that be all right?"

"That'd be fine," Shay said. "If it doesn't work for him, we'll just order from room service."

"We have the best burger in Washington. Ask to have it lightly cooked. If you check with the concierge, he will help you with dog-walking routes."

On the way to the elevators, Harmon said, "I could *really* get used to this."

"What's the black-card thing?" Shay asked.

Harmon said, "It's supposedly unlimited charging, no questions asked. . . . I don't know if it really is or not. Basically, it's an expensive way to impress desk clerks and waiters, if that's one of your concerns."

"Not one of mine," Shay said. "But . . . trying it out for a night isn't uninteresting."

They settled in their rooms, and Harmon knocked on Twist's door after a while, and Twist asked, "Now what?"

Harmon said, "I've got an idea."

"Another one?"

"Yeah. I know this guy. . . ."

Shay went with Harmon to the Sixx Restaurant and Lounge at the Pentagon City shopping mall. Before they left the hotel, Harmon told her to leave the pistol and knife behind. "The guy we're meeting is sorta old-fashioned when it comes to teenage behavior, so try to keep your mouth shut. You know, as much as possible without your head exploding."

The man who showed up at the Sixx was a tall, wide army sergeant in full dress, with a dollar-bill-sized arrangement of ribbons above the left pocket of his uniform. Shay and Harmon were already sitting in the most shadowed booth in the restaurant when the sergeant showed up, and Harmon slid out to shake hands and then do a bit of shoulder bumping and backslapping.

Harmon said, "Chet, this is my friend Shay Remby, and, Shay, this is Sergeant Major Chester D. Landy. Chet speaks directly into the shell-like ear of the army chief of staff."

They both said, "Pleased to meet you," and Landy slid into the booth across from them. A waitress came, and the two men ordered beer and steaks, and Shay got a lemonade and a cheeseburger. Harmon and Landy spent twenty minutes talking about people they had known in Iraq and Afghanistan and about a fight in what Landy referred to as "that other place," with an uncertain glance at Shay.

"You know Andy died?" Landy asked.

"Ah, man . . ."

"I talked to his wife, and she said he just quit. Stopped taking treatment. Took him about six weeks, but he managed to die."

"I might have done the same, though I'd probably have found a quicker way," Harmon said. They then both glanced at Shay, and Landy changed the subject again.

When the meal came, they nibbled around the edges for a few minutes, then Landy asked, "So, what's this about?"

Harmon looked at him steadily, then said, "I'm going to ask a favor of you, but you'll have to decide whether or not to do it. If it's taken the wrong way, it could hurt your career."

Landy smiled and said, "Hard to tell yet whether there's much wiggle room. What's the favor?"

Shay leaned across the table and said, "Harmon asked me to keep my mouth shut, but I have a really hard time doing that. I'll try, but if you have any questions, I've got all the details right back to the beginning."

"Give me the two-minute version," Landy said.

Harmon: "An ex-SEAL named Thorne is in Washington, right now, with a computer-assisted sniper rifle, and he's going to try to shoot the president."

"You're . . . ," Landy said.

"Serious. Yeah," Harmon said. "He works for Singular—the company that's blowing up now for doing experiments on humans. I used to work there, too, but now I'm trying to bring them down. It's not right what they're doing. Singular is well protected, though. Thorne has some feds running interference for him. Some of them probably in on it, some probably not. So I need to inject the information at a high enough level that somebody actually does something about it, and soon. We believe he could be planning to make the attempt in the next few days."

"What do you want me to do?" Landy asked.

"We were hoping that you'd relay this to the chief of staff, and that he could get the White House to take it seriously. That's our biggest problem—that the whole thing sounds crazy—but I have seen Thorne make one hit after another on a seven-inch target at twenty-two hundred yards."

Landy blinked. "You've actually seen that?"

"Just a couple days ago, practicing at a measured distance for the shot. Look, talk to somebody who really knows his guns. He'll have heard about this sniper rifle; it's made by North Texas Ballistics. Look for North Texas Ballistics in the news."

Landy was silent for a few seconds, then shifted uncomfortably and said, "If I didn't know you . . ."

"Yeah, I know, sounds nuts," Harmon said. "I'd react exactly the same way if the shoe was on the other foot. But we can give you a checklist of people to call, people to talk to, news reports to look up. There's a guy in the FBI we've been feeding information to. We believe the danger is imminent."

"I'm ordering a pot of coffee. Give me the whole version."

Harmon tipped his head at Shay and said, "She knows it all."

Shay started at the beginning.

31

Thorne and Denyers hooked up at the Manassas airport an hour after Shay, Twist, and the others arrived in Gerald Armie's Gulfstream. Thorne had been in Jacksonville, checking into a motel, talking to the maids, establishing an alibi far away from Washington, D.C.

"You ready to do this?" Denyers asked when they were in his car.

"Why? You want to call it off?"

"No, but I won't kid you," Denyers said, "I'm scared."

Thorne nodded.

Twenty miles up the road, Denyers said, "Your most vulnerable point will be after the shot, before you've gotten rid of the rifle. You've got to be really careful about driving—you can't even afford to be rear-ended. I'm worried that you have to drive too far before you get rid of the gun."

"Let's stick with the plan. I'm good with it. Nothing will ever be perfect," Thorne said.

"I'm just sayin'. . . ."

"I know what you're saying. But I took the driving courses just like everybody else. Nobody's gonna hit me."

"Gotta signal lane changes. . . ."

"Earl . . ."

They got to Denyers's house, parked in the garage, let the door come back down before either of them got out.

They went to bed early, popping some sleeping pills to drag themselves under—Thorne was looking at a twenty-seven- or twenty-eight-hour day—and got up at five in the morning. They both popped amphetamines to kill the sleep aids, and by six o'clock, they were on the road.

They left Denyers's car in a camera-free parking garage, exited the garage in a nondescript four-year-old Toyota soccer-mom van with perfectly good plates registered to a nonexistent person. Denyers carried that person's ID with him, and the insurance certificate in the door pocket went to the same name and address. The Fender guitar case was in the back.

"What are you going to do with the money?" Denyers asked Thorne. They'd both get twenty-five-million-dollar paydays from Royce if they pulled off the hit.

"Hide it," Thorne said.

"Hard to do now," Denyers said. "The IRS looks at everything."

"Lots of ways to do it, though. Here's one: you take the

twenty-five and go to, say, Nigeria, and you introduce yourself to the guy who approves foreign businesses, give him a little taste of the money. Then you set up a business that, say, trades in oil futures. That's big in Lagos. I set up Thorne Trading, make a mil the first year, two mil the second, four mil the third, and so on, pay my U.S. taxes, and when Royce's money is nice and squeaky clean, I come home."

"That's a lot of years in Lagos," Denyers said.

"Give me some credit, Earl. I'm not going to actually *live* there," Thorne said. "I'll rent a place somewhere secure and safe and obscure. Switzerland. Lichtenstein."

Denyers said, "Huh."

"What are you going to do with yours?"

"My old man is almost eighty, and he's in bad health," Denyers said. "My mother's dead. I inherit it all. Right now, his estate's worth maybe a mil, but he's pissed away more money in his life than I'll ever see, even with Royce's payday. When he croaks, I'll open the safe-deposit box and find a nice round twenty-five mil inside, in gold coins. Old gold coins. The bank and I will report it to the IRS, the feds will take their pound of flesh, and I'll wind up with something like seventeen million free and clear, taxes paid, including the value of his actual estate."

"That sounds like an excellent plan, as long as your old man doesn't hang on until he's a hundred and one, or something," Thorne said.

"He won't. I can guarantee it," Denyers said.

"Wow," Thorne said flatly. "That's cold, man."

At ten o'clock, they were parked in a rapidly filling lot outside the Westfield Garden State Plaza in Paramus, New Jersey, one of the largest shopping malls in the state. They had a two-hour wait, which they would spend in the van, mostly in the back.

Denyers had brought along a large mirror and a theatrical makeup kit. The beards didn't have to be perfect, but both of them had experience with disguises. Getting the beards right took a half hour; they'd throw the makeup kit in a Dumpster on the way to the shooting platform.

At eleven-thirty, Denyers said, "Let's go."

"Give it a few more minutes," Thorne said. "Stick to the plan."

They did, and Denyers then said, "I don't know. . . . I'm getting scared again."

"It's now or never, Earl."

Denyers sat staring past the front seat for ten seconds, then fifteen, feeling himself sweat. Then he shook it off and said, "Fuck it, let's go." And, "This beard itches like poison ivy."

As they crossed the bluff that overlooked the Hudson River, the whole of Manhattan seemed to open in front of them.

"There it is," Thorne said, looking across the river. "Looks like a dream, doesn't it?"

"Or the beginning of a nightmare," Denyers said. They pulled into the parking garage, got a ticket. "Get your guitar."

32

Cade woke early, a few minutes after seven o'clock. He'd been up past midnight, and all during the night, ideas and pieces of ideas had been clicking through his half-awake brain. How to find Thorne? He seemed to have disappeared. Probably traveling under false names, Cade thought, with good credit cards under those names. He'd know how to break up his trail if he thought it was necessary.

Cade's subconscious had kicked out another idea overnight: if Thorne was planning to shoot the president, then . . . where would the president be over the next few days?

Harmon was sleeping as silently as if he were dead. He'd told Cade that he'd taught himself never to snore—there were places in his past where a snore would have been a real bad idea—but he was easy to wake. Moving as quietly as he could, Cade opened his laptop.

He typed "President's schedule" into Google.

To his surprise, the president's schedule immediately popped up, the first item in the search, from www.whitehouse.gov. He clicked on "President's Schedule," found an hour-by-hour listing for the next few days, and muttered, "Ah, shit."

Harmon asked, "What happened?" He sounded wide awake.

"I'm a dumb-ass, we're all dumb-asses," Cade said. "The president's daily schedule is on the Net, hour by hour. Guess what? He's going to New York City today, and he'll be out in the open three or four times."

Harmon sat up. "Where?"

"He's giving a speech at eleven at the Sheraton New York—"

"Hotels—security's always tight."

"Then he's at some museum at one—"

"That'll be tight, too."

"And he's going to a Yankees game at four. . . ."

"Yankee Stadium?" Harmon said. "Crap. Lots of time out in the open, and Thorne could get lost there. It'd be chaos, thousands of people stampeding out of the place. . . ."

"Here's the really bad part," Cade said. "Tomorrow the president flies to London. He'll be gone for a week. So . . ."

Harmon got up and said, "Time to get moving."

"To where?"

"To New York. My army pal is going to talk to the chief of staff this morning. I'll give him the latest, but it's still gonna take a while for them to get up to speed. Best thing to do is go to New York and face-to-face with Secret Service guys, try to warn them. . . ."

Harmon pulled on his pants and hurried down the hall. He would have banged on Shay and Cruz's door, but X was barking before he raised his knuckle, so he went and woke Twist.

Twist said, "I don't know what we can realistically do there. . . ."

"Create a ruckus," Harmon said. "The Secret Service can't

ignore that. They can arrest us, but they can't ignore us if we're face to face."

As they cleaned up and got dressed, Harmon suggested to Cade that he stay in Washington: "We'll want you on the Net full-time, and the fastest place is right here. In the car, you're down to using the iPad, and it's too slow."

So Cade stayed in Washington. Cruz and Harmon took one truck; Twist, Shay, and X the other. Shay took the iPad.

"Four-hour trip," Cade told them before they left. "That's if nothing happens to slow you down."

They had to stop once for gas, at the Joyce Kilmer Service Area, Manhattan almost in sight. While Twist and Harmon handled the gas, Shay and Cruz scrambled into the Burger King for burgers, fries, and soft drinks.

Shay ran a bag of food to Harmon's truck, and Harmon waved everybody together. "We're making good time. I updated Chet Landy, but I haven't heard anything back. . . . Did you get Barin?"

Shay said: "We called, but he isn't picking up—I've left, like, four messages."

"Yeah, not good enough. Look, somebody's gonna wind up in jail tonight, and I'm thinking it should be me. If nothing happens, they'll give me a psych exam and put me on a list, and I'll be out. I've been in worse places than a federal lockup. When we get to the stadium, we'll work it until we're sure we've spotted a Secret Service agent. I'll make the approach; you guys watch. If I give you a big head shake, that means they've taken me for a kook. We'll work on a plan B as we drive. . . ."

They got back in the trucks and were moving, Harmon's vehicle in the lead, when he suddenly swerved to the side and stopped.

"What happened?" Shay asked as Twist swerved in behind him.

Harmon got out of the truck and jogged back to them, a cell phone in his hand, his face white, trailed by Cruz.

Twist rolled the window down and asked, "What?"

"I got Cade on the line. I asked him to get the address of the museum, in case we want to take a look at it." He shook his head, pressed the speaker button. "We're all here."

Cade said, "I already told Harmon part of it, but I'm the dumbass again. I saw that the president was going to a museum, but I'd never heard of it. I just looked at the address. Then I decided to look at a satellite view . . . and hell, I'm sorry, but it turns out the museum is an aircraft carrier. It's called the *Intrepid.* It sits on the Hudson River, and the only place to give a speech would be standing on the flight deck. There are about a million windows looking down on it. . . ."

Harmon blurted: "It's not the stadium. It's the carrier." He looked at his watch. "In an hour and fifteen minutes."

"Ah, shit," Twist said. "We gotta go."

They all turned back to their vehicles, and Harmon shouted, "Same plan: I'll talk to the Secret Service at the carrier, make the first approach, but it's gotta be in a hurry! If they bust me, and nothing happens, go to the stadium!"

Twist got back behind the wheel, ran his hands through his hair, and said, "I don't believe this. I really don't."

Harmon was already wheeling out of the rest stop, and they lost him in a minute or so in the heavy traffic.

"Gotta go faster," Shay said.

"If I go faster, we'll pile up somewhere, and that won't help."

Shay got on the iPad and found the fastest route to the museum, straight north and then through the Lincoln Tunnel, which ran under the Hudson River and emerged in Manhattan only a few blocks from the *Intrepid*. She gave directions to Twist as he maneuvered through the growing traffic approaching the river.

Next she called up a satellite view of the *Intrepid*. The ship stuck out into the Hudson like a pier; the satellite view had apparently been taken in the winter, because there were no leaves on the trees.

She looked at it for a few minutes, then asked Twist for their cold cell phone. "I need to call Cade."

Twist handed her the phone and said, "This is worse than I-5. Okay, not worse than the 5, but worse than the 405. Okay, not worse than the 405, but worse— Oh, screw it. . . ."

Shay got on the phone and called Cade.

"Yeah?"

"When we did the numbers on the distance that Thorne was shooting at the ranch, at the target, it was like twenty-two hundred yards, right?"

"I can check, hang on. . . . Yeah. If Harmon's stride was right on, it'd be twenty-two seventeen."

"Go to Google Earth and use their tape measure and see where a twenty-two-hundred-yard shot would be coming from."

"Two or three minutes," Cade said. "Call me back."

Shay hung up and called Harmon on the walkie-talkie: "Where are you guys?"

"Coming up on the Lincoln Tunnel. Traffic is a goddamn nightmare."

She told him about the question she had for Cade, and Harmon said, "I should have thought of that earlier, dammit."

"I'll get back to you," Shay said.

She was looking at her watch, giving Cade the full three minutes, but he called back before she had a chance to call him.

"Okay, first of all, if he was rehearsing this shot at the ranch, then it's not coming from the New York side. It's coming from across the river in New Jersey. I'm liking the town of Weehawken."

"You're sure?"

"Pretty sure. The shot's so long that if it were coming from the New York side, the shooter would have to be all the way up by Central Park, that far away. There's just no sight line that long from the New York side: you'd have to shoot through buildings."

"I don't know where Central Park is," Shay said.

Twist: "A long way. Cade's right, a mile-long shot in Manhattan doesn't make sense."

"Something else," Cade said. "If the shot comes from that side, from New Jersey, it'll take forever for the Secret Service to get there from Manhattan. Even if they call some Jersey cops, the shooter will probably be long gone."

"How do you know it's this Weehawken place?" Shay asked.

"Because there's pictures on the museum's website that show other high-profile speeches, so I can see where the president will probably be standing. The only place you can see that speaker's stand from the Jersey side would be from Weehawken. There are three buildings at about the right distance, and high enough to shoot at the deck. But one has big windows, facing in just the right direction, at exactly twenty-two hundred and seventeen yards."

"Which one is it? You have an address?"

"No address, but I'll get one. What I have is a screen grab of my numbers on top of a map. You on the iPad?"

"Yes."

"I'm sending you that shot . . . now."

Twist said, "You need to call Harmon and tell him exactly what you just told us. The shooter's gonna be on this side of the river."

"Doing that right now," Cade said, and clicked off.

Shay said to Twist, "We've got to get off this road. We need to stay on this side of the river."

"Give me a route," Twist said.

Harmon called a minute later: "We're locked into the tunnel approach. We can't turn around here. You gotta get there, you gotta hurry. Hurry, hurry. . . ."

33

The approach to the building that would act as a shooting platform was intricate. There was almost no place you could go in an urban area in the United States where you wouldn't be caught by a video camera. Almost.

Denyers had left his own car in a parking garage without cameras, and they'd exited in the Toyota minivan—no exchange to be seen there. They'd driven the common-as-dirt van to New Jersey, gotten bearded up in the shopping mall lot, and, from there, driven to another camera-free automated parking lot, where they would trade the van for a Toyota Corolla, which Thorne would drive to Florida after the shot.

They were now both in full disguise and wearing thin flesh-colored rubber gloves. The gloves were hot but necessary.

After the shot, Thorne would drop Denyers a half mile from the parking lot with the van. Denyers would walk there, down several residential streets without visible cameras, still wearing his disguise.

He'd then drive the van back to Washington, where it would eventually be sterilized and dropped in a very bad neighborhood, the doors unlocked, the keys on the front seat.

Thorne would continue on, change plates in a camera-free car wash, dump the rifle and the old plates in the ocean, then drive straight through to Jacksonville, where the car would be sterilized and abandoned, the doors unlocked, the keys on the front seat. . . .

They both were confident that the trail could not be traced—and if by some wild chance it were, it would end with some doper who'd seen the chance for a free car.

The building that would be the shooting platform had an automatic door on the underground parking garage. Denyers produced a remote control and clicked it once. The door began to open.

The building was supposed to be a medical complex, but the doctors had gotten it eighty percent built and then run out of money. Now they were all suing each other—and the building was largely deserted.

"You're sure there's nobody here but the guard," Thorne said as he pulled forward into the garage. The door folded shut behind them.

"I'm sure."

"And he'll be behind his desk in the lobby."

"Most likely. Could be running a check on another floor; he's supposed to do that from time to time. But we set off the alarm just now when the garage door opened. I expect it'll take him about a minute to get down to the parking level," Denyers said. "Get the guitar. And put on your ball cap, just in case."

Thorne put on his hat and got out and popped the side door on the van, and at that moment, they heard a door open and a guard came through. He was a tall, affable-looking black man wearing a gray uniform and a New York Giants baseball hat.

He smiled and said, "Who're you guys?"

Thorne came around the van and said, "We're here to kill the president."

The guard's smile faltered. "What?"

Thorne lifted his hand, which had a pistol in it, and shot him twice in the heart.

They dragged him into the stairwell, leaving behind a thin track of blood, took his keys, and stuffed the body under the bottom flight of stairs, out of sight unless you looked for it.

That done, they climbed the stairs to the lobby. "Hope you're right about the elevators being turned on," Thorne said. "I don't want to be running up and down twelve floors."

"Elevator key should be on that ring, too. . . ."

They came out in the lobby a few seconds later, heard music, then saw movement behind what was to have been a nice reception desk but right now was several slabs of raw plywood.

A young woman stood up from behind the plywood, looked at them, and asked, "Where's Damien?"

"Who're you?" Denyers asked.

"His girlfriend. Dr. Robles said it'd be okay if I visited him. . . ."

Thorne shot her twice in the heart, and as she toppled to the floor, Denyers said, "Goddammit. Hope nobody's expecting her somewhere."

Thorne looked at his watch. "We're shooting in twenty minutes. No one expecting her would worry if she's only twenty minutes late." He nodded at two partly eaten chicken sandwiches. "Besides, they were only halfway through lunch, so she wasn't going anyplace right away."

They dragged her body behind the desk and covered her with a leaning sheet of plywood, and Thorne said, "I'm going up. If somebody else shows—"

"I got it," Denyers said. He took a pistol out of his pocket, put it on the desk, and took the security guard's chair. Just another rent-a-cop. With an itchy beard.

Thorne disappeared into an elevator with all his gear.

The guard and his girlfriend had a radio tuned to some easy-listening rap. Now *there* was a category, Denyers thought, and he pulled the radio over with his gloved hands and looked for something different. He eventually landed on an NPR station playing Mozart's *Eine kleine Nachtmusik,* a big hit in Denyers's preferred genre.

A little night music: the perfect background accompaniment for a presidential assassination.

Twelve stories up, Thorne looked down the hall, walked to his right. Nothing was finished. The floors were rough concrete, the drywall was unpainted, there were no toilets attached to the plumbing. Two doors down, he stepped into one of the roughed-in rooms, no walls at all, just aluminum framing threaded with white plastic tubing and wiring that led to bare, switchless electrical boxes.

Everything smelled like damp concrete and plaster.

He had the guitar case, with the gun and scope, and a duffel bag, containing the gun's bipod, an adjustable stock support, the computer, and a yoga mat. He stepped over to a window, which opened horizontally and only about six inches. Two inches was enough.

When it was open, he took the rifle out of its case, handling it as though it were the crown jewels. The scope was firmly attached to the weapon, metal on metal, and it had been heavily padded in its travels since the last sighting-in. Still, even the slightest movement between the gun and the scope would cause a missed shot.

He attached the rifle to the bipod, and the stock to the stock support, and moved them to the window, placing the muzzle of the gun about an inch behind the open window.

He cranked the stock support up—the deck of the *Intrepid* was slightly below him—until he had a rough aim point. He stuck the computer cable into a USB port on the rifle's stock, carefully turned on the scope, and brought the computer up.

A single click and he was looking at what the scope was seeing, but on the computer screen. What he could see, at a sharp angle, was a portion of the *Intrepid*'s flight deck. Even with the naked eye, he could see the bright colors of dozens and probably hundreds of people gathered on the deck. He could also see an American flag, which hung limply from its flagstaff. No wind drift to worry about. Perfect.

But the rifle was set up too high—he reached over and slowly screwed the stock support even higher, which brought the gun's muzzle down, and then slowly moved the muzzle to the left until he was focused on a woman who was sitting in a chair on the speaker's stand, talking to a man standing next to her. She was wearing one of those red-orange dresses that political women favored, and it made an excellent setup target.

When everything was perfect, he slowly adjusted the scope's magnification until all he could see was the red dress and about three or four feet on either side of the woman. Then he screwed the stock support a bit lower, which raised the muzzle, until he could focus on the teleprompter the president would be using.

From Thorne's perspective, the president would be standing slightly to the left of the teleprompter, and he moved the rifle stock a tiny fraction of an inch until it was aimed through the space where the president would be standing.

He took a cold cell phone from his pocket and called Denyers, who answered on another cold phone. "Let's go to Denny's and get a cheeseburger," Thorne said, which meant that he was set.

"Sounds good to me—see you in fifteen," Denyers said: the coast was clear.

He checked the sight again on the computer screen: a luminescent green cross hovered just to the left of the teleprompter. Still locked on.

To fire the rifle, he had to pull the trigger, then key Command-F. The computer would signal the rifle to fire when the selected target was exactly positioned.

Far across the river, and down below, he could see people in masses, clumping in front of the speaker's stand, and a couple of dignitaries hurrying to their chairs on the stand. He looked at his watch: one o'clock.

The president was on his way. . . .

34

Cruz spent most of his time looking stoically out through the wind-shield, giving occasional traffic alerts: "Driver two cars up is merg-ing left" or "There's a biker up ahead moving between lanes."

Harmon, on the other hand, seemed to Cruz to be freaking out, jamming the big SUV into the smallest cracks in the traffic, moving slow drivers over by leaning on the horn, ignoring the multitude of upraised fingers and shaken fists. And he was sweating—the first time Cruz had seen that.

Nothing Harmon could do, though. By the time they got into the tunnel itself, it was eighteen minutes to one o'clock. Once in the tunnel, the traffic smoothed out and the phone reception got better.

They didn't have an iPad, like Shay and Twist, and were relying on Cade to get them through traffic.

"When you come out of the tunnel, you will actually have gone too far; you'll have to go back west to get to the river, and then north," Cade said. "I don't see anything definitive on traffic, but

I've had a New York radio station up, and they say things are starting to clog up because of the presidential motorcade."

"How far is it from where we come out of the tunnel to the *Intrepid*?" Harmon asked.

"About . . . nine blocks. But three of those are the long New York east-west blocks, and six of them are the short north-south blocks. . . ."

"Faster to run or faster to drive?"

"Run, I think. Though it depends on where you bail out of the car," Cade said. "But traffic . . . Actually, I can't tell you from here. It's confusing, but I'd bet you could run it faster if there's any traffic at all."

Harmon pulled the gun out of his cargo pocket and said to Cruz, "If the New York cops catch you with this gun, they'll put you in prison. First chance you get, find a Dumpster or a sewer and throw it in. Sewer would be better. Wipe it first." He shoved the gun at him.

"What are you doing?" Cruz asked.

"I've seen these motorcades before. They create a first-class clusterfuck, and there'll be cops everywhere. If we stop rolling, I'm going to run for it. You gotta get over here in the driver's seat—do not take your sweet time."

Harmon was talking so fast that Cruz had a hard time keeping up. Cruz said, "Man, you gotta slow down, you're gonna have a stroke."

"We're talking about the *president*," Harmon said. "The *president* . . ."

The traffic in the tunnel ground to a stop. They couldn't see movement ahead of them, and Harmon said sharply, "Now!"

"What?"

Harmon yanked his door open and shouted, "Run!" and then Cruz realized what he was doing and yanked his own door open, and they both ran around the truck, nearly colliding at the back bumper. The car behind them honked once, and then they were back inside. Fifteen seconds later, they began moving again.

When they could see daylight up ahead, Harmon got on the phone again with Cade, who said, "Take the exit heading north, go north."

Cruz spotted the exit, and after a couple more slowdowns, they were back in the light, out of the tunnel, but the streets were jammed with traffic. Harmon said, "I'm running. Don't forget to ditch the gun. Take the phone, stay in touch with Cade. I'm running."

They were a block north when they slowed again, and Harmon popped the door and was gone.

The idea of an assassination scared Harmon to death. He'd fought in wars in a number of countries where assassination was simply the way politics was done, and he wouldn't have wanted to live in any of those places.

So he sprinted toward the Hudson. He was both large and fast. He could run five miles in thirty-five minutes wearing boots and carrying a pack and a gun, and now he was wearing running shoes and carrying nothing at all.

But he wasn't running on a track; he was running on sidewalks and in the street, in traffic.

He made the turn onto the West Side Highway, and the sidewalk traffic suddenly got heavier. He dodged around a guy in a wheelchair and nearly bowled over an old lady and her dog. She screamed at him, and a fat man in a black T-shirt, walking the opposite direction, put out an arm and shouted, "Slow down, a-hole," but Harmon blew past him.

Up ahead, the traffic on the West Side Highway was being diverted to the east, the highway blocked off. Harmon could see people moving off the sidewalk and into the street as they got closer to the *Intrepid.*

No sirens yet, and the motorcade usually arrived with screaming sirens all around.

About the time he thought he'd manage to get close to the ship, he found a thick rank of people stretching across the highway—and found himself up against a waist-high mesh fence with cops every six feet.

The closest one was a heavyset young guy. Beyond him, and a little back from the line, was an older guy with what looked like a buck sergeant's stripes—in the army, anyway. He was the only cop around who looked like he might have some rank.

Harmon pushed and shoved his way through the crowd, ignoring the complaints and curses as he plowed toward the sergeant, saying, "Gotta get to the cop, gotta get to the police."

He shouted at the sergeant, "Hey, Sergeant! Sergeant!"

The younger cop turned toward him and said, "Get back there! Get back!"

Harmon: "I need that sergeant! Sergeant!"

The sergeant heard him and stepped over. "What's the problem?"

"I gotta talk to the Secret Service and I gotta talk to them right now."

"Uh-huh."

"I gotta talk to them!" Harmon shouted. "Right now . . . Listen, just get me to a guy. Just get me one. . . ."

The sergeant turned and looked over his shoulder and said, "I'll see if I can find somebody to talk to you. But I need you to calm down."

Harmon looked at him, then at the fence, and suddenly went over it, a half vault. The young cop and the sergeant both grabbed him, and he pulled them away from the fence, the sergeant saying, "Hey! Hey!" and more cops heading toward them. Harmon turned to the sergeant and said, "In about six minutes—"

The sergeant was twisting Harmon's arm around behind him and shouting to somebody else, "Cuff him!" and Harmon pushed back and said, "In about six minutes, a crazy former SEAL named Thorne is gonna try to shoot the president. You hear that? In six minutes, he's gonna try to shoot the president. . . ."

One of the cops clamped a handcuff on Harmon's left wrist, then bent the right arm back: Harmon didn't fight it, just kept chanting at the sergeant, "Gonna try to kill the president. I need the Secret Service."

With two cops holding Harmon now, the sergeant wiped his face on his sleeve, pulled off Harmon's mirrored aviators, and said, "What the hell are you talking about?"

"Man, I'm a former Delta guy. Another guy I know, a guy named Thorne, is set up to shoot the president using a computer-assisted sniper rifle. You don't have to believe me, but you have to get me to a Secret Service guy. Then you can put me in jail or whatever you have to do, but right now, get me to the Secret Service."

The sergeant looked at him for a moment, then said to the cops, "Bring him this way."

"Gotta hurry, gotta hurry," Harmon said.

They took him to a glassed-in cube that might normally have been a ticket station, where a lounging cop was keeping an eye on another man, who sat on a plastic chair with his hands cuffed behind him. The other man was unkempt, long hair gelled almost straight up, steel rings piercing his nose, cheek, lips, and ears.

They pushed Harmon into a chair, and the sergeant said, "I'll see if I can find somebody."

"Hurry!"

The sergeant walked away. Harmon looked at the lounging cop and asked, "What time is it?"

The cop looked at his cell phone, then looked back at Harmon. Not talking.

Harmon said, "Please."

The cop looked at his cell phone again. "Twelve-fifty-six."

And then they heard the sirens.

"Oh, shit," Harmon said.

He started to stand up, but the cop pulled a Taser from his holster and said, "You stand, you get a billion volts in the neck."

Thirty seconds later, the sergeant came back through the door towing an apple-cheeked guy in a gray suit, with a bug in one ear. He looked like he was about fourteen.

"What's the problem?" he asked.

Harmon opened his mouth, then said to himself, *Calm down.* He took a breath, and said, as evenly as he could, watching the crowd churning through the glass opposite him—the president was walking toward the elevators that would take him to the ship's deck— "My name is Dallas Harmon. Until a couple of weeks ago, I was a security officer with Singular Corp. That's the company that has been in all the trouble on the West Coast for doing human experimentation. I won't tell you about all of that, but I will tell you that Senator Dash was on their board of directors, and when the top people at the company thought they were getting in trouble, they killed her."

"Senator Dash committed suicide . . . ," the agent said.

"No, she didn't. She was murdered. There's an FBI agent named Brian Barin who is working the case out of the FBI's Los Angeles office, and more agents from the Phoenix office are now digging up bodies at Senator Dash's ranch in New Mexico."

The agent, who'd been leaning against the doorframe like he had more important places to be, suddenly straightened up and stared very seriously at Harmon. "Barin . . . All right, I'll call him, then. But what about the president?"

"I don't have time to explain how it connects, but I can tell you that there's a former SEAL out there named Thorne who's equipped with a computer-assisted sniper rifle, and he's planning to shoot the president. Right now. He's another former security officer from Singular, and he's been convinced that if he makes the shot, he'll be covered by the people who take over for the president." Harmon took a breath. "Now, all you have to do is delay the speech while you check me out. Talk to your lead guy out here, and don't let the president get up on that speaker's stand."

The young agent did the same thing that the sergeant had, squinting at the very fit, sweating man and something about him was convincing: the agent lifted his hand to his mouth and said, "We may have a situation here."

He listened to his earbud for a moment, then lifted his hand again. "We have a guy here—"

Just then, a band began blaring in the background: "Hail to the Chief."

"He's going up on the stand!" Harmon shouted at the agent. "He's going up! You gotta stop him, stop him!"

The Secret Service man took a step toward the door, his hand still at his coat sleeve, and Harmon bellowed, "Run, dummy, run! Run!"

The agent, still talking, ran out of the cube. The cop watching Harmon had gone wide-eyed, and Harmon decided to take a chance and sprinted after the Secret Service man.

He'd gone ten steps when the Taser hit him in the back of the neck and he went down. . . .

35

New Jersey, the part of it they saw, toward the end, was a jungle of concrete, beat-up buildings, and billboards, swarming with cars. There were just as many cars in Southern California, but the California highways seemed more orderly, more planned, while the Jersey roads looked like they'd been designed by somebody's otherwise unemployable nephew.

Shay and Twist were fighting their way north, parallel to the Hudson River but well west of it.

"We're not going to get there in time to do any good," Twist said, giving in to despair. "We're way late, we screwed this up. . . ."

"*We're* not supposed to be doing this at all," Shay said. "Why doesn't goddamn Barin call us back?"

"GET OUT OF THE WAY!" Twist shouted at a slow-moving car that had them trapped. From the back, X barked once, and again. Then Twist said, "Hang on," and he passed the slow car on the shoulder, and suddenly, as though that single move were the key to everything, the traffic seemed to part in front of them and they were moving fast.

They didn't have to slow down again before they got to Weehawken, and then they were over the bluff and coming down toward the river and a series of tall buildings that stood along the waterfront.

"Eight minutes to one," Shay said. "Go left, go left. . . ."

Cade called: "Harmon just bailed out of the truck and he's running to the *Intrepid*. There's a chance he'll get there in time to talk to somebody. Cruz is going to find a place to park, if there is such a thing."

"We're coming to the building, I think. We're a block away," Shay told him.

"Careful . . ."

They turned a last corner and saw the building—but the driveway that would lead around to the left, to the front of the building, was blocked by yellow metal barrels hooked together with chains.

That drive was empty except for a demolition pile of pink insulation and broken plasterboard; newly installed windows on the back of the building still had labels on them. "It's an empty building," Shay said.

Twist: "What better place to shoot from? No witnesses around . . ."

Another driveway went down to the right. "Gotta be a parking garage," Twist said. He went that way, but at the bottom of the ramp, they faced three brown steel gates, all down, and card readers for which they didn't have a card.

"Dammit." Twist reversed back up the ramp, back to the barrels, and said, "This is where we get out."

"Yes."

• • •

Shay opened the back door for X, touched the gun at her hip and then the knife at the small of her back. Twist was already running as hard as he could around the building toward the entrance.

The front of the building faced the Manhattan skyline, which was like nothing else in the world, but Shay had eyes only for the entrance as she and X outpaced Twist and got to the side-by-side doors of greenish glass first. She yanked on one, then the other. Locked. Twist looked through the glass and said, "There's a guard in there."

He began banging on the glass with his cane, and the guard waved them away, then put up both hands, a "Wait" sign, and climbed off the stool he'd been sitting on and walked up to the door. He was a pudgy man with a black beard, wearing a baseball cap and sunglasses; though the lobby was dimly lit, and Shay got a vibe. . . .

The man had one hand slightly behind his butt as he approached the door, and Twist blurted, "He's got a gun."

Shay shouted, "X!" and at that moment, the man on the other side of the door hit the lock bar, and the door popped open and his gun was coming up, and Shay screamed, "Kill him!" and X was in the air.

The dog hit Denyers high on the chest just as Denyers's gun went off and Twist shouted something and went down. Shay and X were in the lobby as Denyers rolled across it, hands trying to simultaneously beat away the dog and cover his face, and he fired the gun again, and then X had his gun arm and was dragging him, screaming, across the floor. And then Denyers lost his gun, and Shay shouted at X, "Down, X! Down!"

X backed away, just a few inches, peering down into Denyers's face, still snarling, all wolf teeth, right there.

Denyers groaned, "I'm hurt."

He'd been bitten on the neck and arms and was bleeding but not gushing. Shay kicked Denyers's gun to the other side of the lobby, trained her own gun on him, backed up to the doors, which had automatically closed, and turned to see Twist sitting up on the other side of the glass, blood spreading on the pavement beneath him.

She pushed the door open, and Twist said, "Hit . . ."

Then, suddenly, X again attacked Denyers, and when Shay whirled, she saw the CIA man with another pistol, but the dog was all over him, and she ran back and kicked Denyers in the head, then grabbed his gun arm and wrenched the gun free, feeling Denyers's trigger finger snap as she did it, and shouted again, "X, down!"

X backed away, and Denyers groaned again, his face bleeding heavily now. "One more time and I kill you," Shay snarled at him. "You hear that?"

"Yes."

Twist had managed to drag himself into the lobby and said, "I'm hit in the leg. The bone is broken. . . ."

There was a trail of blood behind him, but Shay thought, *No time.*

She said, "I gotta go up, I gotta stop Thorne."

"Go. . . ."

Shay looked around, spotted a Subway sack on the desk with some napkins. She ran that way . . . and saw the body of a woman behind the desk. *No time. No time to think about it.* She grabbed the napkins and ran back to Twist, saying, "There's a body behind the desk; if he moves, shoot him."

Twist, pale as a sheet, held up a cell phone. "I'm calling 911. . . . Hurry."

Shay ran to the elevators, shouting at Denyers, "What floor? What floor?" But she could see that one of the elevators was up on twelve and the rest were at the lobby. She pressed the call button, and there was a *ding* when the doors opened. She and X got in. She thought for one second, then punched 10; an overheard *ding* could kill her.

The tenth floor was a construction mess. Out of the elevator, gun in her hand, Shay ran hard to the exit sign at the end of the hall, looked up, listened just for a second, as Harmon had taught her, then ran up the two flights, keeping X in a heel with a slap on her thigh.

On twelve, she peeked around the doorway. Heard nothing. Bent over and whispered to X, "Find him! Kill him!"

X surged down the hall. Shay went after him, leading with the muzzle of her gun.

Two doors down from the elevator, Thorne's eyes were fixed on the computer screen. The president had just climbed up on the speaker's stand and was shaking hands with the celebrities and other politicians on the stand with him. Thorne had to wait until the president settled at the podium before he could select him as the target and pull the trigger.

At the distance he was shooting from, it would take a bit more than two seconds for the bullet to arrive at the target. In two seconds, a man could easily move ten feet or more, even at a stroll. The target had to be relatively fixed, and the podium and teleprompter would do that for him.

The president was wearing a dark suit, which stood out neatly against the bright colors of the crowd on the other side of him. He shook a few more hands, then stepped to the podium, then moved past it, arms in a V, waving to the crowd.

And then back to the podium.

The scope had a video screen much like those on digital cameras, where the operator could select a person to follow with the focus—or even a part of a person to follow with the focus.

When the president had settled in to speak, Thorne moved the fluorescent green cross to the center of his back and pressed the K key, which was "Select Target." An orange outline immediately sprang up around the president's dark jacket. Too big an area: the rifle could fire when targeted on the lower back. That'd probably be fatal, given the large fragmenting .338 slug, but not a sure thing. Using the computer's touch pad, Thorne manually narrowed the target area to a four-inch patch in the middle of the president's back, the kill zone.

The president moved to one side, and the patch followed, but the cross remained where it had been.

What was that? Footsteps in the hallway? Focus. . . .

He went back to the rifle and, as gently as he could, reached across and pulled the trigger. The rifle was now ready to fire.

When he hit Command-F, the rifle would fire as soon as its sensor decided that the target patch was motionless and centered on the targeting cross.

Thorne's fingers hovered over the keys.

I will live forever. . . .

Command . . . F.

• • •

X paused at the doorway and looked back at Shay, and she screamed, "Kill!" and X launched himself into the room like a wolf and, a quarter second later, hit the squatting Thorne in the face.

The gun fired, but Thorne had the sickening impression that just as it did, his left arm brushed the gun's stock.

Just brushed it . . .

The dog was all over him, savaging his face, but Thorne had been in desperate fights before, and he ignored the pain and focused on one thought: *Gun.* He was aware that he was screaming but let that go as his free hand, the one away from the dog, found the gun in his waistband and pulled it and automatically fired it. He had no idea where the slug would go, but the muzzle blast should give him a tenth of a second, and that would be all he'd need to swing the gun around and kill the animal.

And it worked: X froze for just that sliver in time, and Thorne's hand came around, and though one of his eyes was clogged with blood, he could see out of the other one, and the pistol was coming up—

And his hand exploded and the pistol flew six feet away, clattering on the hard floor, and he registered the fact that he'd been shot, and he batted the dog with his bloody hand. . . .

The dog was back on him, and an ankle appeared near him, and a girl's voice was screaming, "Stop! Stop it or I'll shoot you!" and he thought, *Amateur hour . . .*

His hand snaked out, and he had the ankle, and he pulled as hard as he could. There was another shot but no impact, and the girl came down, and in some tiny corner of his mind, he registered the red hair. . . .

The dog was ripping at the back of his neck, and Thorne grabbed a chunk of red hair and yanked again, almost blind now from the blood, but he could feel where she was, and she had that gun. . . .

Thorne grabbed her hair and yanked hard, hit her four or five times in the side, hard, and Shay, already on her knees, fell on top of him, and X peeled off a piece of Thorne's scalp, and Thorne was screaming like a man falling out of a tall building, and he was clawing his way up her arm, where he got hold of her gun and was ripping it away from her. She tried to hold on but he had a hundred pounds of muscle on her, and she felt the gun slipping out of her control.

Because of the way they were lying, in a pile, the dog alternately ripping and howling, Shay's free arm was useless, flailing around, and she hit him with it, but the blows bounced off the top of his head and she knew she wasn't hurting him. . . .

The gun was going. . . .

And she thought, *Knife*.

She found the familiar handle at the small of her back, gripped it with one bloody hand, and as Thorne pulled the pistol free, she struck with it, half blindly, and connected.

The knife, once a carpenter's file, now carefully ground down to a blade guaranteed not to break on bone or tendon or ligament, punched a hole in Thorne's chest.

Thorne's body went rigid, still clutching at her, began to shake, shake hard, and then . . . stopped.

• • •

Shay rolled away from him, onto her back. X came over, whimpered once, and licked her face.

Her nose hurt, and both her sides were on fire. She tried to sit up, but her head swam and darkness crowded her vision down to a tiny pinprick. . . . *Better to lie still.*

The first responders, two young men with drawn guns, found her on the floor, Thorne dead beside her, X hovering over her.

X snarled at them, and Shay said, "Don't shoot my dog."

36

Nobody told her anything.

Ambulance people and men in suits took her out on a gurney. Shay saw there was blood on the lobby floor but saw no sign of Twist or the bad guy; three people in white crime scene suits were hovering over the body behind the desk. She saw X: he was on the end of a chain, with a full head muzzle, and he whined as she went by. She'd cooperated with that—the first cops said it was either the muzzle or they'd shoot him. She'd kept the dog quiet while they muzzled him, but where they took him after the lobby, she didn't know. They took her to a hospital.

They cleaned her up, gave her an MRI, then put her in a large single room with metal walls and built-in restraints on the bed and told her to sleep. Which was impossible.

She asked repeatedly about Harmon and Twist and the president, but nobody would tell her anything.

A balding doctor who might have portrayed a wise old medic in

a bad soap opera did tell her that her nasal septum—nose bone—
had been cracked in the fight and she'd need a nose support for a
week or so, but it'd be fine when her giant black eyes went away.
She also had cracked ribs on both sides, and he recommended she
avoid laughing. That had been a kind of doctor joke, she decided.
So not funny.

A lot of suits came to talk with her, and she told them everything:
every last thing. Then she told them again. And again. For hours.

She asked if Twist was being treated in the same hospital, and
finally one doctor on an overnight shift gave her a quick nod behind
the backs of the security people.

And then a tiny, efficient nurse who'd been doing the blood
pressure checks and changing out the drips from what seemed like
the beginning leaned down and whispered into her ear one very
good thing. . . .

"They say now that you saved the president's life."

On what she thought was the morning of the third day, someone
wheeled Twist into her room; he was sitting up on a bed, one leg im-
mobilized in a fat white cast. She would have flung her arms around
him if either of them could have gotten that near to the other.

Shay asked, "Your leg?"

"Busted by the bullet," Twist said. "Maybe the best news of my
life."

"What?"

"The orthopods here say my original injury was badly fixed.
They say they can rework everything. Might have a few extra screws
and bolts, but they tell me I should be able to run again . . . real
running, no cane."

"That's amazing, Twist," she said.

"What about you? Your face . . ."

"It'll heal," said Shay. "Broken nose, couple ribs. I've been asking about you, but nobody would tell me anything."

"Nobody would tell me anything, either. Then this guy"—he pointed up at the orderly—"just came and got me."

"You've got a visitor," the orderly mumbled.

Shay asked Twist, "What happened to . . . that guy in the lobby? The guy who shot you?"

"I don't know. They took us both out on stretchers; I haven't seen him since, and . . ." He shrugged.

She glanced at the orderly, then asked, "Cruz? Cade? Harmon?"

Twist shook his head. "No idea."

A visitor arrived: Harmon pushed through the door with a package under his arm.

He had a rosy healing scrape on his cheekbone, and he said to Shay, "Jesus. You look like shit."

"Thanks. So do you," Shay said. And, "Please, please, tell me that's not a box of chocolates under your arm."

Harmon looked embarrassed and said, "Yeah, but, uh . . . they're for Twist."

He handed the box to Twist, who said, "Thank you," and looked pleased, and added, "Nothing like a visitor bearing chocolates."

The orderly said, "He's not the visitor. I didn't know he was coming."

Two seconds later, a muscular man in a blue suit, with a bug in his ear, pushed into the room, looked at the orderly, and tipped his head, and the orderly left. Another two seconds, and President Terrance Berman walked in.

Shay said, "Ohhh." Then the president, who she would have said looked taller and thinner on TV, said cheerfully, "So. You're the people who saved my life."

The president shook hands with all of them, looking each of them square in the eye and saying simply, "Thank you." It was so heartfelt and sincere that Shay found herself near tears.

The president lingered next to her. "I understand you turn seventeen next week. Happy birthday. But you're too young for this stuff. Go back to school."

"I'll do that," Shay said.

"College, too," he said. "When you get a letter from the secretary of education, don't throw it away. Uncle Sam's got a scholarship in mind."

Twist said, "Uh . . . sir . . . nobody exactly told us what happened."

"Well then, I'll tell you," the president said. "I was standing there with my mouth open when my teleprompter exploded and I was swarmed by the Secret Service, and then I was running down some stairs and got shoved into a limo. A woman in the crowd took the bullet." He grimaced. "She lost her arm."

"Oh no," Shay said.

"Sadly, yes. I visited with her a few minutes ago. The bullet was the size of a brick. Well, that's an exaggeration. But if it had hit me in the back, as intended, I'd be dead."

"Wow," Shay said.

"Yes, wow," said the president. "Again, my thanks. To all of you."

"President Berman, sir," Shay said tentatively, unsure of title etiquette, "we know Thorne is dead, but what about the guy in the lobby?"

"The man in the lobby was a CIA operative who was trying to help you out," the president said, a slight tone to his voice. "Thorne was a deranged man, acting alone."

"What!"

"Shocking, I know. Listen, here's the story: you good citizens alerted everyone to the Thorne threat—the FBI and also the army chief of staff. News spread to the White House. The CIA agent, who was in New York with my entourage, was in a position to get across the river in a hurry. You all met at the building where Thorne was, but Thorne had already killed the security guard and his girlfriend and managed to wound both the agent and Twist. You, Shay, had remained in the car until you heard the gunfire, and when you rushed to help them, you found that Thorne had already taken the elevator up. You took another elevator up. After a vicious struggle, you and your dog managed to overcome Thorne, who died in the struggle, but only after he managed to get off a shot. Your dog, by the way, is fine."

They were all silent, a bit stunned.

Shay couldn't leave it alone. "But . . . you know why they were shooting at you in the first place, right?"

The president lifted a finger to his lips. "The story I've told you is what a very thorough investigation will find and what the public will know. But I assure you, the guilty will be punished. We are not in a place where all the guilty can be *publicly* punished. I hope you understand that. I would rather it not be known that a top official in the CIA and a billionaire who contributed to the campaigns of pretty much every major politician were tangled up in a conspiracy to assassinate the president, and the actual assassination of a senator, in order to cover up a despicable and horrific scientific enterprise. I'm not sure the American public could stand it. I'm not sure I can stand it."

"But they'll be punished?" Shay pressed. "The guy in the lobby, and Royce, and Dr. Janes . . . and *all* of Singular?"

The president nodded. "Yes. I promise you. Every single one."

Shay said, "And the vice president?"

The president put a finger across his lips again.

Twist: "But the whole point . . ."

The president: "Trust me."

Then he was gone, like a mirage, leaving an empty space in the room. Shay could hardly believe he'd been there. Two doctors hustled in, now free to tell them when they'd be released, and another Secret Service agent showed up with some papers to sign—"You agree not to talk about this with anyone. It's all being declared top-secret. . . ."

Twist: "What if we don't want to sign?" That was the hippie painter anarchist talking.

"Well, we have some very, very quiet places in the federal housing system where you could spend a few years reconsidering. . . ."

"Where do we sign?" Harmon asked.

While that was going on, the president was taken down to his waiting limo. Another large man in a gray suit was waiting in the backseat, and when the car eased into traffic, the fourth car in the motorcade, he handed a slim file to the president, who opened it and found what looked like a chemical analysis. "Just tell me what it says. In English."

"During his debriefing, Denyers told us that the vice president handled the gun case—the guitar case that was used to carry the gun."

"Yes."

"His prints are on it, his DNA. No question."

"Shit."

"Yes, sir."

"I guess I knew that," the president said.

"This is a problem," said the man in gray. "We have to resolve it."

"Yes."

"I've spoken to some of our advisors. They're suggesting that the vice president should resign to devote himself to the fight against his late-stage colon cancer."

"And the fight will be ultimately unsuccessful?"

"You can bet on it, sir."

37

The excitement about the assassination attempt was extreme for about two weeks and then began to fade.

The murder of Senator Dash was a suicide.

The vice president had cancer and, doing the right thing, as always, resigned.

The cover-up held.

The Singular scandal was used as a diversion from the assassination attempt, and the news media bit on it, especially when the FBI announced that DNA from twelve bodies had been recovered from the burn pit at Dash's ranch. Ian Wyeth, the St. Louis neurosurgeon who'd done most of the surgery in America, had disappeared. The FBI leaked word to the media that he was probably hiding in Indonesia, although some thought he'd gone directly to North Korea. Lawrence Janes, director of research at the facility in Eugene, Oregon, was also missing and was more firmly placed in North Korea by unnamed FBI sources. Nobody ever mentioned Varek Royce.

The FBI may or may not have been lying, but in any case, the statements were wildly inaccurate. And the CIA knew exactly where the three men were.

After cooperating with the investigation with countless more hours of interviews, the whole group was reunited in Los Angeles at the Twist Hotel. Even Harmon. Even X.

Shay clung to Odin when she finally saw him again, not minding the ache in her mending ribs. Her genius, good-hearted, single-minded, reckless brother. They'd survived. She'd been afraid he wouldn't—that's why she'd gotten involved in the first place. But he seemed stronger now. Older. And sadder for the loss of Fenfang. She'd been worried he wouldn't survive that, either, but she saw now that he would.

Odin's leg was healing, and he and Twist took long cane-assisted walks to get their strength back.

Twist was his usual high-intensity self. He had a second operation to remove some braces in late September, and by mid-October, he was walking two miles a day.

By mid-November, he was jogging. With his cane, which he spun like a majorette's baton.

"There's more than one use for a good gold-headed cane, as you know," he told Shay. He demonstrated by whacking it against a plaster wall in the hotel, leaving a substantial dent.

He was beginning a new cycle of paintings that were all about speed.

· · ·

On a cool, still October day, Odin, Shay, and all the rest of them, joined by Fenfang's sister, Wei Wei, who'd flown in from China, took Fenfang's ashes in a bronze box down to the Pacific Ocean in Malibu. They walked out waist-deep in the water, and a Buddhist priest from Silver Lake said some words.

Shay cried when the ashes were spread on the water, and was offended when Cade and Cruz were surprised.

She cried a second time when she learned that the president had called Marcus West's parents to tell them that he had died a hero, protecting others and helping to bring down Singular.

Fenfang's cousin Liko was among the prisoners they'd rescued from Senator Dash's ranch, and Wei Wei was able to see him, but he didn't seem to know she was there—his prognosis was poor. Robert Morris was in even worse shape and was gone on the last day of October. His wife sent a note to Shay, thanking her for the rescue; Shay cried a third time.

And that was the end of the crying.

A government man who simply said he was an "aide" told Shay and Odin privately that the government had confirmed the death of their mother. When the human experimentation had begun, Kathleen Carter had gathered several of the prospective subjects and tried to flee to China. She was killed during the flight.

When Odin asked, "Was she shot or something?" the aide's eyes switched away.

"The exact circumstances of her death . . . aren't really known," he said.

Shay looked at him for a long moment, until Odin asked, "What?" and Shay said, "They told this guy to go easy on us." To the aide: "Mom committed suicide, didn't she?"

The aide said, "I didn't . . . As we understand it, she would not allow herself to be captured. She feared that she'd be used in an experiment. Whether she actually committed suicide or not, there's no way to tell. The North Koreans lie about everything—but the talks they had with the Chinese were very direct, and the Chinese think they were telling the truth."

Odin: "When you say the talks were very direct . . ."

"I'd deny saying this, but what I mean is, the Chinese kicked them so hard that the North Koreans are now wearing their asses for hats."

When the aide went away, Odin draped his arm around Shay's shoulders and said, "We always knew." They were both dry-eyed. Their mother had been gone so long she seemed almost like a myth, like a fictional figure.

"Now *we're* what we have left," Shay said. "Just us. It's enough."

But Singular wasn't gone, not yet.

On a quiet Thursday evening in early November, Royce, Wyeth, and Janes took the elevator to the roof of their new facility in Honduras, carrying glasses and a full pitcher of margaritas. The new lab was being built in a former military installation that looked out over the Gulf of Fonseca toward the Pacific Ocean. The building was silent: the dayworkers, who were doing the rehabilitation, had gone home.

Royce was pulling strings back in the States, calculating the possibility of going back; his best sources said he hadn't yet been tied to the assassination attempt. If he couldn't return, he'd already determined that he and his money would be welcome in Singapore. But what he really wanted was a younger, athletic, and anonymous new body. Wyeth thought he might have it in three years. "We've still got all the computer files. And it won't take long to get the lab up and running."

"And this time, we won't be exposed to any snooping," Royce said as they settled into the lounge chairs on the roof. "I've told our friend exactly what's at stake, and all *el presidente* said was, 'I want in.'"

Janes said, "We're gonna need more experimental subjects."

"Also not a problem," Royce said. "*El presidente* says Honduras has all kinds of annoying peasants that he'd like to see the end of. All we need to do is give him a number and he'll deliver them. We should have been here from the beginning."

They were sipping their drinks, staring at the starry sky. Royce said, "I just saw a star go out."

"Probably a plane," Wyeth said.

Royce couldn't see the plane because it was painted night-sky gray and had been designed not to be seen—not even by radar.

As Royce spoke, two one-thousand-pound bombs called JDAMs—Joint Direct Attack Munitions—were on the way down to the Honduran facility. Royce, Janes, and Wyeth never felt a thing. A few seconds after the star winked out, they were just a bunch of hot molecules in a fiery cloud.

The president, it seemed, had been serious about scholarships—for Shay, Odin, Cruz, Cade, even Emily. Danny Dill was happy back in Arcata—and happy for the government not to think of him at all.

317

Odin was weighing MIT against Cal Poly. He wanted to be near Shay. But Shay couldn't seem to figure out what to do with herself. She was fidgety and restless.

So was Harmon.

Shay and Harmon decided to go to Moab and check out the desert tower that Harmon had dared her to climb. They'd stop in Hopi country for a couple of days first to let X get acquainted with his puppies and to pay a proper visit to Harmon's friends.

They drove to First Mesa, picking over the remnants of the whole Singular conflict as they went. Shay was frustrated that she didn't know more about what might happen to Varek Royce, Dr. Janes, Wyeth. Denyers. The vice president. They'd seemed to vanish.

"You're never going to know, so you might as well try to forget about it," Harmon said. "But I promise you, they'll be taken care of, one way or another."

At First Mesa, Harmon couldn't stay away from the sole white puppy in the litter, and the white puppy couldn't stay away from him, hanging on to the cuff of his jeans as X looked on with what might have been—probably was—doggy amusement. When Harmon went inside to supper, the white pup managed to get inside with him and find its way onto his lap.

After two days at First Mesa, Shay and Harmon left early on a cool, sunny morning, leaving X with his family, for the three-day round trip to Moab. X had been showing signs of separation anxiety, and Shay had to sit with him for a few minutes, reassuring him that she'd be back; Harmon sat with the white puppy.

When they got in Harmon's truck, he said, "I cannot, *cannot,* with my lifestyle, have a dog."

"It's too late. That puppy's your dog, whether you like it or not. And what is your lifestyle anyway?"

"Hmm," Harmon said. "What's yours?"

"Good question."

The drive to Moab took five hours, and then they hooked out into the desert, to the Needles.

Shay stood at the bottom of the tower and looked up.

"Piece of cake," she said.

"We'll find out tomorrow," Harmon said.

38

They were both sweating heavily as they did the last pitch up the vertical wall at the top of the needle. "Had to be a last piece like this, didn't there?" Shay said as she clung to foot- and handholds the size of marbles.

"It's how you find out how good you really are," Harmon said. He was tied into a bolt thirty feet above her and ten feet to the right. "The bottom four hundred feet kicks your ass. When your ass is thoroughly kicked, this wall comes along . . . and then you find out whether or not you're a . . ." He swallowed the last word.

"You were about to say *chicken,* weren't you?" Shay asked. She blew a few strands of hair out of her left eye.

"You get up this far, we already know you're not a chicken," Harmon said. "We've got another fifty feet. You have to make that move—you saw me do it."

The next move depended on the momentary friction between a sticky rubber climbing shoe on her left foot and the rough, slanting sandstone of the wall. If she stuck for a fraction of a second, she could catch a protrusion with her left hand, then another with her right, then slam her right foot into a solid edge. If she missed, she'd be hanging from the end of the climbing rope, four hundred feet above the Colorado Plateau.

If she was lucky. Some of the preset bolts they'd encountered on the way up were a little shaky.

"Gonna have to move . . . ," Harmon said. She could see herself, a tiny speck of blue and red, in his mirrored aviators.

He hadn't finished the sentence when Shay launched herself. Friction! Grab! Pivot! Grab! Right foot slamming into edge! She stuck there like a spider, breathing hard, the scent of blood in her nose. Harmon was looking down at her, and she said, "You weren't about to say *chicken*. You were about to say *pussy*."

"I thought better of it," Harmon said, not denying it. "Let's go up. From where you're at, it's a walk in the park."

He was lying. Though it wasn't as difficult as the forty-foot pitch below, it wasn't anybody's stroll through anybody's park. When they finally crossed the top of the wall, they stopped to catch their breath amidst a collection of red boulders. They were past the hard parts but still fifteen feet below the very top of the needle. "Let's go," Harmon said after ninety seconds and a few swallows of water for each of them. "We've got a meeting."

"What are you talking about?"

"You'll see," he said. "And maybe I should apologize in advance."

They climbed the slope to the top. A hundred yards away, a Black Hawk helicopter sat on a flat slab of red stone. A chunky, square man was sitting on the stone reading a book. A taller, thinner man wearing a flight suit was wandering around on the other side of the chopper.

"What's this?" Shay asked.

"A meeting and an easier way down, if you want it," Harmon said. "C'mon."

They walked up to the slab of rock and found that the chunky guy was sitting on a plaid blanket and had a picnic basket and a cooler with him; he'd been reading Joseph Conrad's *Heart of Darkness*.

Harmon said to Shay, "Meet my friend Richard, who works with the Central Intelligence Agency. He's a man of some importance, but not so high up that he's lost all contact with reality."

Richard nodded and asked, "Roast beef or turkey?"

Richard wouldn't talk until they had sandwiches and drinks, and then he dug into the picnic basket and handed Shay a stiff brown envelope. "Open it."

She found, between two pieces of cardboard, a diploma from Hollywood High in Los Angeles. "What?" She read it again. "It's dated next May."

"That's so we can get your senior picture in the yearbook. We'll get your face in the choir and a couple other places, too. If you want us to."

"What's this about?" Shay asked.

"First, you're advanced enough in all your studies to graduate now, so the diploma's at least semi-legit," Richard said. "You won't have any trouble getting into college. Believe me."

"That's nice, but we're not meeting up here so you can tell me that."

Richard looked at her for a moment, scratched his neck, and said, "Look, we've got this problem, and your name . . . came up."

"What problem?" Shay asked suspiciously.

Richard leaned back against a boulder, getting comfortable. "There's this Russian guy who's right at the top of the Kremlin hierarchy. Like a lot of those guys, he's got a place in London, and a bank in London, and a wife and kid in London, in case everything goes sideways in Moscow."

"What does that have to do with me?"

"Shut up for a minute and I'll tell you," Richard said. "This guy is *very* secure—bodyguards, electronic sweeps, best possible encryption on his phones, randomizes his movements so you can never tell where he'll be, or when. Travels in a convoy, with watchers front and back. He has a study in the middle of the house, without windows, so we can't even read his window glass."

"Read his window glass?"

"Yeah, you put a laser . . . Never mind."

Harmon made a rolling movement with his fingers, as in, *Get to the point.*

"Okay. He has this eighteen-year-old son named Yuri. A real little asshole. He's already working toward full-fledged alcoholism, not allowed to drive in England anymore, so he now has a driver to take him around to the clubs. Anyway, he also likes women he can . . . He likes women younger than himself. Innocents he can impress. 'Cause he doesn't have a lot going for him, except Daddy's money. He has a distinct taste for redheads. . . ."

"Wait. You want me to go to England and seduce this guy?"

"No, no, no, heaven forbid," Richard said. "We'd never ask a teenager to do something like that. That'd be immoral. Maybe illegal. Might even be in bad taste."

Harmon said, "Dick, you're protesting too much."

"We really don't want you to do that," Richard said to Shay. "What we'd like you to do is to get to know him just well enough to get asked to a party at his house . . . at his father's house. He and his friends party in Yuri's rooms on the first floor, at the back, which are effectively sealed off from the rest of the house. But Yuri's bedroom has a private bathroom. We know this from the previous owners. There's an electric wall outlet in there. We need somebody to get in there, unscrew the cover plate, pull the outlet, and rewire one of *our* outlets in there."

"It doesn't blow up, does it?"

"No. This bathroom is right below Yuri's father's study, and it's on the same electric circuit. Our . . . outlet . . . will give us access to some of what he does up there."

Shay stared at him, still suspicious, then asked, "And I don't have to screw Yuri?"

"No, no, no . . . though you have to find a way into his private bathroom."

Shay looked at Harmon, and he shrugged. "They asked me. I said I'd set up a meeting. You can say no and go to Hollywood High. Probably *should* say no."

"Hollywood High," she said. After a moment: "Sounds . . . boring."

Richard said, "We'd buy you a few thousand dollars' worth of classy clothes, entry into Yuri's clubs, stick you and your dad in a nice two-bedroom flat in Soho so your dad can take the train up to his radiometric archaeological seminar at Oxford on Monday, Wednesday, and Friday evenings . . . giving you time to party."

"My dad?"

Richard tipped his head at Harmon. "We'd want somebody experienced close by, in case we need to extract you in a hurry. The

Russian security guys can be a little rough . . . and we might not have totally mentioned to the Brits that we're thinking about doing this."

Shay cut her eyes at Harmon, neither surprised nor unhappy that he should be in the mix. She crossed her arms and came back at Richard with the confidence of someone who understood her power. "How much?"

"How much?" Richard said, perplexed. "You mean . . . money?"

"Of course I mean money. You can't buy me with a couple of outfits."

"No, no, no, of course not," Richard stammered. And then, "What do you want?"

"Whatever Harmon gets."

"Done."

Shay lay back on the blanket, got comfortable in the sun, and closed her eyes. A fly buzzed around her nose and she brushed it away. After a minute, she said, "I had this knife. The Secret Service has it now."

Richard said, "I know about that."

"I'd want to take it with me," Shay said.

"Sure," Richard replied.

"And X," Shay said. "My dog comes, too."

JOHN SANDFORD is the author of more than thirty-eight bestselling thriller novels, including the Lucas Davenport Prey series and the Virgil Flowers series. He was a journalist for many years and won a Pulitzer Prize for his work.

MICHELE COOK is a former reporter, who specialized in crime and social justice. She and John met when they both worked at the *St. Paul Pioneer Press*. Michele is also a produced screenwriter.

John and Michele live and write in Santa Fe, New Mexico.